the
Laughing Side
of the
World

the
Laughing Side
of the
World

Book Nine of the Latter Annals of Lystra

Robin Hardy

Westford Press

The Laughing Side of the World:
Book Nine of the Latter Annals of Lystra
2nd edition
Christian fantasy/romance

ISBN: 978-1934776728
Copyright © 2011, 2014 Robin Hardy.

Westford Press
mail@westfordpress.com

Cover image © Kiselev Andrey Valerevich

Descriptions of many medieval foods were taken from Cindy Renfrow, *Take a Thousand Eggs or More: A Collection of 15th Century Recipes* (Unionville, NY: Royal Fireworks Press, 1991). See the Appendix for more information.

The Latin verses quoted in Chapter Seven are taken from "The Passion Play" (Benediktbeuern) as reproduced in David Bevington, *Medieval Drama* (Boston: Houghton Mifflin Company, 1975) p. 204.

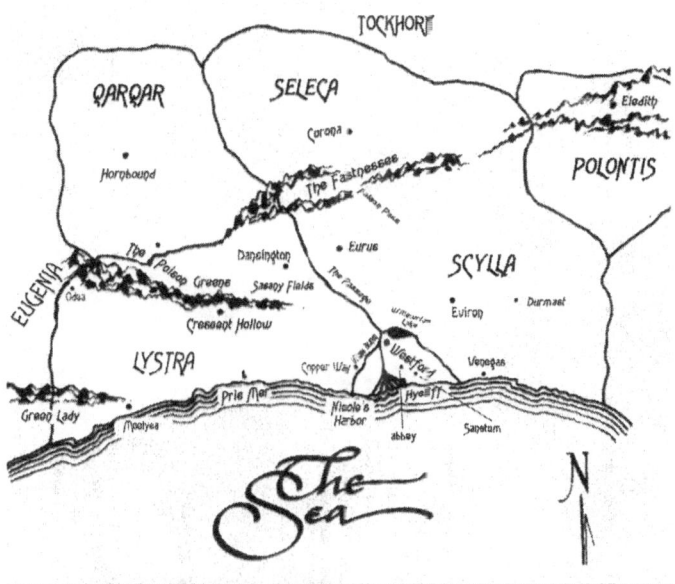

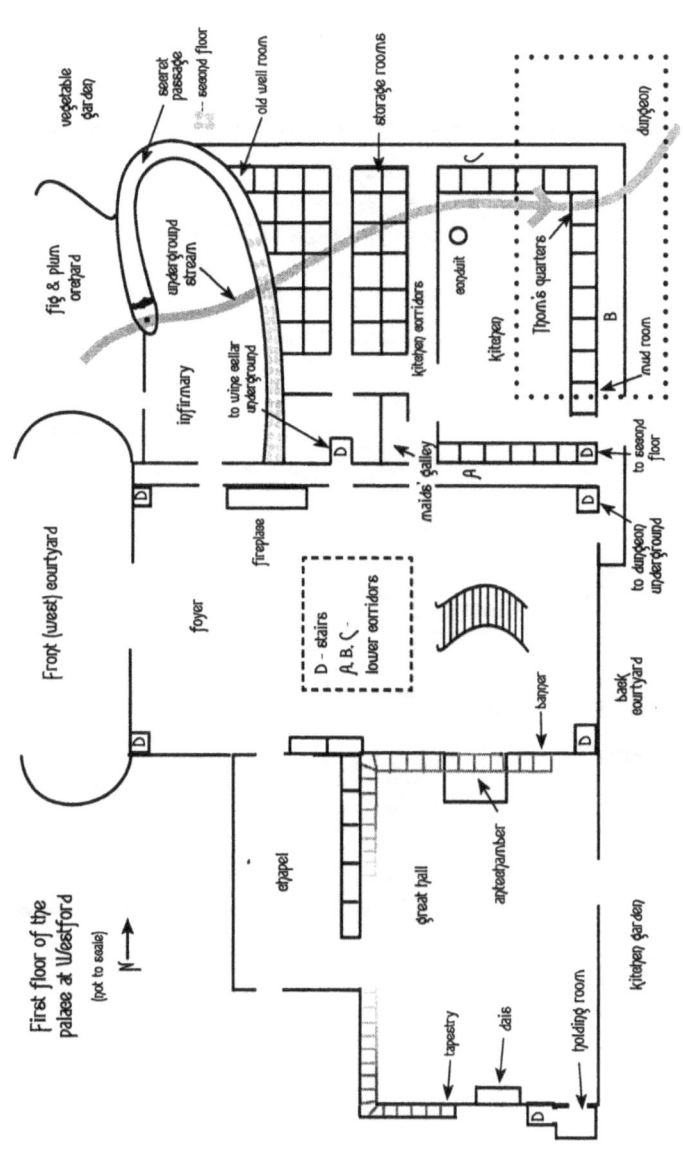

First floor of the palace at Westford
(not to scale)
N →

Front (west) courtyard

foyer

chapel

great hall

tapestry

dais

holding room

kitchen garden

antechamber

banner

back courtyard

D - stairs
A, B, C -
lower corridors

fireplace

infirmary

to wine cellar
underground

maids' galley

A

to second
floor

to dungeon
underground

secret
passage

second floor

old well room

underground
stream

storage rooms

kitchen corridors

conduit

kitchen

Thorns quarters

B

mud room

dungeon

vegetable garden

fig & plum orchard

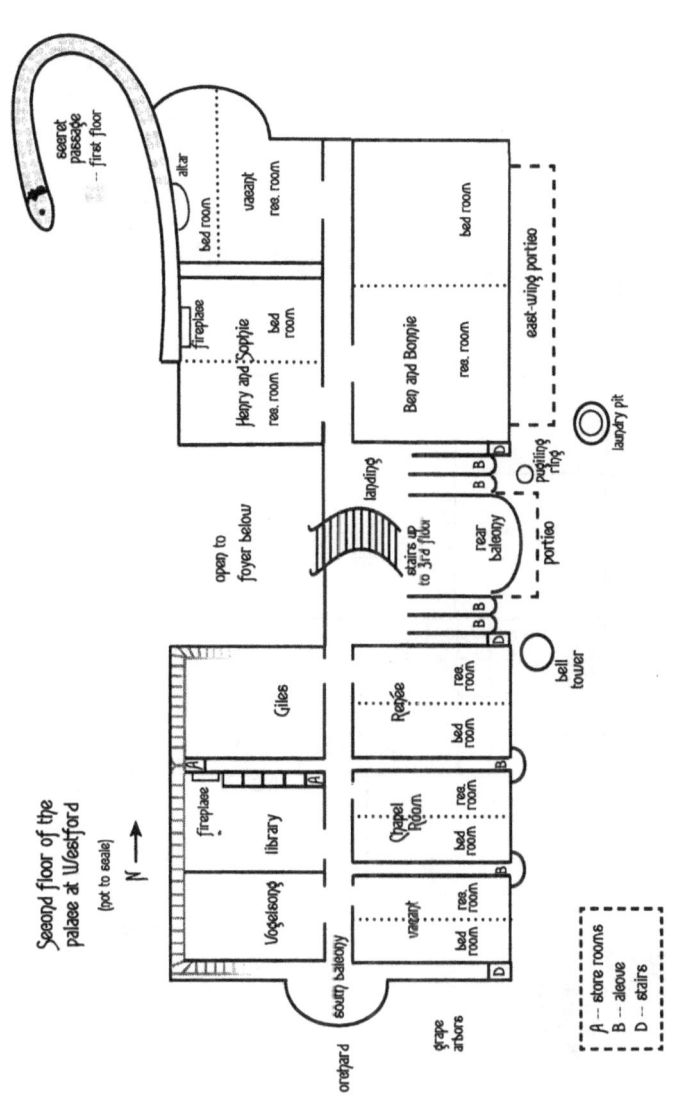

Second floor of the palace at Westford
(not to scale)

N →

secret passage
--- first floor

altar
bed room
vacant
rec. room

fireplace
Henry and Sophie
rec. room
bed room

Ben and Bonnie
rec. room
bed room

east-wing portico

laundry pit

landing

open to foyer below

stairs up to 3rd floor

rear balcony

B B

B B

D

railing ring

D

portico

Giles

Renée
rec. room
bed room

bell tower

fireplace
library

Chapel Room
rec. room
bed room

B

Vogelsong

vacant
bed room
rec. room

B

D

south balcony

orchard

grape arbors

A — store rooms
B — alcove
D — stairs

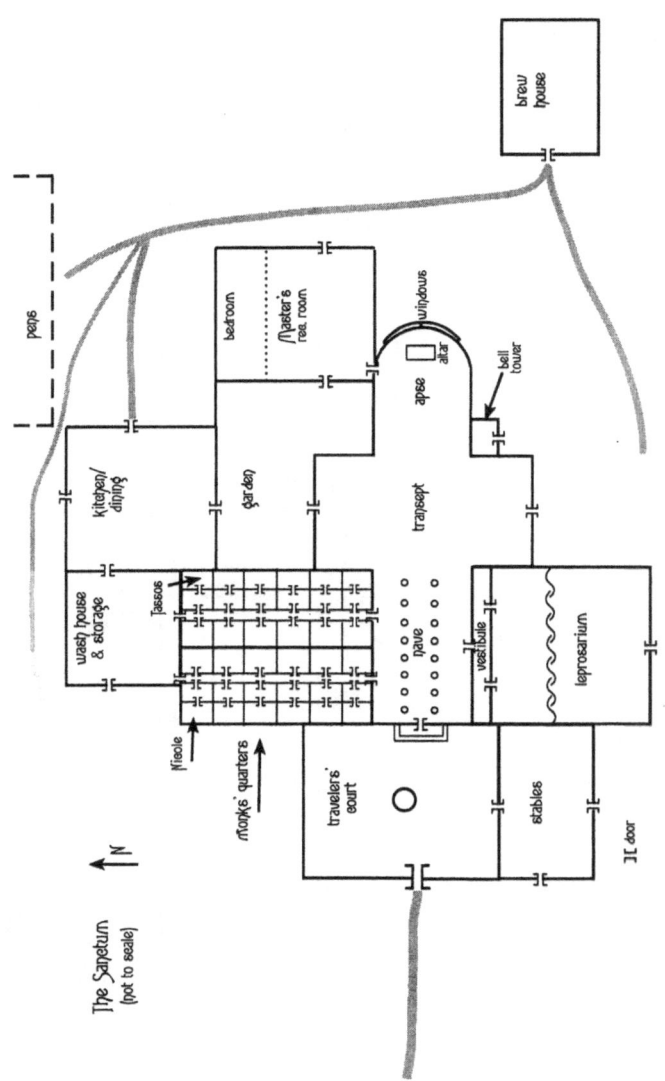

The Sanctum
(not to scale)

N

brew house

shed

bedroom

Master's
res. room

window

altar

apse

bell
tower

kitchen/
dining

garden

transept

wash house
& storage

presses

nave

vestibule

leprosarium

alcove

monks' quarters

travelers'
court

stables

IC door

When I look over beyond the line,
and beyond death,
to the laughing side of the world,
I triumph.

> From Samuel Rutherford's letter
> to Robert Cunninghame,
> August 4, 1636

I

With sunrise spread over the rolling hills to her left, Nicole set out from the palace of Westford on a sturdy dun mare. She took to the market road, sparse of traffic at this hour, and kicked the mare to a leisurely lope—as fast as Nicole could compel her to go.

She was leaving everything of a life of privilege behind: her status as Surchataine of Lystra, her fine clothes, her servants, her newly married daughters. The only part of her life that lay ahead on this road was her heart—her husband Ares, who had preceded her by only hours.

At the sound of thudding hoofbeats behind her, Nicole reined up and twisted in the saddle. And she saw a large man on a great warhorse pursuing her determinedly. The muscled flanks of the animal rippled under its burden; its head bobbed in the effort of producing the speed its rider required.

The man himself was unconvincingly attired in a coarse monk's habit, too small and too tight, that rode up over the threadbare breeches on his thighs. The robe, incidentally, was identical to the one that engulfed

Nicole, who wore a simple cotton dress underneath.

As escape was now impossible, she waited for her pursuer to come abreast of her. "Surchataine," he said, saluting gravely.

"Oswald, what are you doing?" she exhaled in a gentle reprimand. He was the senior of two Seconds to the Commander of the Lystran army.

"With the Commander's permission, Lady, I have delegated my duties to the Second Paramore. You shall not travel to the monastery unescorted."

"But Oswald," she murmured, eyes glittering, "there is a flaw in your disguise. You look nothing like a monk." With heavy features, curling hair that was prematurely grey, and a short, bushy beard, he looked like nothing but a veteran soldier.

"Lady, you look less like a monk than I," he responded.

This was true. There was no chance of hiding her feminine features, even at the mature age of 34. And neither had she trimmed her long auburn hair, given her priority of pleasing Ares over maintaining a disguise.

There was a further giveaway in their disguises due to ignorance. Both she and Oswald carried behind their saddles something that should have immediately disqualified their entrance into the brotherhood they were about to invade: satchels of provisions prepared by the finest kitchen staff in the Southern Continent.

Smiling, she turned the mare's head to resume her southward journey. The monastery/leprosarium that Ares had built, known as the Sanctum, was half a day's ride from Westford, within view of the coast. "So how shall we two unlikely monks worm our way inside, Oswald?"

Guiding his horse to walk beside hers, he mulled, "It may help to know why Surchatain Ares chose to start the Procession of Unlikely Monks to begin with, Lady."

"Oswald, Henry is Surchatain," she reminded him.

Ares, after the last of a series of attempts on his life, abdicated the throne to concentrate on uncovering the would-be assassin and his conspirators. Twenty-four-year-old Henry, raised by Ares though not his own, had been vested with the rulership less than a month ago. And a few days following, he married Ares' daughter Sophie.

"It would not do to salute Ares upon finding him at the monastery," Nicole added.

"No, Lady, it would not," Oswald agreed gravely, glancing up and down the empty road, because a guardian kept on watch.

"As to why he went," she sighed, "you know that Father Birondo, who has been serving at the palace for—how many years?"

"Nine," Oswald answered immediately. "Nine years. Surchatain Ares appointed Father Birondo after removing that treacherous lackey of Lady Auer's. She put her nephew up to challenge the Surchatain for the throne, and her priest acted as spy for them."

Nicole stared at her companion in mild awe of his recall, then resumed, "Yes, well—dear Father Birondo is one of the Order of Preaching Brethren, who now serve at the Sanctum. Since Ares had so much time on his hands while pretending to be dead, he spoke a great deal with Father Birondo and a few of the other monks.

"They told him that they had grave concerns for the well-being of the Sanctum under their Master, Father

Manworren. Thus Ares decided to go see for himself what the situation was—and give Henry a chance to settle into his position without interference."

Oswald's heavy brows drew down. "Did he not tell you what these concerns were?"

"Not specifically," she admitted, with a trace of unease.

"And the Surchatain had no objection to my lady's joining him?" he asked pointedly.

She puckered her lips. "Not once I explained to him that I was coming regardless."

The shadow of a smile crossed Oswald's face, then he squinted in thought again. "What does the Surchatain know of this Manworren? And why did he appoint him Master of the Sanctum?"

"Ares did not appoint him; he preferred not to interfere in the internal affairs of the order, especially after the uproar when Ares decreed that all petitions for anathema had to go through Westford. He was much afraid of its abuse," she said.

"The practice lends itself to be abused," Oswald observed.

"I suppose it does. At any rate," she continued, "I assume that this Manworren rose to his rank in the customary manner, but as to what he is doing now—well, that is what Ares wanted to see."

Oswald did not reply right away. He was guiding his horse to the side of the road to allow the passage of the vegetable seller's one-horse cart en route to the palace at Westford.

The vegetable seller, a serious businesswoman, saw and recognized the Surchataine and the Second, but acknowledged neither. Her only concern this morning was the price that Georges, the old dinner master, would offer for September turnips and overripe melons.

Once she had passed, Oswald repositioned his horse beside Nicole's. "Does my lady know how the Surchatain proposed to gain entrance for himself without being recognized?"

It was a good question. The deep scar that cleft the right side of Ares' face made him known by sight almost anywhere in Lystra or Scylla.

Recently, in fact, a wanderer who was of middle age and sturdily built, having been told that he resembled the Surchatain, took it upon himself to slash his own face in approximation of Ares' legendary scar, and allowed it to heal open. Then he stole himself some black clothes somewhat comparable to Ares' dress blacks and began traveling up and down the coast impersonating the Surchatain.

News of the imposter soon found its way to Westford, but as he was apparently using his disguise for the sole purpose of eating excellent meals, drinking fine wines, and bedding many women, Ares declined to assign already taxed resources to tracking him down.

After succeeding with this deception for some months, the imposter was finally killed by the jealous husband of one of his dupes. The husband, upon traveling to Westford to claim the throne, was highly vexed to find it already occupied by the genuine article.

"Ares didn't mention how he would get around being recognized," Nicole admitted, downcast.

Oswald eyed her. "That does not sound like the Surchatain, to leave such a detail to chance."

"No, it doesn't," she agreed.

"Therefore, I would say that he intended no disguise."

She looked over at him. "What do you mean?"

"That he intended to present himself to Father Manworren as Ares," Oswald said. "It is rare enough for a living Surchatain to abdicate willingly. The last time it happened, according to Counselor Vogelsong, was because the Surchatain desired to enter a life of contemplation, as his youngest son had done before him. So it has happened. A man reaches a certain point of life that he desires only rest." Though no one knew Ares' exact age, he was 51, and for the last 17 years he had borne the weight of Lystra on his shoulders.

In recounting this bit of history to the Second, however, the Counselor had failed to mention the sequel to the story of the abdication. After six months of peaceful monastic life, the former Surchatain got wind of the fact that his hand-picked selection for the throne, his firstborn, had renounced his religion and compelled his subjects to do the same.

So the old Surchatain laid aside his robe and donned armor. He defeated his son in battle, blinded him, put him in prison, and installed his son the monk on the throne. The father then returned to an untroubled life of contemplation.

At Oswald's conjecture, Nicole felt a pain in the pit of her stomach. If her husband intended to enter a life of monastic contemplation—entailing celibacy—he had not told his wife this. "Ares assured me it was to be a ruse."

"Then that it is, Lady," Oswald said. After a moment's silence, he added, "It would be helpful to know all that the Surchatain confided to my lady."

Nicole thought back, watching the shifting sheen of her horse's mane under the early morning sunlight. "Not a great deal, really," she confessed. "He spoke in the most general terms about—the responsibilities of power, and walking by the light given us. He seemed to feel that because he was told there were problems not only by Father Birondo, whom he trusted, but several other monks, that the compulsion was laid on him to do something about it, especially as he was no longer Surchatain. I gathered that he would not know exactly what to do until he arrived, and saw what the situation actually was."

"And how was he to accommodate my lady in the monastery?" Oswald asked.

"He was going to sneak me in," she replied with the flash of a grin. "There is a travelers' court in the very front, with a well and stables, so I was to stop there and rest till I knew what he might do."

"At last, a whiff of a plan," he grunted. "That'll do. Then you shall be the Lady Nouri, and I your bodyguard Forcht, on your way from Venegas to Westford."

Venegas was a small coastal town in Scylla. Surchatain Magnus had expended large sums attempting to build a harbor there comparable to Nicole's Harbor or Prie Mer. Due to the exponential increase in trade all along the southern coast, he was somewhat succeeding, despite the inhospitable cliffs.

Unlike the coastal towns of Lystra, however, Venegas was a town of strangers, of passers-by. So it was a reasonable risk for the Second to choose that as their starting point.

"Then what are we doing wearing these ridiculous robes?" Nicole laughed. "Perhaps we should discard them."

Oswald considered that, but rejected it simply because he did not wish the Surchataine to be seen in a peasant's dress with no covering. "We were robbed on the way, Lady, but a passing band of Preaching Brethren chased the villains away before they could do further harm, and then gave us these robes."

"Robbed? In Lystra? Ares would take great offense at that story," she observed.

"No, Lady, we were robbed while yet in Scylla," Oswald clarified. "The Preaching Brethren were on their way to minister in Venegas."

One of the responsibilities of the Brethren was to send out bands to teach and evangelize in all surrounding areas. Unfortunately, neither Nicole nor Oswald knew that Master Manworren had been sadly negligent in this directive.

"That is rather convincing, Oswald," she said in admiration.

"Forcht, Lady Nouri. I am your servant Forcht," he reminded her.

"Forcht," she murmured, nodding.

Increased daylight brought an increase in traffic, so Nicole and Oswald suspended scheming for a while. Knowing that the Sanctum would not provide hay, they departed the road to let their horses graze, then resumed their travel.

Shortly, they passed the abbey, established probably a hundred years ago, where nuns cared for orphaned children. Ares also sustained the abbey by Westford's wealth—a practice that Henry would not presume to change even had it occurred to him that he could.

Having awakened this morning in time to catch Nicole in the corridor as she was leaving the palace, Henry stood in that same corridor long after she had left. His curling blond hair hung over his hazy grey eyes; the blond stubble on his face added to the look of wildness that had stamped him ever since his wilderness sojourn.

Nicole's departing words—*"Stand forth, Henry; you will not fail"*—still reverberated through his skull. But their confidence was almost drowned out by the drumming of the fear: Ares was gone. He had really left. Henry was alone on the throne.

Even during his exile to the outpost in Odea four years ago, as painful as that was, he knew that all would be well, for Ares—Henry's guardian since birth—ruled in Westford. The abandonment he felt today was nothing like Henry had experienced since the time he had been captured and sold into slavery, when he was 13.

Yet even then, Ares ruled, and because he ruled, he had found Henry and rescued him. But now Ares had stepped down, thinking to leave Henry in his place, and the world fell apart.

In blind desperation, Henry turned to the back stairwell to ascend to the eastern parapet on the roof of the palace. This was the most deserted spot in a place teeming with people, and the daily ascension of the light was a natural time of reverence for Henry. He would not have known to call it *worship*.

Here, he brought out his fears in a motley procession before the Surchatain of heaven and earth, and he leaned on the parapet, suspended over the world, to let the wind whip his hair and blow away the phantasms.

It was Commander Thom, Ares' closest friend, who finally found the young Surchatain at the eastern parapet. Approaching, the Commander saluted and said, "Surchatain, the Lady Sophie was somewhat distraught upon finding you missing this morning, and the Counselor Vogelsong has some matters that require your attention." His impassive face and cool blue eyes offered no subtext to the message.

After a moment, Henry turned to regard his erstwhile superior. Henry knew that once upon a time Ares had been Commander, and Thom his Second in Command, but that was part of such a distant past that Henry might as well try to imagine them as children—these men who seemed to him as gods.

"Thom, I'm scared," he whispered.

Thom shifted, appraising him. Then he said, "The night that Magnus attacked us from the north with his trebuchet, and Ulm attacked us from the south, Ares had only the—most tenuous evidence that either would occur that night. He set the Green Regiment, under himself, in defense of the palace, and the rest of the army he sent south to meet Ulm.

"But there was no direct indication that Ulm's ships would debark then and there. In committing to this course, Ares had great fear, and there was cause for it: he alone made the decisions that would determine Westford's survival. He had no one to rely on for counsel; nothing to base his decision on but his faith that God would not lead him astray."

Thom paused while Henry called up the events from

dusty memory. "That was the night of Sister's wedding. I was seven or eight years old. Melva was with us. The whole cause of the warring was her."

"Yes, Surchatain."

"And I'm told I fell asleep under a table in the banquet hall," Henry said.

"Yes. You also know the outcome—that Magnus was persuaded to leave with Druella as prize, and that the combined armies of Lystra and Calle Valley withstood Ulm's invasion. Ares was proved right.

"But I have come to believe, in the years since, that the timing of the invasion was based on Ares' decision to prepare for it. Not the other way around," Thom said.

Henry blinked at him. "What?"

"Ares put himself so completely under the yoke of Christ, that the fact he believed that Ulm would attack that night, and arranged his defenses against it, moved his Master to prompt the attack *for that night*, so that Ares would succeed in meeting it. Had Ares chosen another course, I believe that God would have incited Ulm to attack in such a way as to come up against Ares' prepared defenses. I have no proof of this, of course, and a man would be a fool to presume such protection, but still, I believe this to be the case."

"If that's so, then why wouldn't God prevent Ulm from attacking at all?" Henry exclaimed.

Thom regarded him. "Because that would deprive Ares of the battle that proved him worthy to rule."

Henry stared at him, then looked back in despondence to the distant horizon. "That was Ares."

"Who placed you under Christ's headship, and your obedience indicates your desire to remain there. Thus, I believe you are under the same protection," Thom ended.

Henry turned back to study Thom's steady gaze, then gestured. "I suppose I had better go get dressed, then."

"Surchatain." Thom extended an arm in an invitation for Henry to precede him downstairs.

Nicole and Oswald approached the front gates of the travelers' court of the Sanctum. A score of travelers leaving the court, bound for Westford, had passed them on the road, so that only a handful remained here now.

A large signboard at the right of the gate, written in beautiful calligraphy, read: "Welcome, Traveler, to the Well and Shelter of the Sanctum. May it please our Guests to observe Peace, to refrain from Begging, Fighting, or Licentious Behavior while within; to Keep Animals in the Stalls provided; to see to your own Provender, and to know that our unworthy Court is intended to be but temporary Shelter on your Way. Peace be unto You." In smaller letters below was plainly written: "If you cannot read, have this Notice read to you."

Upon reading the sign, Nicole and Oswald eyed each other. "I had not taken into account the *other* travelers that might sojourn here," she observed.

"Then we shall. If the Lady Nouri will precede her humble servant Forcht," he said by way of reminder, nodding to the open gates.

"Thank you, Forcht," she replied.

So they entered, and dismounted to look around. It was a nice large courtyard paved in clay brick, about fifty feet in length. All four sides sported an overhanging roof five feet in depth, with benches placed sporadically along the walls, and firepits every ten feet or so. A large, fresh-water well equipped with rope and bucket stood in the center of the courtyard, and a screened latrine, amounting to a hole in the ground, was discreetly tucked in the back corner.

Oswald glanced at the four visitors presently occupying the court (three in one group and one by himself) and pointed Nicole toward a desirable corner with its own firepit, well away from the latrine. "If my lady will make herself comfortable."

"Thank you—Forcht." She remembered just in time, and he nodded gravely.

Oswald unpacked everything from the horses, then led them into the stables while Nicole settled against the wall in the corner of the court. The closest bench terminated a few feet from the firepit, enabling one to sit near a fire while remaining within easy reach of a bench. It was, all in all, a considerate set-up for wayfarers.

Since summer was hanging on through September with great tenacity, Nicole made no move to begin clearing the pit for a fire. While waiting for Oswald, she opened a satchel to remove sausages, fried spiced onions, bread and cheese.

A shadow crossed her preparations, and she looked up at a brown-robed figure that had stopped in front of her. Before she could blurt in a whisper, "Ares?" the man lowered his hood and smiled upon her. It was not her husband.

He was clean-shaven, as most of the Brethren were when not constrained by a particular vow, and his hair was short and tonsured—as she could see when he bowed his head to her.

Immediately before he spoke, she realized why she had leapt to the conclusion that he was Ares: this monk was Polonti. Not full-blooded, perhaps, but then neither was Ares full Polonti. But the race of Ares' ancestor Roman was clear in this man's face, hair, and build.

He said, "Greetings, Lady. It would be an honor and benefit to our modest Sanctum if my lady would consent to abide in a room within for the evening."

She declined, "Oh, I don't wish to cause any inconvenience. Your court is quite adequate."

He persisted, "Lady, we earnestly beseech that you avail yourself of a room within the walls."

This time she hesitated. Was he acting on Ares' behalf? If he was, she decided, Ares would find some way to make that known to her. Caution was required of her now. "You are too kind, but I require no special treatment."

His flat face settled into grim lines. "I must insist that my lady accept our poor offer of protection."

She regarded him in surprise. Was he issuing a threat or a warning? "Since you phrase it thus, I will. But I must wait until my bodyguard returns from the stables."

He bowed again. "That is reasonable, my lady." So she began repacking provisions into her satchel.

He stood waiting, then said, "Forgive my ill manners. Your servant is Brother Tassos. May I inquire my lady's name?" It seemed to her that he asked almost reluctantly.

She glanced up. "I am Lady Nouri of Venegas,

traveling to Westford." She stopped there, knowing the perils of too many words.

"Ah. I see." He looked at her robe, but did not press for an explanation.

At that time Oswald came back into the court. As he advanced to her corner, Nicole stood, and he settled a cool gaze on the monk with her. Before either man could speak, Nicole said, "Forcht, this kind monk is Brother Tassos. He simply insists that we take lodging inside for the night."

Oswald turned his deep-set eyes to appraise the monk, then bowed stiffly to her. "As my lady wishes."

He bent to take up their saddles, bedrolls, and provisions. No tack would be left in the stables within easy reach of traveling thieves. There was a minor tussle when Nicole insisted on carrying her own satchel; at her look he relinquished hold of it.

Nicole turned to the monk. "Kindly show us to our rooms, Brother Tassos."

"My lady greatly honors me." He led her up short, broad steps to doors that opened from the travelers' court directly into the nave of the church. It was nicely constructed with polished oak floors, a few tapestries on the side walls, and stained-glass windows at the apse.

Although thoughtfully designed, it was considerably less ornate than some of the other great churches around the Continent. In selecting materials, Ares had been far more concerned about functionality than beauty. The church proper was constructed of stone; the surrounding buildings were mostly wood.

Almost immediately upon entering, Brother Tassos turned to open an arched door on their left. It led into a corridor lined with doors on the left and right.

Proceeding down this corridor at a smart pace, the monk brought Nicole and Oswald to the last door on the left. As the corridor ended at another door, Oswald reached for its handle. Tassos held up a prohibitive hand. "I regret that this door is always barred on the other side."

Looking at him, Oswald attempted to open the door anyway. When it didn't budge, he uttered, "You appear to be right about that."

Withholding comment, the monk reached instead for the latch of the smaller door on his left, and opened it. Nicole looked into a room with a pallet and washstand. Without window or candle, the room was dim even at midday.

"Forgive the inadequate accommodations, Lady Nouri," the monk pleaded. "We will have a chamber pot and amenities brought at once."

"It is quite suitable as is, Brother Tassos," Nicole insisted. Oswald brought in their gear to pile it in an orderly fashion in the corner. He looked at a second door in the cell, opposite to the one they had entered by, but did not attempt to open it.

"Your room, sir, shall be directly across the corridor, here," Tassos offered.

Oswald came back to the corridor to look down on him from his towering height. "My place shall be at my lady's door."

The monk hesitated in mild confusion; Nicole forestalled an argument by saying, "We shall make ourselves invisible, dear Brother. Please accept our gratitude for the shelter."

He turned to her again. "The gratitude would be ours, Lady Nouri, if you would consent to dine with our Master, Father Manworren, at this time."

"Now?" she asked, as it was yet afternoon.

"Yes, Lady, whenever you are ready." Tassos bowed again, which began to irritate Oswald.

"Well, then, certainly. Allow me to make myself presentable by means of your washstand, then Forcht and I will be greatly honored to be received by the Father," Nicole said.

Tassos glanced at Oswald, who was likewise beginning to irritate *him*. "I shall send a brother with amenities, and another to lead you to the dining area. The layout can be confusing," he explained.

"Certainly," she agreed, and he departed.

When he had gone, Oswald took that opportunity to enter her room and open the second door, which had no lock or bar. It opened into an identical cell that could be reached only by this one door.

Although the tiny room was also equipped with pallet and washstand (dry), it was obviously unoccupied. Nicole whispered, "Had you the chance to see the plans of this place, when it was being built?" This was about four years ago.

"Yes, Lady, at length," he grunted.

"As did I," she murmured in satisfaction.

She knew, for instance, that the monks' quarters, where they were now, was tucked in the northwest corner between the nave and the transept of the church. There was a garden courtyard directly east that enclosed the north arm of the transept, and the kitchen/dining area sat north of the garden.

The lepers, isolated in their own quarters in the southwest corner of the nave and transept, posed no great danger to visitors who kept themselves to approved areas. (Unseen lepers were presumed to be noninfectious.)

Oswald noted, "Then my lady will recognize that this room"—gesturing into the empty one behind hers —"sits on the northwest corner of the monks' quarters, and its two walls face the outside." In gesturing, he inadvertently ripped the arm seam of the robe. So he peeled it off and tossed it in a corner of the inner room.

She looked at the wooden walls. "Wasn't it supposed to be all stone?"

"Yes, but they were so long in constructing it that the foreman seized a load of pine to finish the dormitories. My lady should also know," Oswald whispered, closing the door, "that I found a horse in the stables which I know to be from the palace. It's Burl, a fast gelding, and smarter than most. He is a favorite of the Surchatain."

"Then Ares did arrive," she whispered back.

"Yes, Lady; I'm sure of it."

They returned to the corridor to wait, and a monk presently brought a chamber pot, fresh water, scented soap, and clean cloths to Nicole. Then he and Oswald waited in the narrow corridor while she refreshed herself.

Since the windowless quarters proved rather stuffy, and the disguise of the robes pointless by now, Nicole left hers with Oswald's, both folded neatly, before accompanying the monk down the corridor.

The two dormitory corridors were supposed to

terminate with doors at either end to provide exits in the event of fire, but if the second door of the other corridor was also barred, that meant the two corridors opened only into the church. This disturbed Nicole, as it made the rooms less like quarters and more like prison cells.

Following Tassos, the visitors entered the nave and turned left, admiring the smooth marble columns leading up the center aisle of the church.

When they reached the transept, Nicole almost betrayed her knowledge of the Sanctum's layout by turning toward the northern doors, which led out to the garden courtyard and kitchen/dining hall beyond.

But Oswald, seeing that the monk was not leading this way, discreetly impeded her turn. The monk glanced back as his guests bumped into each other. "Pardon my clumsiness, Lady Nouri," Oswald uttered.

"The fault is mine, Forcht," she said, blushing.

They proceeded clear to the apse with its carved altar and retable before turning to a narrow door on its north side. This opened into an opulent, spacious room. Nicole's immediate perceptions were that of large glass windows (presently standing open), tapestries, shelves of leather-bound books, woven rugs on polished oak flooring, and exquisitely carved furniture.

Such luxuries were not provided for in Ares' stipend to the Sanctum, and had he seen them, he would have immediately confiscated them for the palace treasury and dealt with their procurer.

The obvious occupant of these quarters advanced with outstretched hand to her. He was a handsome man, about Ares' age, with silvered hair, clean teeth, and delicate, manicured hands. He wore a beautifully embroidered robe of white silk and a large gold cross that rivaled the adornment of anyone at the palace.

"Lady Nouri, I am your humble servant Father Manworren. Thank you for accepting my humble offer of shelter. I require my monks to keep an eye on the travelers' court for beautiful women who might prove too great a temptation to other travelers—so Brother Tassos has plucked a jewel from the mire. May I show you to our humble table?" He indicated a large scrolled table heavy with gold dinnerware, and two ornate chairs.

"You are too kind, Father," she murmured, blinking in shock.

2

Father Manworren gestured to the monk who had led in the guests as if he were a servant, not merely a subordinate. Bowing, this brother pulled out from the table one of the two heavy, padded chairs, and the Father urged, "Please, Lady Nouri, be seated."

She accepted the invitation, regarding in mounting astonishment the details of wealth that adorned the table alone: the splendid gold ware, the ornate ivory pot of fresh chrysanthemums, and the embroidered, tasseled runner dividing the round table. The monk pulled out the second chair for Manworren, and Oswald shifted to place his great frame behind her.

Nicole glanced back at him, then said, "May I presume on my lord's kindness to set a place for my bodyguard? He requires sustenance to serve me."

The Father's lips twitched in displeasure as he glanced at the large man standing behind her chair, but he said, "Whatever the lady demands shall be law in this humble place."

Nicole regarded him; obviously, the Law had already been established for this humble place, and she did not consider her demands adequate to displace it. But the problem that Ares had come to address appeared obvious. How had such flagrant abuses gone on for so long?

The Father's eyes flicked up to the monk, who left through a side door to carry in another chair, placing it to Nicole's left. Grunting, Oswald sat.

A small army of brown-clad brothers began setting the table with food and drink. First, as at the royal table, the wine was poured into golden goblets (though years ago Ares had withdrawn the gold in favor of pewter for everyday use). Tasting it, Nicole discerned a rare and expensive Valley vintage.

Next, monks brought out dishes of flampoyntes bake, prenade, greens, fresh bread, and rapeye. Nicole was almost insulted: such dishes might have excelled even Georges' efforts.

"I am overwhelmed by your kindness, Father," she murmured. "Surely you had been expecting some personage of note, to have prepared such dishes."

He waved. "These slight efforts of my staff are simply their daily practice, Lady. I am laboring to mold ignorant men into worthy servants, and it is a difficult undertaking."

Servants? she wondered. *Yours?* Again, this was not the purpose of the Sanctum. But she picked up her fork to taste the flampoyntes. "I judge you to be succeeding."

Oswald watched in disapproval; his instinct was to prevent her eating anything that he had not tasted first, given Ares' frequent bouts with poisoned food. But since that would have been an inexcusable affront to their host, she did not allow it. So Oswald lowered his head and began eating with as much decorum as such large hands could manage.

Manworren replied to her, "I am honored that such unworthy efforts please my lady." He watched her so fixedly that Oswald stopped eating to pin him with an answering stare.

Not looking in his direction, the Father blinked. "Excuse my curiosity, Lady—you are traveling from Venegas?"

"Yes," she admitted. "I have—departed a rather uncomfortable situation, which I do not feel free to discuss. But I am on my way to Westford, where I expect to find friends. More I cannot say, so I beg your indulgence."

A runaway lady? An abused wife, perhaps? Or one turned out due to indiscretions? The Father's eyes gleamed at the possibilities. "Say no more, Lady. But let me urge you—even command you—to accept accommodations here, poor as they are. Whatever your situation, you have found a friend in this unworthy person."

"You are too extraordinarily kind," she said into her goblet. "But I had hoped," she paused, lowering the goblet, "to present my petition to Surchatain Ares."

His fixed smile vanished. "That would scarcely be advisable, Lady."

She raised her luminous hazel eyes to meet his. "Why is that, dear Father?"

At the palace, the young, green Surchatain Henry sat huddled with Counselor Vogelsong over a letter, attended by Commander Thom and his Second Paramore. Although the Counselor's work chambers on the fourth floor, where they were now gathered, was paneled to inhibit eavesdropping, and a guard stood outside the door, the Counselor spoke in a low voice to introduce the matter to Henry.

"Apparently, Lord Roschlau is not content with the grant from the palace to print pamphlets on his greenstone mining debacle—he is set to foment discord. A nobleman sympathetic to us forwarded this letter, copies of which are being circulated everywhere. Our noble friend says that Roschlau's man handed it to him himself."

Taking the parchment, which had been sealed, Henry sat back to read: "To all nobles of Lystra who are weary of the odious burdens of the house of Ares: With the abdication of the sick and elderly Ares comes the appointment of the grandson of the Usurper Talus, a green and stupid youth who has earned no confidence nor right to rule his betters. Make your desire heard to end this disgraceful episode and place a Worthy Noble on the Throne."

Squinting in a manner that he hoped indicated concern, Henry handed the letter over to Thom, who read it and passed it along to his Second. Henry told Vogelsong, "I appreciate that this disturbs you, but—I do not see how this is treasonous. It's not specific enough. The Law is clear: treasonous speech must embody a specific threat. All he does here is insult me."

"That is true, Surchatain," Vogelsong admitted. "But we must not ignore such venom, else it will poison the city toward you. Somehow, we must find a way to answer it."

Paramore turned the letter over to study the broken

seal. "This is not Roschlau's seal," he observed.

"It isn't?" Henry said, reaching for the letter, which the Second handed to him. "Whose is it?"

"I do not know," Paramore said. "But Roschlau's seal is that of an eagle."

"Let us consult the Book of Seals," proposed the Counselor.

Rising from the table, he went to select a heavy volume from a shelf of large books that covered one wall. He shook back a luxurious sleeve to do this, and Henry glanced humorously at Thom.

Since Ares' abdication, Vogelsong had taken to wearing somewhat finer robes than he was previously wont, with matching hats. Had he known that this new vanity would earn him the sobriquet of "Giles the Younger," he might have toned down his choices. Giles, the palace Steward, was as famous for his fussy finery as for his unblinking eye over the treasury.

Vogelsong plopped the great Book of Seals on the table, then sat to begin leafing through it. Leaning forward, Henry held the two halves of the wax seal together so that Vogelsong could compare the imprint on it with the sketches of seals in his book.

"Does the book contain the seals of all the nobles of Lystra, or just Westford?" Henry asked.

Vogelsong replied, "Let us not speak nonsense, Surchatain. Nobles are not scattered through the province like ether—they inhabit only the major cities of Westford, Crescent Hollow, Prie Mer, Eurus, and Nicole's Harbor. This book covers those cities, in that order."

"Ah," Henry said placidly.

Vogelsong, squinting at the wax pieces, was

obligated to don a pair of gold-rimmed spectacles, which cemented the comparison of him to Giles in the minds of all who were watching. Vogelsong even replicated Giles' manner in the small action.

"Hmm. I do believe that is the figure of a woman, with a lily, it appears."

"Yes, Counselor. It is a woman's seal," Henry affirmed.

"That should make the looking easier," the Counselor mused. He turned pages deliberately, scanning sketches. Thom and Paramore moved to stand behind him and look over his shoulders. "Hmm. Hmm," Vogelsong murmured.

Thom suddenly placed his forefinger on a sketch midpage. Henry leaned over to look at the page upside down. "That's it! That's the one. But that's . . . impossible."

"Lady Auer," Paramore mused. He looked back and forth between the sketch and the seal fragments. "Impossible or not, it matches."

"Impossible," Vogelsong echoed Henry as though not hearing the Second. "Lady Auer was banished years ago for inciting her nephew to challenge Ares for the throne. She fled to Eurus, where Surchatain Magnus swore that she . . . was. . . ."

"'Dealt with'?" Henry suggested.

Of that episode, he remembered only the short, sweet fight between Ares and his much younger challenger. In defeating him without killing him, Ares had employed a surprise move that had since become a staple of the Greens' training.

"So." Thom looked off into space, stroking his short,

prematurely greying beard (for an officer's life is a hard one). "The possibilities here are two: either Lady Auer not only lives, but has regained possessions and influence, or someone has found use for her ghost."

Paramore tossed the letter back to the table. "Her ghost, or her seal. Someone who came across it is using it as a shield to engage in treasonous activities. And it strikes me that this is exactly Roschlau's style."

"Her brother, the young challenger's father—was he not given her possessions when she was banished?" Vogelsong mused.

"Lord Backvold. Yes," Thom replied. "But I have been watching him for all these years, and his loyalty to Ares is beyond question."

"Who gave the letter to you?" Henry asked Vogelsong.

"Lord Davignon's man," the Counselor replied.

Henry snorted, "Well, he's out as a conspirator, too. Even after Ares came back from the dead, Davignon is still dreaming up ways to marry Nicole. He wants to insert himself in the ruling family, not overturn it."

"Agreed. This is clearly not Davignon's doing, either," Thom said, studying the letter. Then he observed, "The writing is very plain. Not the ornate lettering you see from a nobleman's secretary."

"Perhaps they wanted to make sure it could be read by anyone," Vogelsong offered. Henry took up the letter to study it again.

They were silent a while. "It is difficult to answer something so—unspecific without giving credibility to it," Paramore pointed out. "The last thing we want to do is crystallize their complaint for them."

Henry, still holding the letter, started laughing. "No, but perhaps we might muddy their waters!" His elders regarded him, and he said, "Counselor, how very difficult would it be to carve a likeness of Lady Auer's seal?"

"Child's play," Vogelsong scoffed. "But it is illegal to forge seals."

"Of a deposed traitor?" Henry asked. "Whose seal has already been compromised?"

"The point is valid," Vogelsong admitted.

"And how difficult would it be to reproduce such a simple hand?" Henry said, gesturing to the lettering.

The Commander leaned down to him in interest. "What are you thinking of saying in such a document, Surchatain?"

"Oh, anything. Anything at all," Henry blustered. "The more nonsensical, the better. We could put out a letter ranting about the price of salt. We could complain about brightly colored hose on men with fat legs. We could compose anything, as long as it would not be taken as a direct attack on anybody."

"Just a lunatic's ravings." Thom said. "Not to be taken seriously."

"Well, there is definitely a problem with men wearing colored hose who shouldn't," Henry hedged.

"I shall begin drawing up such missives imme-diately, Surchatain," Vogelsong proposed with crisp enthusiasm.

"Secretly, Counselor," the Commander cautioned. "And they should be dispersed secretively—left in a tavern or public house with the seal broken. No one should be able to trace them to the palace."

"Wait, here. I'm Surchatain; let me compose them," Henry said, reaching for a quill.

Paramore suddenly pulled up a chair to sit. He folded his hands gravely on the table and said, "I wish to register a complaint against householders that throw slop out of upper windows without looking to see if anyone's in the street below."

"A valid complaint, worthy Second!" Henry noted, dipping the quill.

"Is it too serious for our purposes?" Vogelsong asked, and Paramore looked at him darkly.

"No, no; we might use such a complaint to redirect the people's anger against their sloppy friends and neighbors instead of me," Henry said.

Thom sat as well, and the four were soon pouring their deepest grievances into letters to go out under the Lady Auer's seal.

"Why would it be inadvisable for me to present my petition to Surchatain Ares, Father?" Nicole asked innocently.

"Being from Venegas, I suppose you have not heard the news, Lady Nouri." Father Manworren leaned back in the padded chair, caressing the soft folds of his silk robe. "Surchatain Ares has abdicated the throne in favor of the young Chatain."

"Surchatain Ares abdicated?" Nicole asked. Her surprise at this news was convincing, for she had not expected to hear anything like the truth from him.

"Yes, Lady, most regrettably. I was particularly distressed to see him go, as our little Sanctum was established by his beneficence," the Father said.

Nicole paused, feeling her way along this strange conversation. "Perhaps his successor will hear me."

"You should not place your hope in him, for little is known of the young man's character, nor what his rule might entail," Manworren sensibly advised.

Nicole glanced around the luxurious room to reorient herself according to the evidence of the Father's character. "But what has become of the old Surchatain, then?"

"That, I do not know, Lady Nouri," he replied. "Please, I beseech the lady to eat. The flampoyntes bake is best appreciated hot."

"I am grateful for your kindness," she replied, distracted, and dutifully began to eat while Manworren watched in almost proprietary satisfaction.

After some minutes of quiet eating, Oswald leaned toward her. "Forgive your servant, Lady, but I am bound by my promise to remind you of your vow to minister to the lepers for a day, in gratitude for your safe— departure."

Nicole jerked her head up to stare at him. "That's right! Oh, Forcht, I'm so glad you remembered!"

She turned to their host. "Father Manworren, my dear bodyguard is correct. Please show me to the lepers' quarters, so that I may fulfill my vow."

"Oh, Lady, no, no," he objected reflexively.

She looked pained. "You would not have me guilty of vow-breaking, would you, Father?"

"Of course not. Only—in these circumstances, it is not possible. There are no more lepers here," he said.

"No more lepers!" She put down her fork, and Oswald stared at the Master. "But—that's why the

Sanctum was built!—according to what we heard in Venegas," she covered herself quickly.

Father Manworren shrugged. "Yes, when it was first established, we had many applicants for relief. But the plague has since passed, and those who were here either died or moved on. We have had no new applicants for months."

"I see," she murmured stiffly. While it was true that the plague had lessened, she knew it had left behind thousands of victims that would never be whole again. The leprosarium should have been full to bursting. To put off any suspicions created by her reaction, she began diligently spooning up the rapeye.

When she was through eating, she pushed away the golden bowl and said, "I am so appreciative of your hospitality, dear Father. Perhaps you would not object if my bodyguard and I explored this lovely place?"

"Say no more, Lady." He rose from his chair; Oswald, though not finished, promptly did likewise. "Allow me to conduct you through our unworthy hovel myself, Lady Nouri," Manworren added.

He drew back her chair himself. When she stood, his hand hovered at her back, but with Oswald breathing down on him, he did not presume to touch her.

"How kind of you." She accepted the Master's invitation, directing a peeved glance at Oswald. A guided tour from the leech was not what she wanted at all, but there was no shedding him now.

Father Manworren opened a door into the enclosed garden and began leading her along the curved brick walkway while Oswald followed.

"It's lovely, Father," she murmured, genuinely

impressed, while they passed lush plantings of roses, lilies, and iris foliage that surrounded orderly beds of medicinal and kitchen herbs. A pair of medlar trees graced the center pavilion around a well. Though not as large as the kitchen garden at the palace, it was every bit as well tended, and Nicole felt right at home in it.

"Oh, nothing special at all, but it's my little joy to care for," he said modestly. Nicole glanced away from him to look at the monk who was on his knees on the brick weeding the herbs.

Turning down the path at a right angle, the Father led them to another door which opened into a large kitchen/dining hall. The first thing she noted was how well equipped the kitchen was, with a large oven and roasting pit.

The latter was fitted with a copper chimney and a contraption of cranks and gears to turn three spits simultaneously. And even though the Father and his guests had eaten for the day, three monks were still at work preparing dishes. They paused only to bow hastily before resuming work.

Nicole looked aside at the dining tables. She remembered from the plans that there was supposed to be seating to accommodate sixty Brethren at a time, but the tables and benches that remained now could seat half that, at most.

Glancing down, she could even see the holes in the flooring where permanent furniture had been removed to make room for the additional work tables and sophisticated cooking equipment.

"All this is rather tedious, I fear," Father Manworren apologized, leading them out through another door into a grassy exterior yard with a row of mulberry trees.

To their left were large pens for sheep, goats, and pigs, also being tended by brown-robed brothers, but these the Father ignored in his tour. Oswald, however, studied each monk they passed.

Crossing the yard, they turned right along a walkway to look south past the Sanctum to the Sea. Wary of storms, Ares had situated the complex inland a few miles, but still within easy walking distance of Hycliff. Nicole looked out to the beloved stretch of grey-green, now quite tranquil, and sighed to live in peace near it again, with Ares. Where was Ares?

"As you have seen the church and the travelers' court, I regret that there is little else of our Sanctum to show you, Lady Nouri," the father said. "Which is just as well, for night comes." Long shadows from sunset on the other side of the Sanctum darkened their path.

"I would so like to see the leprosarium, Father," Nicole said. "If I at least visit it, and leave a royal inside, I can say I attempted to fulfill my vow."

The introduction of the topic of money weakened him. He proposed, "Perhaps we may step inside the doorway, but the leprous air remains, and I do not wish my lady exposed to any danger."

"I shall not press farther than you allow, good Father. Please lead on," she urged.

So the Sanctum Master took them back through his quarters to the apse of the church. By this time, a monk was lighting the candles along the walls of the nave, and the Father took up a three-pronged candelabrum to provide additional light.

The party proceeded down the nave until he stopped

at locked double doors opposite the entrances to the monks' dormitory. Handing Oswald the candelabrum, the Father produced from inside his robe a key with which he unlocked these doors.

He opened them out into the nave. His guests were left staring at a second wall, a wooden one, that stood just four feet from the entrance.

Nicole impulsively stepped into this space—whether by delusion or revelation, she felt the presence of Ares. Looking up and down at a narrow corridor that extended to her right and left, she saw two more doors, about ten feet apart, set in the wooden wall.

Nicole looked back as her host reclaimed the candelabrum from Oswald and explained, "This is the vestibule, Lady Nouri, which prevents the malignant air from infecting worshippers in the church. While we had lepers under our care, there were tables set here with saffron candles which burned away the leprous fumes."

"I see," she said. He went down the vestibule a few paces to her right to open a door and extend the candelabrum. Nicole had to squeeze in beside him to look, for she wanted to see and he neglected to step aside.

It was a large room, at least fifty feet in width, with wooden walls and floors, but no windows. It was completely devoid of any furnishings that she could see, except for a brown curtain that hung ceiling to floor, wall to wall, partway through the room—about twenty feet from the doorway where Nicole stood now. A mildly disagreeable odor penetrated this barrier.

Oswald, having entered by the second door, walked on in, reaching out with the clear intention of shoving aside the curtain to reveal what lay beyond it.

Father Manworren said, "I would not do that, friend." Oswald paused, regarding him. "A few bodies of deceased lepers remain to be interred. They are highly contagious." Although skeptical, the Second did not defy him.

"Your alms would cover their burial, Lady," Manworren offered.

"Certainly. Forcht." She nodded to the carrier of the purse. Oswald then brought up a pouch that had been hanging down the front of his shirt, suspended by a cord around his neck. He opened the mouth of the pouch to bring out one royal while many more remained within. This coin he placed in his lady's hand.

Nicole, in turn, offered the gold coin to their host, carrying through with the charade of donating a measly royal to someone who outfitted himself and his quarters like a Surchatain.

She explained, "We were fortunate that Venegas trades in royals as well as cruxes"—the coinage of Scylla. "A royal will be accepted as true gold anywhere on the Continent." That last assertion may have carried an irrational tinge of pride for a Scyllan lady.

Manworren bowed deeply, his hand closing over the small gift. "Your servant humbly thanks his lady."

A bell began tolling, and he straightened. "Forgive me, Lady; that signals the dinner hour for the Brethren. I must go lead them in prayer. Come."

He ushered his guests back out to the nave and locked the door to the lepers' vestibule behind him. Nicole and Oswald watched a silent procession of perhaps two dozen monks, heads bowed, slowly proceed in two lines up the nave to the transept, where they turned out toward the kitchen.

When the monks had passed, Nicole turned to curtsy. "Thank you for your kind hospitality, Father. I and my bodyguard shall retire to the quarters you have so generously provided."

"Rest well, Lady." Manworren nodded, then turned up the nave himself.

Nicole and Oswald watched him go, then she whispered, "Did you see Ares?"

"No, Lady," he whispered back. "He is not among them."

"In the dormitory, perhaps?" she whispered.

They looked at the pair of doors leading to the monks' quarters. "While they are at dinner, you search the rooms off the left door, Lady; I will take the right," he whispered.

So she darted to the left-hand door to enter the western corridor and begin opening cell doors. (Monks were entitled to no locks.) The doors on her left led to double rooms, as hers was, but the doors on her right opened to a single cell. She opened every door down the corridor—18 in all, for she even checked her own set of rooms.

Then she met up with Oswald at the entrance to the nave. "Did you find him?"

"No, Lady. If he is not here, or in the travelers' court, or stables, or church, or kitchen, or Master's quarters, then he must be—"

"Behind the curtain in the leprosarium," she whispered.

"Yes, Lady."

B

At that time, at the palace of Westford, the bells had just tolled eight, the dinner hour. "Surchatain Henry and the Lady Sophie," Georges announced. Henry then entered the banquet hall, escorting his wife, as their guests bowed behind their chairs.

A row of tables placed end to end accommodated approximately sixty guests every evening, summer and winter, in war and peace time, due to the unabated efforts of the old dinner master, Georges.

He had now entered his thirty-first year of service in Westford, placing food in front of four Surchatains, and it was a widely repeated proverb that as long as Georges served, Westford would never starve.

Pointedly, he had been training a replacement for years, and the man had already taken over several of Georges' responsibilities, such as overseeing the kitchen mistress and her servants. But it was unthinkable that anyone should announce the Surchatain save Georges himself.

As Henry and Sophie sat at the head of the table, their guests sat, and Henry waved for the wine steward.

While the steward hurried up to fill the pewter goblets, Henry glanced down the table.

Ben, Captain of the Blue Regiment, sat around the corner to his right. The Captain was placed so high at the table, even above his Commander, due to the fact that he was married to Sophie's sister Bonnie, who occupied the place directly across from him at Sophie's left.

The girls were sixteen-year-old identical twins, both newlyweds. Sophie, though not yet Surchataine, wore her long auburn hair curled around a tiara while Bonnie, as the wife of a captain, had to make do with a jeweled clip.

In compensation, however, she wore a low-cut, voluminous gown and obvious makeup. Sophie's dress, in contrast, reflected her mother Nicole's simple, modest tastes. Ben regarded his wife's décolletage and rouged cheeks, then lowered his eyes. There would be words later.

Next to Ben sat his Commander, Thom, and his wife Deirdre. Next to her sat the Commander's junior Second in Command, Paramore. In his mid-thirties, he was as yet unmarried, because women frankly bewildered him. Being attractive personally and of high rank in the army, he was unknowingly the object of a fierce competition among the ladies of Westford to land him in matrimony. Their simpering attention he also found incomprehensible.

Beside Paramore sat the Steward Giles, also a longtime administrator, having begun his career under Surchatain Cedric, Ares' predecessor and Henry's father. Giles, spreading like a peacock in his successful transition to service under yet another Surchatain, was finding ever more lavish and outlandish outfits to celebrate his status. His ring of kinky silver hair supported his velvet hat like a crown.

Beside him sat his pale-by-comparison wife Genevieve, and next to her was the palace priest, Father Birondo. Not even the strongest spectacles could help his eyes much any more, but he sat with both his hands unobtrusively on the table before him, and the wine steward, in pouring his cup, was always careful to place its base just at his fingertips. Evangeline, Oswald's sweet little wife, watched to make sure the father's fingers found it safely, for she sat next to him in her husband's absence.

On the other side of the table, as previously mentioned, Bonnie sat around the corner on Sophie's left. Next to Bonnie sat Counselor Vogelsong and his wife Elida.

It was Giles' cross to bear that the younger Vogelsong had been given seating above him. Not to mention a Counselorship. Giles remembered when he was only an amanuensis. Bah. The only saving grace in the situation—and it was considerable—was that the Counselor had begun to confer ever greater responsibilities on the Steward.

Next to Elida, and totally eclipsing her in radiance, was Henry's half-sister Renée, twelve years older than he. Having married and shed three husbands, the blonde Lady Renée was very wealthy. She worked hard to remain beautiful, and succeeded, despite her age and her overuse of makeup.

Tonight, she was regarding Giles with a mixture of envy and derision. The ridicule that his excessive taste in clothes elicited was to her a warning, for Renée, who appreciated opulence, would not suffer to be laughed at. But at the same time, the courtiers who used to look first to see what she was wearing, now looked first to Giles. So Renée was torn between courting attention at any cost and retaining a shred of dignity.

Next to her sat Faguy, a longtime supporter of Ares' and the latest target of Renée's affections, despite the fact that she had spurned his offer of marriage years ago (which, to be fair, she probably did not remember). The palace physician Savary sat next to him, and beside Savary sat Wulfredia, lately the Chataines' chaperone before they were married, but now the doctor's assistant. Giles' senior assistant Stengi sat next to her.

The rest of the places at table were occupied by the captains and their wives, followed by the nobles and wealthy merchants who had found favor with Renée, Sophie, or Bonnie. Surchatain Henry, following Ares' wise precedent, stayed as far away as possible from seating squabbles.

Several people were burning to speak, but it was considered an unforgivable breach of protocol to introduce any conversation before the food was given due attention. So they watched intently for an opening as servants brought in savory dishes.

Taking advantage of the plentiful summer harvests in Westford, Georges served bolas with oat crisps as the first course. Then came broth saake with chicken, followed by maumenye royal.

Littering the spacious tables were also various dishes of fresh and steamed vegetables. Such menu choices reflected Ares' and Nicole's tastes; since the present ruler had expressed no desire to change anything, Georges set the menu in favor of continuity and the wise use of what was on hand.

"I have the most thrilling news," Renée announced just at the moment when two other parties were making preliminary indications of opening the conversation. "Darling Faguy and I were married today."

This elicited the attention she desired from all around the table. Henry almost spewed his mouthful, but choked it down to mumble, "Well done, old boy," to the pensive husband.

Giles stared at Faguy in transparent jealousy; half the table knew of his bouts of flirtation with the lady, who accommodated him for amusement.

His wife Genevieve, who rarely spoke at the table, said, "Our very best wishes to you," directing a smile of genuine goodwill to the newlyweds.

Bonnie craned her neck to stare down the table at Faguy as if she'd never seen him before, clearly searching for hidden attributes that might account for Renée's insanity.

Sophie exclaimed, "Oh! Congratulations, dear Aunt Renée! I'm so glad you've found someone who truly loves you."

Faguy, abashed, mouthed something while several noblemen at the lower end of the table forlornly watched their hopes of becoming the wealthy lady's husband get lopped off at the root. Doctor Savary inexplicably turned to regard Wulfredia at his left. She brushed a blond curl from her pink cheek and smiled at him.

The Counselor's wife Elida, perhaps finding courage from Genevieve (or from the fact that she herself was seated one place higher than Renée) turned to the new bride on her left and said, "Oh, yes, our very best wishes, dear lady. We must have a little celebration for you."

"Why, how sweet of you, dearest," Renée gushed, flicking her a sidewise glance. Then, turning to her seriously, Renée inquired, "Now what was your name again?"

Bonnie snorted; Elida's mouth dropped open; poor Vogelsong, entirely missing the insult, answered straightforwardly, "That is my wife Elida, Lady."

"To be sure." Renée's painted lips puckered.

Sophie glanced worriedly at Henry. Attentive to her silent plea, he deduced that this was one of those times that Ares would deploy a word to contain Renée. Scanning the table, he saw Lord Roschlau seated about halfway down.

So Henry called loudly, "Lord Roschlau! The Counselor tells me your mining pamphlets have been approved! Have you printed any yet?"

Roschlau started, then replied, "Yes, Surchatain, a few."

"Excellent! Excellent! Would you by chance have any to show me?" Henry asked genially. At this point, Thom leaned over to discreetly whisper to Ben, who listened and nodded.

"Well, Surchatain—" Roschlau slowly rose while the lower half of the table watched enviously. "I do happen to have a few with me."

"Let's see one," Henry insisted, waving him forward.

So Roschlau approached the head of the table with a

bow and withdrew from his coat a handful of folded parchments.

Henry took one to open it. "Here is the story of this nobleman's courageous, heartbreaking venture to mine greenstone from the Sasany Fields. He assented to record every perilous detail for our warning and instruction. Quite a moving story," Henry critiqued, glancing through it.

"You are too generous, Surchatain," Roschlau said uneasily.

"No, no, it's a worthy tale. Certainly essential to the palace library, don't you think, Giles?"

"If the lord would be so kind as to donate a copy," Giles simpered.

"Nonsense. How much are they?" Henry turned to Roschlau at his elbow.

"One silver piece each, Surchatain. Quite reasonable," he huffed to Giles.

Henry instructed, "Buy us three copies, Giles. You have some coins on you, don't you?"

"Certainly, Surchatain." With ringed fingers, Giles reluctantly drew out his purse to withdraw three silver coins. Roschlau hastened around the table to present him with three pamphlets in exchange for the coins.

"As a matter of fact," Henry said, "I'd strongly recommend it to everyone here." He raised his grey, knowing eyes around the table, and a score of nobles began reaching for their purses, requesting pamphlets.

Roschlau, moving eagerly from seat to seat, soon sold out of his stock on hand and began taking names. Meanwhile, Giles counted the pamphlets changing hands, for tax purposes.

During this enterprising interlude, Henry leaned toward Thom to whisper, "Have our letters gone out yet?"

"Just this evening, bound for taverns and public houses across Westford," Thom whispered back, in Ben's hearing. "Thirty of them." Henry sat back; Thom smoothed his beard away from his mouth and Ben lifted his goblet in satisfaction.

"How shall we unlock the door? I presume that the Father has the only key," Nicole whispered to Oswald. They stood in the candlelit nave across from the locked door of the vestibule leading to the leprosarium.

Scratching his beard, Oswald regarded the lock, then glanced up the nave in the direction the monks had gone, and would presumably soon return. "We could bash the Father on the head and take the key, or we could smash the lock, Lady."

She choked back a laugh. "How dare you mock me, beast? Dear Oswald, I'm serious."

"Forcht, Lady," he reminded her. "Eh, if my lady is set on getting in a room with dead lepers, then we'll essay it by different means."

Taking one of the candles from its stand in the nave, he nodded her back into the monks' dormitory. He led her down the narrow, dark western corridor to the last room on the end, that had been assigned to her.

Entering, he escorted her back to the second room, on the northwest corner of the dormitory. He handed her the candle and knelt to rummage in his pack, bringing out a short-handled axe—essential for chopping the firewood that a traveler required.

Then he cleared everything from the corner of the room and bent to tap on the boards of the back wall here and there with the axe. Finding a suitably weak spot, he aimed one blow and the plank split its entire length.

He reached into the opening to pry off the wood, revealing meadow grass, the night sky, and a portion of the road curling off in the distance. Nicole shielded the flickering candle flame from the sudden breeze.

Removing a second board created an opening large enough for her to slip though, but the dislocation of two more boards was required to make the hole sufficient for his girth.

Once he and she were both outside, he somewhat set the boards back in place with his axe so that the gaping hole would not be quite so obvious.

"Now then." Nicole turned, hand still cupped over the flame. "The travelers' court is behind that wall. It will be closed for the night, don't you think?"

"Yes, Lady. So we should have no difficulties going around it."

They embarked on a path over the meadow and across the road, passing the front of the travelers' court and stables. Turning back toward the Sanctum, they came to the western wall of the leprosarium, abutting the stables.

Oswald glanced around in the darkness, but all was still, so he used his axe to probe for weaknesses in this wall. Being of soft pine, it offered several likely points of entry. Upon the judicious application of Oswald's axe, two boards came away at once.

Nicole started forward, but he restrained her. "Lady, I request that you allow me to enter before you."

"What do you fear I'll see?" she murmured, sinking back, but he nodded and inserted the axe blade to pry off another plank.

Once he had squeezed through, he gestured for her and her light. She ducked through the hole, bringing up the candle with one hand and her sleeve with the other, to cover her nose. The odor was nauseating.

Oswald took her candle to extend it around the room. It appeared to be barren but for three blanketed forms which lay on the floor against the south wall.

"Lady, I strongly request that you remain here," he said, and she did not argue. She watched his candle advance to the forms and dip as he bent to uncover the upper portions.

She watched further as the candle traveled around the room, even entering the vestibule, before its bearer returned to her side. He gestured her out, and she quickly enough retreated through the opening.

Oswald followed, then handed her the candle so that he could begin replacing boards. "Strangely enough," he said, "they appear to be lepers that died. The Surchatain was not among them."

"Then where could he be?" she exhaled.

He shook his head, using the flat part of the axehead to tap boards back into place. "There may be more to the Sanctum than the Father has shown us," he muttered. "Such as a prison."

"But we saw the plans! There was no such secret room!" she insisted in a whisper.

Taking the candle to see that the outer wall looked undisturbed, he replied, "Not in the original plans, no, but the Father has had four years to adapt them. He has obviously done much besides that the Surchatain never intended."

"Then what shall we do?" she murmured in aggravation.

"I suggest that I return you to your room to sleep, Lady Nouri," he grunted. She gestured in resignation.

Nicole passed a difficult night. It was not the strangeness of the room, nor the hardness of the pallet that disturbed her; but she experienced troubling dreams of Ares in a monk's habit, passing ghostlike from one room to the next. As hard as she tried to follow, she could not keep up; and when she tried to call his name, nothing passed her lips but a moan.

Early the following morning, she was gently awakened by the monastery bells' tolling of matins. These bells were neither as large nor loud as those at Westford, but they had a sweet tone, and listening to the steady ringing imparted some reassurance to her. This tradition had survived the Father's changes, at least.

It seemed natural, then, almost compelling, that she should sit up in the darkness to pray for a while. She prayed for those she had left behind at Westford, for their protection and wisdom, but she also prayed for Ares, Oswald, and herself in this strange endeavor.

When she had prayed all she could, she reached out to finger the cracks of the broken boards in the dark room. Sunrise did not penetrate to her corner of the Sanctum, so she got up cautiously, feeling her way first to the washstand, where she emptied the used water into a crack in the floor. Then she found her way to the door.

When she attempted to open it, it lodged firmly against something massive on the other side. Oswald, who had been sleeping in the outer room against the door, sat up. "Does my Lady require breakfast?" he mumbled.

"Just fresh water, Oswald," she whispered. She handed him the empty ewer from the washstand.

"Forcht. Right away, Lady." He rose to find his way out of the room to the equally dark corridor.

Some minutes later, the advance of flickering candlelight heralded his return. Nicole opened the door wide for him to enter with a full ewer, which he emptied into her wash bowl.

Giving her charge of the candle, he bent for the chamber pot. "I shall go tour the grounds this morning, Lady Nouri. Eat, by all means, but please do not leave the rooms till I return."

"Certainly, Forcht," she said carefully.

"Very good, Lady."

While he was gone, Nicole bathed with a bit of old cloth and ate bread and cheese from her pack. She sat in the outer room with the door open to listen, but heard only a few monks leave cells on the far end of this corridor.

With the aid of wood splinters which she arranged on the floor, she calculated that, given two monks per cell, the dormitory could house as many as 72 of the Brethren. Obviously, there were less than half that here now, who appeared to be housed in the eastern half of the dormitory, for the most part. She wondered why that was so.

In due time Oswald returned. "Has anyone come by, Lady?"

"Not yet, O—Forcht. Have you eaten?"

"No, but by your leave, I will now," he said as he sat on the floor to open a pack.

Nicole closed the door to the corridor and sat with him. "Did you discover anything of interest?"

"One or two items, Lady." He paused to bite off a mouthful of sausage and chew contemplatively. "First, Lady, I saw the Father emerge in nightdress in something of a rage that the morning bells had wakened him."

Her brows drew together in disapproval. "All monks are wakened by the bells to pray at matins, and called to prayer by the bells throughout the day. That is everywhere understood."

He glanced at her wryly, thumbing a bit of salted cod into his mouth. "Well, Lady, we have seen that the good Father understands the Brethren's duties differently than such uninformed folk as you and I do."

"Hmph," she sniffed.

"And then," he went on, "I thought to see if I might buy hay off the Brethren for our animals, and the Surchatain's horse; but I thought first I might go check to see that they were still in the stables after all."

"Were they there?" she asked quickly, preempting his explanation.

"Not only there, Lady, but fed and groomed, all three of them. All three had been provided fresh water and hay," he said, eyeing her.

Her mouth hung open. "What of the other horses?"

"The few that are there are not so well-tended as ours," he noted.

"Ares?" she breathed in a whisper.

He shrugged. "'Twasn't you or I. Could have been

one of the Brethren, as a service to guests, but I do not know who."

There was a knock on the door; Oswald hefted himself up to open it. Brother Tassos, who had ushered her inside yesterday, stood in the corridor.

With a bow, he said, "Lady Nouri, Father Man-worren requests the honor of your company at breakfast this morning."

She glanced at Oswald, who promptly began packing away the food. Taking her cue from his willingness, she stood. "It is our honor to accept his kind invitation, Brother Tassos."

She waited until Oswald had removed everything to the back room (and stacked it in such a way as to obscure any telltale light seeping in through the damaged wall).

Then she told Tassos, "We shall accompany you, Brother." He bowed in response, his eyes flicking up at Oswald, who was clearly *not* invited.

Because Tassos carried his own light, Oswald left the candle, extinguished, in the room before he and Nicole accompanied the monk out the corridor and up the nave.

Today, Nicole knew to follow him clear to the apse. With sunrise an accomplished fact, the two large stained-glass windows in the rounded apse, facing east, filled the whole church with glowing light that made the little candle flame superfluous.

Approaching the picture windows, Nicole basked in their brilliance. In designing these windows, the Cres-cent Hollow artisan had recommended two depictions: one of Ares in battle and one of him on the throne.

Ares had mulled over his sketches for a long time, because the man was gifted and Ares greatly appreciated his work. *"What do you think?"* Ares had asked her. *"I love them,"* she had said.

Finally, Ares had approved the drawings, with minor changes: the scar on the face of the Warrior Surchatain was removed, to be replaced with bright red scars on his hands. The crown was also taken out, replaced by a wreath of thorns. The artist had accepted these changes without murmur.

Brother Tassos now led her and Oswald to the door of the Master's quarters, at which he knocked. Upon hearing the command to enter, Tassos did so, standing aside to bow and say, "The Lady Nouri and her bodyguard, Master."

"Ah." Manworren advanced with outstretched hand. "How lovely you look this morning, Lady. I hope you rested well. I grew aggrieved, during the night, when I considered the rudeness of the quarters given you."

"Oh, no, don't give it a thought, Father. I am quite refreshed." She allowed him to barely touch her fingers before withdrawing them. "As we were prepared to stay the night in your court, for you to give us rooms was beyond kindness."

"It is inadequate for someone of your status."

Her heart skipped a beat—had he somehow learned her identity? Levelly, she replied, "Whatever status I once possessed no longer exists." She spoke the truth as she perceived it: although she was still, technically, Surchataine of Lystra, she disliked ruling when it was required of her and intended never to do it any more.

The Father turned away with such a smug look that

she glanced at Oswald for his interpretation of it—did the Father think to have her at his mercy? Oswald raised bushy eyebrows a hair's width, which meant that Manworren should tread very carefully from this point.

"Well, Lady, I beg you then accept the hospitality of this inadequate table." The Father gestured to the golden place settings on embroidered table cloths.

"How kind of you," she murmured her now-standard refrain. Oswald seated her, then took the chair beside her. Manworren seated himself, lifting a finger for the wine, cheese tarts, and fritters that silent Brethren began bringing in.

Most of the monks wore their cowl hoods down, around their necks, because, frankly, it was hard to see from under a full hood hanging over one's face.

But a few, out of humility, did cover their heads as they worked, especially around the Master. Several of the half-dozen Brethren who attended the Father's table this morning had their heads so covered. The long sleeves also covered the hands, except when there was risk of the coarse cloth dangling in the food.

While debating what might be safe and advisable to say, Nicole watched one monk fill her goblet and step away. Another noiselessly stepped forward to place delicately browned fritters on her plate, then Oswald's. She could see only the brother's brown-robed form, as his hood covered his head.

But when he extended his arms to spoon the hot, fried fritters onto the Master's plate across from her, his hands were exposed. And when she saw those hands, a shock passed through her from her head to her toes. She knew those hands. They were Ares'.

4

Almost giddy, Nicole threw back her head. "What a wonderful table, Father Manworren! How excellent your kitchen is. I am consumed with envy."

Manworren looked at her in quick interest; Oswald, perceiving the abrupt change in her manner, stopped eating long enough to squint at her.

"I am delighted it pleases you, Lady," the Father replied. "I would have you enjoy these unworthy efforts for as long as you desired."

"Why, Father," she purred silkily, lowering her chin at him. "I see no reason to inflict such an inconvenience upon you." With fork still unmoving, Oswald cocked his head at Nicole's sudden transformation into Renée.

While she was careful not to look at the monk of her desires, she kept him within view. He had melted back to stand against the wall. Then, like a shadow, he moved along the wall until he came to the door leading out to the garden. When another brother entered with vyaund leche—a special egg dish—the monk slipped outside.

"Lady? Did you hear me?" Manworren said with a touch of impatience.

Nicole snapped her attention back to him. "Forgive me, Father, I was distracted by the stunning tapestries behind you. Were they made in Venegas?"

"No," he said, glancing behind him, where there was nothing to be seen but the tapestries. "Actually, they were made in Crescent Hollow." Oswald eyed the tapestries.

"Of course. I should have realized that. Crescent Hollow is famed for its artisans," she murmured, trying to keep her hand steady enough to raise her goblet. "What were you saying, dear Father?"

"I had said, perhaps you would enjoy a day trip to Hycliff?" Manworren repeated himself, placing his spotless napkin across his white robe, over which he wore a stunning embroidered chasuble.

"Why?" she asked blankly. Oswald almost choked in keeping the sudden laugh confined to his throat.

"Merely for amusement, my dear lady." The Father smiled tightly.

Hycliff, sadly run down from its preeminence of a hundred twenty years ago, now sported a few taverns and public halls that the unsophisticated considered high entertainment. No one from Westford went there unless it involved business of some kind, usually shady.

"Oh! I am so dense," Nicole said sweetly.

Manworren relaxed, issuing a polite denial with an airy wave of the hand, and Oswald's lips twitched, which for him indicated convulsions.

"You mustn't feel the need to entertain me, Father Manworren. I know you have pressing duties. Besides, what I most desire is to rest, and perhaps wander about your charming little estate—er, Sanctum," she said.

The implication that she equated him with nobility caused his chest to expand fully three inches. So he decreed, "Anything that you desire during your stay shall be yours, Lady. Anything, I say. I shall order all Brethren to give your word equal weight with mine."

"How unutterably kind of you," Renée-Nicole uttered, with moist lips and limpid eyes. Manworren almost moaned looking at her.

"Now that you have feasted us so thoroughly"—she stood from a table still filled with food, and Oswald shoveled fritters into his sleeve—"I desire simply to linger in your garden. Or sit in your beautiful church. Please do not allow me to interfere with your duties, which must tax you terribly, I know. Thank you ever so much."

With that, she glided out of the door that the special monk had used. Oswald followed her, holding his sleeve closed. Manworren turned in his chair to watch in bewildered disappointment. He had not yet touched his breakfast.

Outside in the garden, Nicole looked all around, but the monk had disappeared. He could have gone right into the kitchen/dining hall, or left into the transept of the church.

Nicole checked to make sure that the door to the Master's quarters behind her was completely closed, then she grasped Oswald's shirt front to haul herself up to his ear. He leaned down, still holding his sleeve. "That was Ares, who served the Father fritters!" she whispered.

Oswald's deep-set eyes popped open. "You're sure of that, Lady?"

"Oh, yes. I know my husband's hands," she whispered, and he coughed. "Os—Forcht, he *is* here, roaming free! What shall we do?"

He removed a fritter from his sleeve to eat contemplatively. "Well, Lady, we do just what you said: abide and watch. It's clear he's working on the sly, but made himself known to you so that you would not worry. So we will let him do what he wishes, and assist him should he require it."

"Yes," she said. She turned to sit on a stone bench beside a fragrant rosemary bush. "Yes, we will watch." And she looked between the two doors on either hand.

"Henry."

At his name, he turned abruptly from the parapet. Still wearing the breeches he had slept in, his hair blown every which way by the strong morning gusts, he regarded his young wife. Sophie had properly dressed before coming up, and the wind whipped her full skirt like a loose sail. Ryal, Henry's page (and the 12-year-old son of Commander Thom) melted back into the stairwell after having escorted her here.

"Dear heart, you shouldn't be up here," Henry said, pulling her to shelter in the stairway door. "The wind's been known to toss grown men over the parapet."

"But you come up here," she said defensively. "It disturbs me to wake and find you gone."

He stroked her silky chestnut hair. "I know; I'm sorry. I wake early and—need to think, but there are people everywhere in the palace, every hour of the day and night. Does anyone know what all these people *do* here?" he blurted.

She sighed, snuggling into his bare chest. "They're friends," she murmured.

"Are they?" he asked tensely.

"I don't see them doing any harm," she said. "Oh, Henry, can you come back to bed for a little while?" Not having appropriated many of her mother's duties, she mostly wanted to play. She was, after all, still just 16.

"A little later," he murmured, kissing her hair. He was thinking hard about what she had just said.

They don't do any harm? The cover that so many people unwittingly provided enabled the poulterer to poison Ares, twice.

They are friends? None of them were spies, or plants, or stooges, looking for ways to undermine Westford from the inside?

He thought about the ranking officer of the outpost at Odea, Captain Yonge. Looking back on his exile there, Henry realized how tolerant the Captain had been of his unruly attitude and his sensitivity about the leper's brand on his hand. The Captain could have put him in prison or expelled him twenty times with cause. But every time Henry got into another fight, Yonge just sent him out on patrol until he calmed down.

One thing Yonge never tolerated was hangers-on: you had a purpose at the outpost, or you departed at once. Time and again he was vindicated in this practice —the loiterers were caught thieving, sneaking in prostitutes, or spying for the slave traders who desired fewer hindrances to entering Lystra.

Henry suddenly groaned, "I wish Ares were here."

"Why?" Sophie seemed affronted. "He made you Surchatain! Henry, *you're* in command now."

He looked at her. "Yes, he did. Yes, you're quite right. So if I want to take off a few hours to spend with my wife, I should, shouldn't I? Well, I shall. Lady, if you will kindly ask the Counselor to cover my appointments for the morning, I will take care of a trivial matter and meet you back in chambers. Is that satisfactory?"

"Yes, my lord." She grinned, chin down.

"Excellent. Come, then." He urged her into the stairwell, and preceded her down to the fourth floor. He kissed her and sent her off toward Counselor Vogelsong's chambers, then hurried on down the stairs. He stopped by his second-floor quarters, the Surchatain's suite, to don shirt and boots, then went looking for Commander Thom.

Meanwhile, Sophie arrived at the Counselor's chambers and nodded to the guard at the door, who promptly opened it to announce, "The Lady Sophie."

She entered as Vogelsong rose from behind his table, piled high with ledgers and documents. "Lady Sophie! This is an honor. What might I do for you?" An amanuensis who had been working at a small side table sprang up to bow.

"Good morning, Counselor. Henry sent me to ask you to cover his appointments for him this morning, as he has other pressing matters to attend," she said gravely.

Her lie was transparent even to him, and Vogelsong sagged slightly. He drew a long breath, looking at her. She was the Surchatain's wife, but she was not Surchataine herself, yet. Her status eclipsed that of a Counselor—barely—but her authority did not.

Therefore, Vogelsong was not required, technically, to accede to her every demand. For the good of Westford, at this time, he knew he must not. But it was foolhardy to make an enemy of her, and, besides, he was truly fond of her. So he decided to fish for her cooperation, instead.

"I am distressed to hear that, Lady," he said carefully, stepping around the table. "The fact is, the Surchatain has appointments with several powerful nobles this morning on matters that should never have been at issue, but—we ignore them at our peril. I would meet with them myself, but, I am only one man, and have enough sensitive diplomatic work for three who are more skilled than I." He gestured to the piles of correspondence on the table behind him.

She looked at his table for a long time while he composed what he hoped was a more compelling argument why Henry *must* make his appointments this morning.

Then she said, "Am I to understand that what you have to tell the nobles is already decided?"

"Yes, Lady," he said.

"Then why should I not meet with them, and make known to them our decisions?" Ares' daughter asked.

His mouth dropped open slightly. "Actually," he mused, "in fact, that may answer it."

"Who is first this morning?" she asked.

Vogelsong quickly went behind the table to retrieve a parchment from atop one pile. "Lord Guibert," he said. "He was made nobility after realizing a fortune mining turquoise and copper in western Lystra."

"I remember that," she said, nodding. "And I always

wondered why everyone bought his turquoise when no one could be bothered to look at Roschlau's."

Vogelsong looked delighted. "Very observant of you, Lady Sophie. It is because Lord Guibert's turquoise is much higher quality than what Lord Roschlau mined.

"If you were to look at samples from each man side by side, you would see that Guibert's are a deep blue, with high luster and little foreign rock. But Roschlau's are a milky light green, brittle and dull. Even the name 'greenstone' should have been a clue to him that it is inferior grade."

"I see," she said, narrowing her eyes in the excitement of learning something new. "So what is Lord Guibert complaining about?"

"Well, it seems that he has heard about the tax relief we gave Lord Roschlau because of the failure of his mines. It would have been best had Roschlau kept the particulars of those concessions to himself, but—Guibert is now demanding equal relief, contrary to the agreement he signed with your father."

"Let me see the agreement," she said.

Vogelsong practically fell over himself to fetch the document from the back of a large book and hand it to her. Sophie read it carefully, then observed, "This is very clear. Have you the records to show what he earned?"

"Yes." With the grace of a dancer, he darted for a ledger which his astute amanuensis had already opened to the relevant page. Sophie came to the table to bend over the book and study the columns of figures.

Straightening, she asked critically, "Are there any other documents which show that Lord Guibert's obligations should have changed in any way?"

"No, Lady," Vogelsong replied, thrilled that she asked.

"Well, this is all quite plain. His request is out of the question," she said.

"Quite. But he must be told in such a way that does not affront his pride," he told her frankly.

"I see. Well, I shall attempt it. Let me borrow your man with the documents—your name is—?"

The amanuensis bowed nicely. "Your servant is Socius, Lady Sophie."

"Send Socius with me, in case Guibert wishes to argue facts," she said airily.

"An excellent plan, Lady," Vogelsong enthused.

She paused uncertainly. "Where am I to receive him?"

"In the holding room, Lady—the small room off the dais in the great hall," Vogelsong clarified. "Socius shall accompany you downstairs; you shall seat yourself at the table there, then Lord Guibert shall be summoned to you."

"Very good," she said, turning.

Vogelsong accompanied her to the door while his assistant gathered the required documents. "And if my lady will return here afterward, we will discuss the next appointment," the Counselor added.

"I will do that," she said.

A guard was summoned who escorted her downstairs to the small room off the great hall, which held only a rustic table and chair. She seated herself, spreading her hands over the inkstains that covered this table. A small thrill shot through her, as she knew that her father had used this room, and left those stains.

Socius opened the ledger in front of her, placing the agreement beside the page showing Guibert's earnings. "Thank you," she said, glancing up at him.

"It is an honor, Lady," he replied, bowing.

Something about his manner invited confidences, so she confessed, "I'm a little nervous."

"No need to be," he said earnestly, leaning down. "You simply must make Guibert understand that you have the weight of Lystra behind you. And I would advise that right away, when he comes in, you first ask him what he wants. I have seen their demands change from moment to moment."

Sophie's hazel eyes widened. "What if he demands something altogether different than relief from taxes?"

"Then say that you must confer with the Steward Giles—not the Counselor, but Giles. That puts the fear of God into them," Socius replied.

"How wise you are!" Sophie laughed, and he bowed again. She nodded at the soldier who had escorted them down. "You may bring in Lord Guibert."

She and Socius waited; minutes later they heard footfalls advance through the empty audience hall to the holding room. The door opened; the soldier saluted and said, "Lord Guibert responding to my lady's summons."

"Thank you." She nodded to the soldier, who stepped back into the audience hall behind the lord. But the door remained open, and the soldier's eyes did not leave the holding room.

Guibert, awash in finery that matched Vogelsong's for costliness (but did not quite aspire to Giles' boldness) stepped forward. His face dropped in surprised disappointment at the girl sitting before him; the soldier tapped his shoulder in a reminder to bow. This he did.

Sophie opened the meeting with, "I regret that my husband was called to attend an urgent matter, but I have been informed of your particulars, and am authorized to hear you, Lord Guibert. What do you want?"

He regarded the evidence on the table in front of her, and cleared his throat. "Hmrhm. Pardon. Is it Lady Sophie or Lady Bonnie I have the honor of addressing?"

Sophie's eyes went hard at the velvet insult. Anyone who was a regular at the court knew how much the twins resented being misidentified; further, it was ludicrous to imagine Bonnie's sitting here.

But Sophie knew not to lose her temper, so she smoothly replied, "My husband is the Surchatain, and I asked you a question, sir."

"Pardon, Lady Sophie." He bowed again, and paused. "Forgive my hesitation. I had not expected the honor of your lady's hearing me."

"Every word shall be passed on to my husband and the Steward Giles," Sophie said. "I am not here on a whim."

He glanced at the amanuensis standing beside her, who gazed back at him. "No, I see that my lady is well-suited for the task," he admitted.

Not being a longtime resident of Westford, Guibert had not the opportunity of watching Sophie grow up at her father's knee and play around him at open hearings, council meetings, and impromptu conferences over dinner. She had so thoroughly absorbed his toughness of will and clarity of thought that they sprang to her service today almost effortlessly.

Guibert pursed his lips, then proceeded to air his

grievance. "Here is the matter, then: I resent the favoritism being shown Roschlau. He has contributed far less to the palace treasury than I, and yet retains his seat at table and the Surchatain's favor regarding this ridiculous pamphlet of his. Now I even hear that he is exempted from taxes!"

"What do you want, Lord Guibert?" she repeated.

"I want equal favor," he said indignantly.

"You want us to treat you as a failure?" she asked.

His mouth dropped open. "A failure? No. How so?"

"Lord Guibert, what influence can someone have at Westford who pays no taxes?" she asked impatiently. When he failed to reply, she turned to Socius. "What councils does Roschlau sit on?"

"None, Lady. Formerly, he used to sit on the apportionment council, but his term expired and he was not reappointed," Socius replied.

She turned back to Guibert. "No one takes him seriously any more. Is that what you want?"

He looked confounded. "It appeared to me that he was receiving special dispensation."

"Lord Guibert, does Lady Rhea flirt with him?" she asked sternly.

He looked at her helplessly. "Lady Rhea . . . ?"

"The lady with the pointy chin who squints," Sophie elaborated. "You can always tell who's gaining status by who she flirts with. She has her ear to the ground to know who's on the way in and who's on the way out. It's uncanny. She started flirting with you after you hit your first lode, didn't she?"

"Yes, and she won't go away," he whined.

"Be grateful. It means you're desirable property.

You haven't seen her flirt with Roschlau in years, have you?" Sophie grilled him.

"No. Not ever," he said thoughtfully.

"Well, then." Sophie sat back, her point made.

He looked at her for a long time. "Do I have any chance of gaining the favor of Surchataine Nicole?"

Sophie looked dubious. "As . . . what?"

"As a suitor," Guibert said.

"Oh, no. I'm sorry." Sophie tried to sound genuine. "You must have missed the announcement of her leave-taking. She left Westford with Papa, and I'm sure she won't come back without him."

"No, I heard," he said a little despondently. "What about with the Lady Renée?"

Sophie looked thoughtful. "Give her a few months to get tired of Faguy, and then make sure she notices you."

Guibert leaned forward. "How?"

"Just . . . be proud, and aloof. Act like you're not interested in her at all. But make sure she sees you on the next boar hunt. She has a weakness for sportsmen," Sophie confided.

A sentry appeared at the door. "Pardon, sir. Lady Sophie, the Counselor inquires whether you are ready to hear the particulars of your next appointment." This inquiry was calculated to impress upon Guibert that her interview with him was no fluke, and it succeeded.

"I believe so. Have we got everything settled for today, Lord Guibert?" she asked sweetly.

He bowed low to her. "Very much so, Lady. Your servant is most grateful for your counsel. May I presume to call upon you again in the future?"

"Certainly." She bestowed a regal smile on him.

He departed with the first soldier, and Sophie turned to Socius with a snort. "They're all fools for gossip."

"Apparently, Lady," he agreed, grinning.

"Well." She rose, smoothing her dress. "Let's go see who's next!" And Socius gathered the unused materials to take back upstairs with them.

Meanwhile, Ryal had enabled Henry to locate Commander Thom on the rear grounds with the Second Paramore and Captain Ben. With his page in tow, Henry interrupted their conference by telling his brother-in-law, "Sorry, old man, you'll have to learn to deal with her without calling in the troops."

The officers glanced at each other, given Henry's assumption that they were in the midst of a war council. "Deal with who?" Ben asked.

"Bonnie, of course," Henry said. Ben's eyes glazed over and Thom eyed the young Surchatain.

But Henry turned to him in all seriousness. "Thom, there are too many people around." And he explained what he had learned from Captain Yonge at Odea.

The men listened as Henry finished, "How can we clear out the people who have no business in the palace?"

Thom inhaled, stroking his beard. "It's difficult," he admitted. "To drive them out without explanation creates ill will that works against us when we need their cooperation. But yes: the loiterers have become more than a nuisance; they are a danger."

There was a moment of silence as they considered their dilemma. Ryal watched without a word. "We need to make it less comfortable for them to loiter," Ben proposed.

"Or make them want to leave," Paramore said.

Thom studied Henry. "As I recall, the last time we saw a mass departure was when you created an epidemic to keep people off the second floor."

"They did rush out, didn't they?" Henry murmured, squinting. "But for an epidemic, we'd need bodies, and I'd hate to start murdering people at random."

He glanced briefly at Ben, who, anticipating whom Henry would not object to murdering, opened his mouth.

Henry hurried on, "Besides, they came right back when they realized there was no epidemic. But . . . those who feared Ares' ghost didn't come back until he showed up at the wedding, alive and well."

Another brief silence followed. "You're thinking of scaring them off with another ghost, Surchatain?" Paramore asked.

Henry glanced around to make sure no one was nearby, then draped a confidential arm over the Commander's shoulders. The others leaned in closer as he whispered, "Are there any more of those monks' robes lying about?"

"Yes, I believe we kept a few," Thom muttered.

Henry smiled. "Excellent. Commander, please call an open audience for ten of the bells."

5

Thom paused. "An open audience at ten of the bells will not give the townspeople much time to drop what they're doing and come."

"We don't need them." Henry waved dismissively. "We don't want to make it seem that we're excluding them, but the ones we want front and center in the audience hall are all these loiterers that are already on hand, conveniently enough."

"What are you going to tell them?" Ben asked, curious and more than a little suspicious.

"Not to worry, friend." Henry patted his shoulder with a bonhomie that only deepened Ben's suspicions. "I'll not bring Bonnie out, nor mention her, nor use her in any way to threaten the masses."

Heedless of rank, Thom began an exasperated reprimand but Henry hastened to say, "Just have a robe sent to my chambers, Commander. And. . . ."

He turned on Ryal behind him, who looked up with sharply attentive eyes. "Find Van Laeke. He's a fine actor. He's in the Red Regiment. Bring him to my chambers."

"Yes, Surchatain!" Ryal exclaimed, and started to dart away on his mission.

Henry caught him by the jacket and pulled him back. "Wait. One more thing. That . . . makeup. Whatever Ares spilled all over himself that turned his hands red. Can you find me some of that makeup?"

Ryal stared at the Surchatain in wordless, frozen horror at this demand, then his eyes narrowed in determination. Neither death nor mortifying humiliation would prevent his execution of his duties.

Ben suddenly interposed, "Go to my quarters—the Lady Bonnie and I are in the chambers that used to be the Chataines'. Find her maid Ninian, and tell her to give you the lady's makeup. All of it."

"Yes, sir!" Ryal saluted in gratitude.

Ben eyed Henry, almost daring him to make a comment, but the Surchatain merely cleared his throat. Thom watched his son scamper off, then rested a contemplative eye on his young master.

Faguy lay on the cot in his modest room on the third floor and stared up at the wooden underside of the floor above his head. Light from a small trefoil window, paned with greenish glass, colored the room with a rather depressing cast. He had heard the bells toll nine at least half an hour ago, but could not bring himself to get up.

He had married Renée. They had just gone to a notary in town and signed their names in his book, then she had gone to the jewelry shop next door and bought herself a necklace to celebrate. They were married, but he didn't share her quarters—there was no room for him among the more valuable possessions crowding her chambers.

Seeing that his wealth had disappeared with his last (and first) wife, he had barely any clothes to send for, and barely anything to buy new clothes with. So his new wife outfitted him with clothes she purchased from the treasury, inviting the nobles here to look on him with contempt as her accessory. And given her demands for his labor in her schemes, he had no time of his own to rebuild the kind of business that had earned him status and wealth in Prie Mer.

Thinking Ares to be dead, he had come to Westford less than a month ago wanting only to serve his widow. But now Ares and Nicole had both left Westford, and Faguy had chained himself to this vixen. Groaning, he rolled over and covered his head.

As the bells tolled ten, Thom ascended the steps to the dais and looked over the crowded audience hall. Judging from the second-tier clothing that predominated in this crowd—not the finery of the nobles nor the work clothes of servants—Henry had succeeded in drawing the audience he wanted.

"Order! Silence!" Thom shouted, and the rustling abated. "Surchatain Henry has called you to hear his pronouncement." He stepped back and looked to the side.

Ryal opened the door to the holding room and Henry emerged, wearing Ares' discarded dress blacks—the black pants and severe black brocade jacket that had come to represent the uniform of the Surchatain.

Briskly, Henry mounted the dais and turned to the

audience. "This foolishness must stop!" he shouted. The crowd went still, watching him with widened eyes.

Henry continued, "First, you repeated among yourselves this ridiculous rumor of Surchatain Ares being a ghost, roaming the palace in a shroud, with hands and feet of blood. Well, you saw how foolish that talk was when Ares was shown to be alive, did you not?" An affirmative murmuring answered him.

He began pacing on the dais. "Now, I am hearing reports of the ghost of the poulterer wandering likewise —that because he attempted to murder Ares, and succeeded in murdering the Second Rhode, his shrouded spirit now wanders the palace, hands stained with blood.

"Granted, yes," Henry waved in concession, "there have been strange sightings, even during the day. And some say that the ghost carries a vial of poison which he attempts to throw upon anyone who sees him.

"Well, I don't want to hear any more of it!" Henry stopped to gesture angrily. "These are but children's stories, and shall not be tolerated! I shall remove from the palace any who repeat such idle tales. You are dismissed!"

Soldiers began ushering the dumbfounded courtiers out and Henry stalked down from the dais to the holding room. There, he whispered to Ryal, "Tell Van Laeke, 'now.'" With a salute, Ryal darted up the back stairs.

The courtiers emerged from the audience hall, talking to each other indecisively. Since most had nothing better to do, they returned to their usual haunts on the grounds and the first floor. (Soldiers stationed at stairways prevented anyone going upstairs who didn't belong there.)

One kitchen servant, a shade smarter than the rest, paused with furrowed brow. Then he went to seek out Georges. He found the old dinner master in the maids' galley, inspecting the new dinner linens.

"Sir," the servant said, bowing, "I've just come from the open audience, where the Surchatain tol' all the people to shut their traps about the poulterer's ghost, and that there's no such thing. What do you say about it, sir?" The other servants in the vicinity paused in their work to listen. Georges' wisdom was respected far and wide.

He raised a white eyebrow condescendingly. "The Surchatain is quite right," he sniffed. "Everyone knows that the only haunting done here is around the old well room. The ghosts of those who perished in the hanging well would never tolerate the ghost of a murderer horning his way in."

The servant nodded in acknowledgment, and the other staff murmured agreement. The poulterer's ghost, indeed! The palace was already well stocked with a better class of spirits, thank you very much. With that, the servants went back to their duties without fear.

Even in daylight, even outside, certain portions of the palace were in perennial shadow due to the oriels, balconies, towers, and old, heavy vines that encumbered the walls. The south side of the palace was particularly shaded this way, and on warm, late-summer days as this, offered prime locations for loitering.

Today, a group of five courtiers gathered near the grape arbors under the second-floor balcony to discuss the Surchatain's strange announcement.

"I wonder why the Surchatain would call an open

audience over rumors of a ghost," one man mused.

A woman in the group was quick to reply, "Why, you see how gossip gets totally out of hand. But *I* think it was very unwise of him to make these silly rumors public."

Dejected at being uninformed, the first man admitted, "I had never heard them before today. Had you?"

"Oh, yes," she said, eyebrow elevated in superiority. "Of course it's all foolishness, but for the Surchatain to come out and *say so* merely fans the flames of unhealthy imaginations."

"You don't believe in ghosts?" another asked her.

"Certainly not!" she bristled. "The thought that—" She was distracted by the splashing of a few drops on her shoulder. Irritated, she looked up at the figure in the shadow of the balcony directly overhead. He wore a brown shroud with hood low over his face, and his bloodied hand withdrew a small flask—

The woman spread her hands, screaming. Her companions quickly looked up, but saw no one. With hands flailing in front of her, she ran toward the front courtyard, screaming all the way.

Nicole sat in the garden of the Sanctum for well over an hour. Though it was lovely, and the day mild, she grew restless when Ares did not reappear.

Oswald had stretched out under a medlar tree to doze, and as she watched him, she started to think that he was using the time better than she.

Whatever Ares was doing, he would not risk exposure by dallying with her in the garden—anyone who saw it was sure to report it to the Master. With a sigh, she finally got up to lean over Oswald and shake his shoulder. "Forcht."

"Um? Lady," he grunted, pulling himself up.

"I think little is to be gained sitting here longer," she whispered.

"Perhaps we might explore a bit, Lady," he offered.

"Yes, let's," she agreed.

He offered her the remaining fritter, now slightly flattened, that he had deposited in his sleeve. She declined it, so he gulped it down before they entered the north transept of the church.

From there, they passed through the nave to the traveler's court, open to the public for the day. Several travelers had stopped in to replenish their water bottles at the well, but they would probably be gone again soon. Nicole and Oswald walked on out through the front gates.

They turned left, following their route of last night around the stables. Only today, they ventured a little farther into the surrounding pasture land. One monk with a scythe was harvesting tall grass for hay, but since he worked with his head exposed, a glance told them that he was not the one they were watching for. So they passed him with a genial nod and turned eastward, toward the leprosarium.

They drew only close enough to see that Oswald had successfully repaired the hole he had made—at least to casual inspection. But in passing the corner, he nodded toward orderly piles of stones and timber. "Master Manworren has plans to build or remodel this wing," he noted.

She shook her head in dismay. "None of which Ares approved. And he would have been astonished to hear that there are no more lepers in need of care."

"We must assume that he has already been astonished by the news, Lady," Oswald observed.

"Quite so," she murmured, smiling.

At the south side of the leprosarium they paused in surprise at a set of doors standing open. She glanced at Oswald, who shrugged. "They'd've been locked last night, as well."

While they watched, a ragged gravedigger emerged from the doors, dragging the three bundles all rolled up together. He tossed them like so much garbage upon his rickety flatbed cart, then advanced with fawning bows to the monk who stood watching from a distance.

That man, covering his face, threw a coin at the gravedigger before he could get too close. He snatched up his wages, then took up the handles of the cart to lug it over the meadow out of sight.

He was paid to dispose of the bodies in the Sea, which would require him to cart them a few miles to the closest dumping spot. But that was too long a trek. And since no one accompanied him, how would they know, or what would they care what he did with the bodies?

Early on in his dealings with the monastery, he had discovered its trash pit—a deep hole dug out of the limestone just out of sight of the Sanctum and constantly kept burning. So it was a simple matter of convenience for him to deposit all bodies there, unknown to the Brethren—or these two guests.

"And that cleans out the leprosarium," Oswald muttered, watching the gravedigger haul his cart away.

Nicole nodded, looking past the departing death cart to the Sea beyond. Since no monk attended the cart, she breathed a prayer for the souls of those who were on their way to a watery grave. And she considered that, when it came time for her remains to rest until called to life again by the angel, she would rather they be consigned to the Sea than the earth.

But—what would Ares want? Where would he want to be buried? This they had never discussed. So she changed her mind: she wanted to live close to the Sea as long as Ares was close as well; but in death, she desired only for her bones to rest with his.

Until that time, she would have been happy to make the Sanctum her new home, were it not for Manworren's perverting it to his own designs. Her love of the Sea had progressed to the point that she heard the lulling of the waves at night wherever she was.

She and Oswald resumed their stroll. Rounding the southeast corner of the leprosarium, they came upon a tidy field of winter barley that had been harvested some time ago.

In the center of the field, away from the rest of the complex, stood a little house. A footpath was worn through the field to the door cf the house, thence north toward the Master's quarters and kitchen. Nicole cocked her head. "What could that building be? I do not remember it from the plans."

"Let's go see," Oswald proposed. Leading along the path, he opened the door and stuck his head in. Once Nicole saw that it didn't get chopped off, she peeked in under his arm.

They were looking into a single room with a warm,

yeasty smell. A large copper cauldron was gently boiling over a low fire. Wooden barrels stood against one wall, several covered with thin cloths. Strainers, long-handled spoons, and buckets were arranged against the third wall.

Sniffing, Oswald observed, "Well, that's good use of the barley. They're making ale, and a nice quantity of it."

The two entered to look around a bit more. Nicole went over to a shelf and picked up one bowl, then another, raising them to her nose in turn. "Yarrow and cinnamon," she told him. These were used to flavor the ale.

"Very nice enterprise," Oswald muttered. When they exited, he added, "But again, not what Surchatain Ares had in mind when he built the Sanctum."

"He stayed the night," she mused as they leisurely followed the path around the rear of the complex. "He could have ridden back to Westford and brought soldiers to evict Manworren. Why do you suppose he didn't?"

Oswald emitted a rumbling chuckle. "The Surchatain has a sly side to him. I never saw that he liked to use force when cunning would do the job so much better."

"True, Forcht!" she laughed. A passing monk, evidently on his way to the brewing house, bowed, and Nicole nodded pleasantly.

When he was out of earshot, Oswald quietly added, "Though if he needed someone to ride back and bring swords, I would be eager to do this."

She nodded. Continuing down the path, she laced her arm under his in a gesture of long friendship.

Father Manworren happened to be watching at his

open window as they passed by outside. Intent on their conversation, they did not see him, nor even glance toward his window. Manworren's brow darkened.

"Brother Tassos," he said, and that monk came to the Father's side with a bow. "The Lady Nouri moves about most freely, as if she were royalty," Manworren observed with a note of displeasure.

"Yes, Master; she does," Tassos agreed, withholding further comment until he might see where this dialogue was leading.

Manworren shifted to watch the visitors progress down the path toward the pens. "It may be that she has compromised herself with such—unhealthy freedom."

Tassos glanced uneasily toward the retreating figures. "I have witnessed nothing unseemly, Master."

"Her behavior with her guardian is loose and troubling," Manworren said.

Tassos' look grew grave. "Shall we send to Venegas to find her husband and inform him of the lady's whereabouts? He must be distraught over her absence."

Manworren considered the plan aloofly, as a connoisseur would evaluate an inferior vintage. "Perhaps. But then we should have to give her up to him, and that does not strike my fancy." With the visitors now out of sight, his eyes lost focus.

"What does the Master have in mind?" Tassos asked. He had long ago given up anticipating his Master's actions.

"The lady, in her freedom, has obviously compromised herself with her guardian," he coolly observed. "To make this public—or, the threat of making this public, should be sufficient to restrict her to more private quarters . . . where she should be constantly under my eye."

Tassos paused, evidently wary of saying the wrong thing. "Shall I summon her?" he finally asked.

"Wait," the father said, and turned away from the window.

Past the Master's quarters, the footpath forked in two directions: one fork led to the kitchen/dining hall, the other led to the livestock pens. Nicole and Oswald chose a third, unmarked route. Just to see what was there, they left the path at the fork to walk around the far side of the pens. But there was nothing so interesting as a new brew house out this way, only rolling grassland.

Then a monk carrying a bucket appeared, coming through the grass toward them. Nicole, recognizing his stride, gasped and gripped Oswald's arm. The Second spotted the brother and quickly glanced around, but no one else was in sight.

The hooded monk drew up to them and bowed. Nicole inclined her head, waiting with suspended breath.

"Greetings, Lady Nouri," Ares said softly. His hood remained low over his face, but she could see the salt-and-pepper stubble of his beard on his jaw. With such a combination of coverings, his scar was invisible.

"My dear brother has an advantage in knowing my name, when I know not his," she said cautiously. There was evidently talk among the monks, and this particular brother's hearing was acute.

"Your servant has no name, Lady; he has taken advantage of the Master's lax discipline to slip in among the Brethren and perform the tasks that they dislike. Thus no one has cared to press for a name," Ares said.

From the odor of the contents of his bucket, it was evident that one of those tasks was emptying chamber pots.

"How shall we assist you, Brother?" Oswald asked. "Perhaps ride back to fetch arms?"

"No, good Forcht. I do not wish to draw resources away from the young man while he is attempting to establish himself. You can do something else for me— but first I must warn the lady that she is being watched constantly," Ares said. Belatedly, Nicole withdrew her arm from Oswald's.

"Is she in peril, Brother?" Oswald asked, his voice a low rumble. While they talked, he was scanning behind Ares, and Ares was watching behind Oswald. As yet, no one else had come into view.

"No," Ares replied. "But it would be best for her to remain in open view in the garden or the church during the day." He turned his hooded face minutely toward his wife. "There are tapestries that are stored away half-finished; perhaps you could ask to work on one of those. And, of course, you will listen as you work."

"Certainly," she assented, a thrill running through her to be useful to him.

Ares tossed back the cowl hood sufficiently for them to see his deep brown eyes, glinting with a hard-edged humor. "And now, Brother Forcht, I will tell you what I require of you."

With great effort, Faguy roused himself out of his cot, washed his face and hands, and dressed in more clothes acquired from the treasury. When Renée had sent him up there to select a wardrobe with her money, he had taken care to pick what was neither most expensive nor most current.

After seeing what he had chosen, she had dispatched her maid to return it all and pick out suits that were most expensive and current. They were all more valuable than he cared to wear, and this also depressed him. He was the kind of man who would rather work in rags than loiter in gold brocade.

Emerging from the room, he paused to repent of his ingratitude. He had found a home among friends, with his needs provided for, and who was to say that he would not find a way to be gainfully employed?

Wasn't it also possible for him to encourage Renée toward the usefulness he desired for them both? He must have some measure of influence with his new wife, for she had asked *him* to marry *her*.

With gentleness, and patience, might he not even convince her to part with some of her wealth on behalf of the less fortunate? Thus encouraging himself, he lifted his head and straightened his shoulders to descend to the floor below, where Renée had her quarters.

As he approached her door, he was overtaken by a whirlwind in rustling blue silk. "Out of my way! I have a crisis!" Bonnie cried, elbowing past him to burst through the door into Renée's receiving room. "Aunt Renée! Ben took away my makeup!" she wailed.

Faguy watched from the open door as Renée's maid Maddie met the distraught young wife with consoling arms. Shortly, the lady herself emerged from her bedchamber to deal with the crisis.

While Bonnie threw herself onto Renée in the extremity of her distress, the lady glanced up to see the unwelcome male presence at the doorway. "Later, darling," she said, gesturing, and Maddie shut the door in his face.

Faguy stood there staring at the scrolled wooden decoration on the door inches from his nose, then turned down the corridor to trot downstairs.

The thought had suddenly occurred to him: surely he could find someone to tell him where Ares went so mysteriously yesterday morning, and why. It suddenly became important to Faguy to know.

Meanwhile, in Renée's chambers, Bonnie was unburdening herself to her mentor. "He sent that little brat—Henry's page—to make Ninian give him all my makeup! He took everything! What do I do? The rouge was blended specially for me!"

"There, there, dear. We'll address it," Renée soothed her.

"It gets worse. Worse and worse. I have to get Giles' approval on all my purchases. Giles!" Bonnie cried. "He'll never—oh, Aunt Renée, will you buy me more makeup?" Bonnie asked in breathless hope.

Renée eyed her. "I could," she said slowly, "but if your darling twit of a husband confiscates that, too, then we haven't accomplished anything, have we?

Renée paused to let Bonnie absorb that, then continued, "This is when a wife must assert herself. You must go find your little captain and tell him in no uncertain terms that he is not entitled to pilfer your personal possessions. And if he is not inclined to listen to you now, he may be more disposed to listen when he comes to bed tonight."

Bonnie smiled sideways at her "aunt" in perfect

understanding. "I'll summon him right away," she declared.

"No, darling." Renée forestalled her. "Summonses are for private meetings. Go to him, wherever he is, now. You need an audience," she purred.

Bonnie jumped up to exit the chambers in focused determination. At the head of the stairs, she accosted the sentry, "Where is my husband?"

Not mistaking her in any way, he promptly replied, "In the Surchatain's quarters, Lady."

Upon which Bonnie marched across the landing to Henry's suite. At the door of his receiving room, she ordered the sentry, "Announce me to my husband."

"Pardon, Lady . . . Bonnie," he began hesitantly, to make sure he had the right one. When she didn't object to the name, he resumed, "The Captain is in conference with the Surchatain and the Commander—"

"*Announce me*," she repeated. These men would make perfect witnesses.

Whereupon he opened the door to say, "The Lady Bonnie."

She stormed into the room. In her wrath, she did not notice Van Laeke taking off the monk's robe, his hands smeared with her costly makeup. Nor did she particularly notice Thom and Henry casually turning to quietly confer while she flounced over to her husband.

"How dare you take my makeup! I want it back!"

Ben, who had seen the horrors of war firsthand as a child, was calm as he regarded his wife's enraged countenance. "I got tired of everyone laughing at you behind your back."

She paused; Thom and Henry glanced over. Van

Laeke was watching in consuming interest. "What?" she said weakly.

Ben shifted. "Everyone is laughing at you for smearing that stuff all over your face like old ladies do. That someone so young and beautiful should want to make herself look old that way—it's hard to understand why you do it. But some people are saying that old women who are jealous of you tell you to do that, to make you look like them."

She stared at him while unprecedented thoughts roiled her brain. Then she blinked rapidly. "Am I beautiful?" she asked in a whisper.

"You are the most beautiful woman in Lystra—when your face is not covered in chalk and colored wax," he said.

"Oh, Ben." She snuggled into his arms, and he pressed his lips to her forehead. So she whispered something to him.

He turned to his superiors, who quickly looked anywhere else to hide their interest in his affairs. "May I be excused, Surchatain? Commander?"

Thom nodded and Henry huffed, "Shoo! Shoo!" waving him away.

As Ben left with his wife clinging to his arm, Henry inhaled contemplatively. "Commander," he said gravely, "I have greatly underestimated the Captain." Thom raised a brow and Van Laeke chortled.

"Excuse me. Brother Tassos?"

The monk turned attentively. "What can I do for you, Lady Nouri?"

"I noticed the beautiful tapestry hanging in the nave,

and commented on it to one of the Brethren. He told me that there are companion pieces as yet unfinished, but he did not know where they are stored. Since you have been so kind as to give me shelter, I would covet the opportunity to work on one, in hopes of showing my gratitude," Nicole said.

Tassos paused. "That would be very generous of you, Lady, only—you should know that the hands that worked them last were leprous."

"That does not dissuade me in the least. I must make some small contribution to the Sanctum, for my own pride's sake," she insisted.

"How very thoughtful of you, Lady," he replied, bowing. He quickly calculated how this might be worked out to the satisfaction of the Master. "I shall have the frame and threads of the one most nearly complete brought out for you. Where . . . would my lady care to work?"

"The garden is a lovely place to work, if the Master would not object," she said.

"I doubt that he could object to so charming a request, Lady." Especially as the Master had windows which overlooked the garden. "Please go make yourself comfortable there, and I shall ask him."

Seeing that he turned away from the Master's quarters toward the nave, she said quickly, "Oh, I don't wish to interrupt dear Father Manworren at his duties."

"Do not trouble yourself about it, Lady," Tassos urged. "The Master is merely visiting with merchants in the travelers' court. He likes to see what they have to sell that may benefit our little monastery. Once I have his permission—and I am certain it is forthcoming—I shall see that everything is set up for your pleasure in the garden."

"You are most kind," she purred.

She turned toward the garden door, watching out of the corner of her eye as he hastened down the nave. He could not believe his good fortune in the Lady's suggesting an excellent way of keeping herself under the Master's eye.

As soon as he was out the front door, Nicole hurried into the garden. Canvassing it to make sure it was unoccupied, she ran to the door of the Master's quarters and let herself in.

She glanced through the main room and the bedroom; finding them also empty, she locked the doors to the garden and the apse. Then she flew to open the back door of Manworren's quarters. Upon her gesture, Oswald slipped inside.

6

Glancing around uncertainly, Oswald muttered, "All right, then, He said small, valuable items." Far out of his depth, he looked at Nicole.

Stepping into the center of the Master's receiving room, she submerged once again into the character of Renée, this time in order to locate the most valuable trinkets at a glance. Spotting an ebony box with mother-of-pearl inlay, she hastened over to flip it open.

"Apparently, he sees no need to lock anything up," she noted, removing the unused key.

"Who would rob the chief of thieves?" he muttered.

From the box she lifted a palm-sized ivory diptych, exquisitely carved. She handed this to Oswald, and he tucked it into the folds of his shirt. Further rummaging, she brought out a jeweled rosary, which also went into her companion's bulky shirt.

Closing the box, she looked around the room. For the last souvenir, she snatched up the gold saltcellar from the sideboard—if the other items were not missed at once, this certainly would be. It was still half full of salt.

After taking possession of that, Oswald slipped out the back door again. Nicole unlocked the door to the apse, then the garden door. She emerged into the sunshine, strolling to the stone bench by the center fountain. There, she sat to serenely wait beneath a medlar tree. It really was a beautiful garden.

As an indication of her admiration of the garden, she began daydreaming about what she would change in it. A partly shaded corner, currently unused, would be perfect for milkweed, she decided. No garden was complete without butterflies.

Oswald, laden with valuables stolen twice over, lumbered around the outside of the apse, passing the glorious stained-glass windows. Scanning the fields and path, he bypassed the small bell tower.

But then he spotted a stepladder obviously for use in the bell tower. Glancing over his shoulder to make sure there were no witnesses, he took up the ladder with one hand, carried it a ways, and deposited it outside the door of the south transept, where it was painfully out of place. Then he went on in. The Surchatain had given him very specific instructions about where to place his little treasures.

Inside the church, Oswald progressed to the apse. But hearing footfalls behind him, he merely knelt before the altar and bowed his head. The Brethren passing him did so quietly, in respect of his evident prayer.

When all was still, Oswald opened his eyes and looked over his shoulder down the nave. Keeping an eye out, he stood to scrutinize the carved retable above the altar.

Now, Ares was taller than most of the Brethren, but

Oswald was a head taller than Ares. So when Oswald withdrew the saltcellar from his shirt, he had no trouble placing it just out of sight atop the high retable.

He retreated down the nave to stand in front of the entrance to the east corridor of the monks' quarters, where he looked back toward the altar. A tantalizing glimmer of gold atop the retable could be spotted from here. Closer toward the front door, it might easily be spotted by anyone with sharp eyes. And the stepladder, dropped in haste outside the church door, could provide a clue as to how this valuable object came to rest above almost anyone's reach.

The front door opened suddenly; Oswald stayed where he was while Master Manworren passed by with Tassos talking to him in a low voice: "I am sure you will see, Master, that there is nothing base in the lady—" Neither looked aside to him or up toward the retable in their haste.

Oswald watched them advance up the nave and exit through the garden door, then he took a survey of his surroundings to ascertain that he was unobserved. He slipped into the door behind him, that led to the eastern group of monks' cells.

Touching his brushy beard, he casually strolled to the end of the corridor and opened the door to the last cell on his right. This, according to Ares' information, was a double room which housed Tassos. As benefiting his station as the Master's assistant, the outer room was furnished with a nice table and chair, a small wine station, and a two-shelf library.

Oswald progressed to the inner room. Being windowless and completely enclosed, it should have been dark as a tomb. But a shaft of light from a poorly patched roof illumined it quite well. Oswald looked around at a cot with a blanket and pillow, a porcelain chamber pot, and a carved washstand equipped with, of all things, a mirror.

Suppressing a chortle at this vanity, Oswald took a step forward, upsetting a bucket (fortunately empty) that had been placed beneath the hole in the roof. He took care to replace the bucket just as it had been, then stepped around it to the cot. No mean pallet for this monk! Upending it, Oswald studied the canvas straps on the underside that supported a thin feather mattress.

He withdrew the rosary from his shirt to thread it between two straps and the mattress. Then he put the cot back where it was and bent to look underneath. The crucifix could just be seen from this angle.

Satisfied, Oswald got up to return to the outer room. Here, the placement of his last treasure was easy. As the tiny diptych opened in two hinged wings like a book, he inserted it between two books on Tassos' shelf. They completely hid it.

After a last sweep of the room, Oswald inched open the door to look into the narrow corridor. It was unoccupied, so he exited Tassos' cell, closing the door behind him. He paused at the nearby door terminating the corridor.

Experimentally, he pressed the latch to see if it would open. It did, but, hearing noises through the narrow crack, Oswald closed it again.

In the original plans for the Sanctum that he had seen, this door was supposed to open to the outside, but there was obviously another room beyond. Not knowing what it was used for, he felt it unwise to traipse through it.

The salient point he had learned was that this corridor was open on both ends, whereas the other—the one closest to the travelers' court—was locked at one end. To prevent easy escape, perhaps?

With the successful completion of his errand, Oswald ambled to the door leading to the nave and again peeked out. This time, he was compelled to wait a moment for a brown-robed figure to pass on by. Then Oswald was free to enter the nave unseen and re-enter the corridor that led to his lady's rooms.

Given that he was supposed to be here, he dropped all stealth to stroll to the room on the far end, where he ransacked his own satchel for a flask of wine and wooden cup.

Thus equipped with a reason for his absence from the lady's side, he brought the refreshment to the courtyard garden, pausing at the entrance to fill the cup and set the flask down. He eyed her sitting on a stone bench with Manworren and Tassos standing on either side of her.

Upon seeing him, Nicole said, "Forcht, isn't it wonderful? Dear Father Manworren has consented to allow me to work on a tapestry for the nave."

Manworren and Tassos looked back as Oswald extended the cup to her. "Good heavens, take that nasty brew away!" Manworren exclaimed in horror.

Oswald paused in surprise—the Valley wine that this cup contained was renown for its sweetness and purity—but the Father had turned on his underling as if he were to blame. "Bring her a cup from my store."

Tassos bowed and hurried into the Master's quarters. A confirming look flashed from Oswald to Nicole in the instant before Manworren turned back around. "I hear that you visited our little brew house," he said to Oswald.

"Yes, Father," Oswald confessed, a bushy eyebrow creeping up at this confirmation that Nicole was being watched.

"Well, you are welcome to it. We sell it to travelers, but it's not fit drink for a lady," Manworren bristled. Accepting that, Oswald drained the cup himself.

Shortly, Tassos and another monk brought out a golden goblet and pitcher of wine, along with a platter of late-summer fruit and freshly baked bread.

Borne by four other monks, the tapestry frame appeared through the kitchen door. It held a six-by-eight-foot canvas, half completed, along with the colored yarns, needle, and pattern on parchment. Nicole directed where the stand should go; Manworren corrected her minutely to keep her in full view of the window in his quarters.

Following, a feather cushion was produced for the lady's comfort in sitting for extended periods of time. Nicole accepted it all with flattering thanks, then threaded the needle and bent over the frame while Oswald made himself comfortable under the nearby medlar tree.

A few moments after the monks had withdrawn from the garden, Nicole raised her eyes to Oswald on the ground a few feet away. Through slitted eyes, he looked toward the Master's open window at Nicole's back.

Seeing Manworren standing in it, Oswald winked at

her, silently communicating, *While he's so busy watching you, he can't watch elsewhere*. Then he closed his eyes again. Smiling, she drew the first stitch tight.

A little earlier that morning, after being informed by a sentry that an open audience was to take place imminently, Sophie and Vogelsong required a few minutes to finish their consultation in his fourth-floor quarters. Even when ten bells sounded, they did not hurry, knowing that they were too important to be left out of anything that required calling an open audience. In fact, being alerted to the impending audience might have encouraged them to tarry a little longer than they would have otherwise.

So they continued to discuss in detail her meeting with Lord Guibert and her upcoming meeting with Lord Hetrick, going over Vogelsong's notes on both lords.

When all had been sufficiently and exhaustively covered, Sophie murmured that they should not keep the Surchatain waiting. Vogelsong gathered his notes to put them away and they started downstairs.

They had almost made it to the first floor when they saw the last of the stragglers leaving the hall. The open audience was over. She and the Counselor watched, stupefied, then she turned to him to exclaim, "He didn't even wait for me!"

"I didn't even know an audience had been scheduled," he returned. Seeing a sentry at the foot of the stairs turn to look up at them, Vogelsong beckoned to him.

The sentry trotted up the stairs. "Counselor?" He saluted. "Lady."

"Has the open audience concluded?" Vogelsong asked.

"Yes, Counselor."

"What was said?" Vogelsong demanded. He was affronted at not only being left out, but at missing the opportunity to be widely seen in his smart new outfit.

"Counselor, the Surchatain only told the people that he was to hear no more talk about the poulterer's ghost, and that anyone who continued to circulate rumors of having seen it was to be put out of the palace," the sentry replied.

Vogelsong and Sophie stared at each other. "That was *it*?" Sophie said.

"Yes, Lady," the sentry said.

A commotion around the front doors caught their attention. These great double doors, ten feet tall, always stood open in good weather to admit light to the foyer.

Sophie and Vogelsong watched several people rush out in confusion, rush back in, blather excitedly, and rush out. Doctor Savary was brought out of the infirmary to examine someone in the front courtyard.

The Counselor gestured to the sentry. "Go find out what is happening."

The sentry trotted down the stairs and took command of the excited courtiers. They clustered around him, dragging him outside, as well. The Counselor and the Lady stayed where they were on the steps, watching.

In a few minutes, both the doctor and the sentry came back in while most of the courtiers remained milling outside. The sentry spoke to the doctor, gesturing to the pair on the stairway, so Savary consented to accompany him up the stairs.

"Counselor. Lady," the sentry said, saluting again. "Lady Pia claims that the poulterer's ghost threw poison on her from the south balcony. She says she'll never set foot in the palace again."

Vogelsong looked in astonishment to Savary. "Doctor? Has she been poisoned?"

"In my opinion," the doctor said tightly, "people need to stop expectorating out of every window handy. Now please excuse me, Counselor. Lady Sophie. I have patients who are genuinely ill." With a short bow, the doctor stalked back down the stairs to the infirmary.

The pair on the stairs stared at each other a moment, then Vogelsong noticed a man standing in the foyer below, watching them. Seeing that he had been noticed, he bowed unobtrusively. Vogelsong gestured. "Ah. There is Lord Hetrick. Let us keep our appointment, Lady."

The sentry escorted them the rest of the way down the stairs, and Hetrick met them at the foot with another bow. He was in his twenties—young, for a lord, having gained his title by his uncle Lord Davignon's machinations on his behalf with the Steward Giles, which certainly involved large sums of money deposited into the palace treasury.

"Thank you for receiving me despite the invasion of spirits, Counselor," Hetrick said dryly.

"Your appointment is with Lady Sophie, Lord Hetrick," Vogelsong corrected him. "I am here merely in an advisory capacity."

The lord's eyes flicked briefly to the young face before him. With the same note of dryness, he replied, "As you say, Counselor."

He then glanced around the teeming foyer. "I request a private place to meet, sir."

"Yes, Lord Hetrick." Vogelsong began to move toward the audience hall, but Hetrick stopped him. "Counselor, I request a *private* place. Even now I hear repeated the significance of Lady Rhea's flirtations."

Sophie gaped at him, reddening, and Vogelsong cleared his throat. "I understand. Come."

Vogelsong turned to trot briskly back up the stairs with Sophie and Hetrick at his heels. They ascended to the fourth floor, where Vogelsong led to his quarters with the paneled walls and the guard standing outside. (He retained his quarters on the second floor mostly for the convenience of his wife Elida.) Upon their entrance, Socius looked up from his work, then stood to bow.

The Counselor walked around him to sit behind his cluttered table. "Please have a seat, Lord Hetrick. Lady Sophie."

Socius sprang forward to arrange two chairs close to the table. After they were seated, Vogelsong said, "Now you may air your concerns to the lady with all assurance of confidentiality." Sophie tried to look mature and important.

"I pray your indulgence if I address you both, given the gravity of my errand," Hetrick said, glancing between them.

"Of course, Lord Hetrick. I lean heavily on the Counselor's wisdom," Sophie said.

"Thank you, Lady," he replied with a nod, then turned to Vogelsong. "I was given to understand that you received an anonymous letter that had passed to my uncle with Lady Auer's seal," he began.

"Yes," Vogelsong said. "You recognized her seal?"

"My uncle did, after some contemplation. He felt he knew it upon seeing it, but he had to consult his register to identify it. Once he showed the entry to me, I took it upon myself to go to Eurus and see whether such a letter might be, in fact, from her hand. What I discovered was that both she and her nephew Athian were executed years ago," Hetrick said.

"You are sure of this, sir?" Vogelsong asked.

"Yes, Counselor. It is recorded in Surchatain Magnus' records. I can even quote you the entry: 'On the fourteenth of July, in the year 8077 from the creation of the world, Auer, formerly lady of Westford, and Athian, son of Backvold of Westford, were executed by the severing of the head for treachery against Surchatain Magnus.'"

"That was nine years ago," Sophie murmured.

This fact rattled her deeply: that something so crucial to today's events happened when she was seven years old. It made her eagerness to counsel nobles look silly, even to her.

"'Treachery against Surchatain Magnus'?" Vogelsong repeated. "Not 'Surchatain Ares'?"

"No, Counselor; it clearly said 'Magnus.' So whoever is circulating these letters is using a dead woman's seal to do so," Hetrick said.

"Treachery against *Magnus*," Vogelsong was still musing. The charge made him wonder if the lady and her son were executed not because of his challenging Ares, but because he failed in doing so.

This suspicion must die on the vine, however; certain that Magnus had gotten away with the murders of his parents long ago, Vogelsong saw no way to hang on him the charge of conspiring against Ares.

"Having made this discovery, *Counselor*"—Hetrick attempted to draw him back to the present issue—"I returned home in haste. This morning, my uncle handed me another letter, pressed upon him by an anonymous hand."

As he spoke, he was withdrawing a folded letter from the purse on his belt. Seeing the Counselor still entangled in vexing questions over past treachery, Hetrick handed the letter to Sophie. She read it, gasped, and almost threw it at the Counselor.

That got his attention. He noted the broken seal of the woman with the lily, then turned the letter over to read: "Whoever shall kill the spawn of Talus is promised a reward of five thousand royals from the hand of the one who writes this."

Nicole sat for several hours working on the tapestry, glad to be doing so. The garden fragrances enveloped her, and no one minded nor molested her. A few Brethren here and there weeded, harvested squash or herbs, or pruned vines, but they stayed to themselves while doing so.

She did notice how they talked to each other. Whenever two were in proximity, she would catch a whisper if she listened hard; glancing up, she might see one's lips move. But since they almost always wore their hoods when they spoke, it was impossible for her to piece two words together. All she could say for certain was that they talked a lot.

Oswald dozed (either in pretense or reality) while

she stitched, but she caught his narrowed eyes focused on the window behind her once or twice. He did not need to make any sign to tell her that Manworren was watching. Tassos came out once to ask if she required any refreshment, any thing at all, which she appreciatively declined.

At length, she shoved aside the frame to stand and stretch. It was now late afternoon. Oswald sat up, and she said, "Come, Forcht, I need to walk a bit."

He got to his feet, shaking himself like a big dog. Immediately Tassos appeared from nowhere to ask, "What does my lady require?"

"Nothing, dear brother, but to stretch my limbs. I hope that the gates to the travelers' court will not be shut for the evening while we are walking," she said.

Tassos was quick to reply, "Certainly not, Lady; do wander wherever you will. When you return, Master Manworren has begged the privilege of your company at his unworthy table."

She hesitated. "That is an undeserved kindness, but. . . ." He watched her anxiously while she went on to confess, "I fear that I may give offense to the good Master. It has been a few days since I bathed."

He almost fell over himself to assure her, "Please do not give a moment's thought to such a concern. For my lady's comfort, we shall fill a tub in a most private corner of the wash house. When my lady returns from her walk, she may bathe in complete comfort and privacy."

"Oh! That would be a most kind and welcome accommodation!" she said honestly. "I accept. Please thank the Master. Come, Forcht."

Oswald stepped to her side, and they exited the garden into the apse. They strolled down the nave without speaking, but at the door to the travelers' court, both looked back to the retable. A glint of gold could be seen atop it. They glanced at each other, then went on outside.

A dozen travelers had stopped in the court for the night, as only a few hours of good daylight remained. Nicole and Oswald passed through the court and turned left to walk past the stables and leprosarium, as before.

They did not speak, choosing to reserve their attention for everything they passed. The south doors to the leprosarium stood ajar amid evidence that the cleaning and refurbishing were fully underway.

The two walkers progressed eastward, passing the brew house, where a monk emerged with three large clay jars on a handcart. He bowed to them in passing; they nodded and watched him pull the cart up the path.

"If he's taking the brew to the travelers' court, there's an easier way. He'd cut his trip in half taking it through the church," Oswald observed.

Nicole laughed, "Oh, dear, Forcht! The Master would never countenance ale in the church."

"Hmph," he said. "Maybe so, maybe no."

They continued their circuit around the apse and the Masters' quarters. Here, Nicole was careful not to look toward his window. She was also careful to walk a respectable arm's length from her bodyguard.

Where the path forked, they came upon their first disagreement: Nicole wished to round the far side of the pens, hoping to chance upon Ares again, but Oswald said, "Lady, to walk so far out of our way again invites suspicion. If we are merely out for a walk, let us stay to the path." Reluctantly, Nicole agreed, and they took a lesser-traveled path between the kitchen and the near side of the pens.

By the time they passed through the travelers' court and re-entered the nave, they found Tassos waiting for them. He bowed, saying, "If my lady will accompany her poor servant, I shall show you to the mean accommodations for her bath."

"Gladly. Please allow me to fetch clean clothes," she said, turning into the west corridor of the monks' quarters.

Oswald accompanied her to her room at the far end, then stood at the door while she retrieved a fresh (very plain) cotton dress, clean underlinens, and a comb from her bag.

The two of them met up with Tassos in the nave, and he led them down the east dormitory corridor. At the end of the corridor, he opened the unlocked door into a large wash house/storage room. Glimpsing wet fabric in tubs and on washboards, Nicole gathered that washing had been suspended while the room was vacated for her use.

"If it please my lady"—Tassos gestured to the corner, where light steam rose from a filled wooden tub. Soap, towels, and a chamber pot sat nearby, and surrounding all were large scrolled screens.

"How very excellent. Your kindness never ceases to amaze me," she said, briskly drawing one screen into place. Oswald extended the other to completely enclose her in the corner.

"I am gratified it pleases my lady. If you will leave your, er, soiled garments there, we shall be pleased to wash them for you," Tassos said to the screens. Turning to Oswald, he noted, "You may wait outside."

In response, Oswald turned his back to the screens, folded his thick arms, and looked down on the monk. Clearing his throat, Tassos withdrew.

After a moment of quiet, Nicole whispered, "Are you there?"

"Yes, Lady," Oswald rumbled.

"Good." She began undressing, then paused. Her corner bath had been set up against the bolted door leading directly to her room in the west corridor.

Doing nothing about it for now, she finished undressing to bathe thoroughly, washing her hair as well. But when she had dried herself and dressed, she leaned down to study the bolt. It was a simple draw bolt. Quietly, she drew it just past the jamb, so it was not apparent that the door was now unlocked.

While she combed out her long hair and plaited it (her only adornment being the embroidered ribbon she used to secure the braid) she peeked out from behind the screen to see what she could of the room. She noted that additional tapestries were stored here, as well as pallets, blankets, and household movables.

All dressed, she pushed one screen aside, and Oswald turned around. "Do you wish to bathe, Forcht?"

He snorted, "What care I who I offend here?" On second thought, he said, "When my smell overpowers the lady, I will dip myself in the brew-house cauldron."

She chuckled, squeezing his arm, then let go of it before exiting to the east corridor.

Brother Tassos met them right away, as before, to lead them through the nave to the Master's quarters. At this point, Nicole was beginning to question the Sanctum's layout. The church seemed to be utilized mostly as a highway of convenience to another destination within the complex, rather than the center that Ares had intended.

Entering the Master's receiving room, Tassos announced, "The Lady Nouri—and her guardian," he ended on a mutter.

Manworren came forward to greet her as though he hadn't seen her in a fortnight. "Dear Lady Nouri! How refreshed you look!" Lust betrayed itself in his eyes as he regarded her damp hair.

"Your hospitality is so overwhelming, I may alarm you by staying far longer than you intended," she replied lightly as he seated her at his lavish table. Glancing over the dinner ware, she saw no replacement for the saltcellar. Had he missed it yet?

"The lady will thrill an old monk with such careless talk," he chided happily, and she smiled at him. His face lost some levity while he watched her annoying guardian take his seat, but then he recovered to wave for the wine.

While the golden goblets were being filled, and the Master turned to issue instructions for the serving of the first course, Nicole studied his slightly altered appearance. His face was clean-shaven, as before, but she now detected a hint of perfume. Also, instead of the religious robes, he wore an elegant suit that would not be out of place at the palace table at Westford.

The preoccupation with fine clothes that permeated Westford was a bondage that Nicole was most anxious to be rid of. She had never been comfortable with judgments based on the threads on one's back, and found the return to plain dress liberating. But, given Manworren's aspirations, she began to wonder when he would suggest something finer for her to wear.

But even she was startled when he turned back to her, effusing, "If my lady finds our pathetic efforts pleasing, so that she would consent to stay for a while, I would consider it a signal honor to dress her more appropriate to her station."

Oswald, glowering, set down his goblet with such a solid *thunk* of disapproval that the Master jumped. He was forced to quickly backtrack. "I understand that the lady dresses as she chooses for travel—"

Nicole chose to rescue him from his greedy misstep. "You are far too generous, Father. I will think on it."

He squirmed like a pleased child, and it was all Nicole could do to refrain from laughing at him. He snapped his fingers at the woefully slack servants—that is, Brethren—who finally began bringing in platters of fried spiced onions and roasted duck. She scrutinized every anonymous set of hands that came within her view, but did not see Ares tonight.

So they began eating. The dishes were wonderful, of course, and it was amusing to watch Manworren watch Oswald shovel in prodigious quantities of laboriously created masterpieces.

But she grew restless, desiring to help along Ares' plan so that she would not be faced with the necessity of dressing like Manworren's mistress.

Shifting, she sighed, "Dear Father, your staff have excelled in their efforts once again. However, it is my shame to have a weakness with roasted meats, and that is salt. May I have just a pinch?"

7

Manworren did not respond at first, being preoccupied with Nicole's hair falling about her shoulders. Then he blinked and repeated, "Salt."

"Yes. For the duck," Nicole said.

She carelessly looked away, and Oswald pretended not to notice while Manworren waved impatiently at Tassos. That brother went to the sideboard and stared at it.

A second later the Father barked, "Salt!"

Nicole, taking a delicate bite, said, "Forgive me, Father; I spoke too soon. The duck is perfect as is; any further seasoning would ruin it."

But, of course, it was too late. Tassos was desperately foraging all over the sideboard, and in its drawers, and even underneath it, for the missing saltcellar.

Brimming with fury at the delay, Manworren turned around. Tassos, pale, looked at him, spreading empty hands.

The Father's eyes latched onto the usual resting place of the precious saltcellar, and its barrenness almost seared them. He turned back around to the table with shallow breathing and ashen face, which his guests studied.

"Truly, Master Manworren, if you offered me salt now, I should refuse it. The duck is sublime. It would be obscene to tamper with it," she insisted.

He looked at her with sightless eyes and uttered a weak laugh. Then he turned back to watch Tassos flounder around the room in panic.

"Search the kitchen!" Manworren ordered, and Tassos fled through the garden door.

The master returned grimly to his dinner, but his guest was now invisible to him. Nicole and Oswald glanced at each other and ate in silence.

Faguy wandered forlornly around the ground-level floor of the palace. Having been to the open audience, and heard the commotion raised by Lady Pia's sighting of the "ghost," he deduced that Henry had found the hauntings useful enough to continue. But Ares was no longer the ghost; not knowing who was, or the reason for the machinations, increased Faguy's sense of severance.

That he was an outsider here was reinforced by every blank face he met—he was known to no one here, save his new wife; he had nothing to do here, save wait on her. So far, he had been unable to even broach the question of Ares' whereabouts with anyone.

Rounding the corner of the lower corridor near the infirmary, he paused at the sound of someone singing. It was the richest voice he had ever heard, full of color and expression. He stood still, soaking in the comforting waves of song:

"Domine Jesu, fili David, miserere mei.
Quid vis ut faciam tibi?
Domine, tantum ut videam.
Respice, fides enim tua salvum te fecit."

An educated man, Faguy understood the Latin at once. It related the encounter of Jesus with the blind man, in which the blind man approaches the Master and pleads:

"Lord Jesus, Son of David, have mercy on me."
"What do you want me to do for you?"
"Lord, that I may see."
"Receive your sight, for your faith has made you whole."

Peeking around the corner to locate the source of this golden stream, Faguy saw a large woman in a plain aproned dress, her blonde curls spilling out from under a small cap. She was singing as she stood over a work table with mortar and pestle, crushing herbs.

At his movement, she paused in her song to regard him. "Please continue," he said urgently.

Her round face took on a worried look. "Are you in need of the physician, sir?"

"No, Lady," he said despondently. "I am merely in need of —someone to tell me where Lord Ares and Lady Nicole went in such haste."

She looked on him sympathetically, but Doctor Savary came out from a side room to study him. Savary said, "You are the one who received the Second Rhode's last words, and raised the alarm that the poulterer had poisoned him. What is your name again?"

"Faguy, Doctor," he said, bowing.

The doctor narrowed his eyes at him while Faguy shifted in discomfort, knowing that he had no business in the infirmary.

Then Savary instructed, "Close the door behind you." Faguy did so at once. Savary whispered, "Both those you seek have gone to the monastery and leprosarium south of here—the Sanctum. There was something awry that he wished to address."

Faguy's mouth dropped open. "Thank you, Doctor. I shall repeat this to no one."

Savary nodded curtly, then paused at the lady's smile of tender approval. "Is the potion ready, Wulfredia?"

"Very nearly, Doctor."

As she returned to her task, Faguy opened the door behind him. "Please carry on, Lady, with my gratitude."

He exited into the foyer, clutching this pearl of knowledge in wonder. The Sanctum! He must go at once. If something was amiss there, Ares might need him. Faguy took a step toward the beckoning, open door to the front courtyard, then looked down at his ridiculous brocades. Go dressed like this?

And . . . what would the Lady Renée say of his leaving? The fact that she had no use for him at this very moment did not imply that he was free to do anything without her consent.

He sagged under invisible chains. But echoes of the song floated back to him like a prayer: *Domine Jesu, fili David, miserere mei. . . .*

A man entered the foyer from outside. Why he

should attract Faguy's attention was not readily apparent. He had a prim little mustache and thin brown hair that extended in wisps past his hat. He was dressed in the kind of faux elegance worn by up-and-comers who had greater ambitions than income, and after a moment, Faguy recognized him as one of Giles' more self-important assistants—Stengi

Faguy watched listlessly as he stopped right at the door, lifted a parchment, and shouted to all within earshot, "I need to see Lord Chernay, Lady Renée, Lord Faguy, Lord—"

Faguy rushed up to him. "I am Faguy. What is it?"

Although irritated by the interruption of his announcement, Stengi said, "Lord Faguy, you and the Lady Renée were wed by notary Spechler in the jewelry district?"

"Yes, yesterday," Faguy said.

"Well," the other harrumphed, "Spechler had let his license lapse for failure to pay notary fees, so all official actions performed by him since June the eighth are null and void. You will have to reapply for a certificate of marriage to another notary."

"He—failed to pay his fees—?" Faguy stammered.

"I have the book right here, sir," Stengi said, tapping a slender volume hanging by a ring at his waist. "He never paid me."

Faguy looked confused. "I was under the impression —that only the Steward may collect fees."

"I often go out in his name, Faguy," Stengi said, bristling in offense at the implication of overreach. "And I am telling you, your marriage is null and void."

Faguy stared at him. When the ramifications of this

revelation dawned upon him, he seized Stengi's shoulders and kissed him on the forehead.

"I say, sir!" the assistant protested, straightening his hat.

But Faguy was leaping up the stairs like a hart escaping the trap. Grasping the banister, he rounded the curve in the stairway, bypassing the second floor on his way to the third—

And then he stopped. He should tell her. He should not count on her receiving such news from the Steward's assistant.

With sinking heart, he turned back toward the second-floor landing. But if he told her, she would want to go straightway to another notary, and could he withstand her?

He didn't know. But his conscience would not suffer him to run off under the delusion of helping Ares when he had left his pseudo-wife in ignorance.

So he approached her door with leaden feet, and knocked. After waiting a while, he was poised to knock again when the door opened.

Maddie eyed him with a smirk and said, "The lady is busy. What do you want?" Open-mouthed, Faguy withdrew his hand. "Well?" she prompted impatiently. He was speechless at the fact that his wife's maid was barking at him as if he were the slop-boy.

"Nothing." He left her at the door and bounded once again for the steps. Heart racing, he flew to his room.

He fell on his knees to look under the cot and retrieve his clothes—*his* clothes, the trousers, pants and jacket he had worn from Prie Mer.

Hands trembling with excitement, he removed the

palace finery, including the pointy, girlish shoes, and dressed himself in these humble work clothes. Then he sat on the cot to put on his worn but sturdy leather shoes. Leaving the brocades and silks on the cot, he hastened back down the stairs as rapidly as his invigorated legs could carry him.

Before leaving the palace, he stopped in the infirmary, poking his head into the door of every room until he found the physician bent over a table of potions. "Doctor," Faguy said quietly, "I have come to tell you that I am on my way to the Sanctum, to see if I might be useful to anyone there."

Savary straightened from his table, squinting at him. "Let me have you supplied with provisions," he said, gesturing to the kitchen.

"No, Doctor; thank you. I intend to beg," Faguy said with a quiet thrill. "I will take nothing, unless you wish to send something by my hand to anyone there."

Savary shook his head. "He's not indicated the need for anything," he muttered. Then he observed, "You will not be riding, then."

"I have good enough transportation," Faguy said, lifting a knee to slap it.

"Then take this." The doctor reached over to a side table, plucking up a handsome old walking stick made of polished oak. "The man who owned it previously needs it no longer."

Faguy hesitated, then accepted the smooth, sturdy stick with the gnarled head. "Thank you, Doctor. This I will take."

He saluted with the stick, and the doctor nodded in return. "God speed."

With that, Faguy exited the foyer, trotting down the wide stone steps to the cobbled courtyard. He left through the tall, open gates, then took to the southbound market road, singing, *"Domine Jesu, fili David, miserere mei. Quid vis ut faciam tibi? . . ."*

Henry, his grey eyes focused and serious, stood in the Surchatain's chambers holding the latest letter bearing Lady Auer's seal. Close by on either side were the Counselor Vogelsong and the Lady Sophie; standing a pace off, to give him breathing room, were Commander Thom and the Second Paramore.

But all were silent while Henry digested the short letter. Presently he looked up, and the Commander regarded the triumph in his eyes. "A reward of five thousand royals for my death. That must mean I'm very important!" he crowed to Thom.

The Commander smoothed his bristles away from his mouth, as he tended to do when concealing a smile. But Vogelsong upbraided the young Surchatain, "This is a most grave matter."

At the same time, Sophie cried, "Henry, it's not funny!"

"No, dear heart." He clasped her to kiss her on the forehead. "But neither is it the end of the world. Ares got death threats all the time."

"Surchatain, I do not ever recall a bounty of five thousand royals on his head," Vogelsong said sternly.

Henry looked up in wonder. "You mean I'm more important than Ares?" Henry could not have been more thrilled had he been named Surchatain of the World.

Over the Counselor's aggrieved sputtering, the

Commander observed dryly, "It may be, Surchatain, that someone sees you as more . . . vulnerable."

"That hurt," Henry said, then sighed. "I suppose you're trying to make me look at it as genuine. Well. The author can't be that hard to track down. Who do we know that has five thousand royals to waste on my poor carcass?"

"We could ask Giles." Thom muttered, "but of the nobles I know who could scrape together that kind of gold, none has the overriding desire to be rid of you, that I'm aware of. They all gained their wealth under Surchatain Ares; since you are so clearly continuing his policies, it would seem counterproductive for them to want you dead."

Paramore asked, "Then, could it be someone who, of himself, does not possess that kind of wealth, but is in a position to receive payment from Lystra's enemies?"

Thom raised a brow at him. "That is a distinct possibility."

"So," Vogelsong said, "it could be anyone with a grievance. Anyone, rich or poor, known or invisible. Like the poulterer."

There was a heavy silence. "Well, there's that," Henry said with finality, tossing the letter onto his scrap paper pile.

The others quickly looked at him. "Surchatain, how shall we answer this?" Vogelsong said, again sounding like a chiding schoolmaster.

"How? I don't see how," Henry admitted. "We have enough ears listening in the public houses and taverns; I'm not going to start dragging people off the street and interrogating them. Ares got these things all the time and paid no attention to them. It is a course of action that I like."

Vogelsong looked vexed, but Sophie watched quietly. Henry's dogged adherence to her father's example was comforting to her. Then Paramore said, "Be that as it may, why should we not—step up our counteroffensive?"

The others looked at him in interest. "What do you mean?" Thom asked.

"Well, our counterfeit letters, Commander," Paramore said. "If our enemy is blustering threats under the dead lady's seal, then perhaps we should, too."

"But who would we threaten?" Vogelsong asked.

Henry's eyes had locked onto Paramore in a pensive, half-smiling gaze. "I like the way this man's mind runs," the Surchatain murmured. He looked off in contemplation. "Offer . . . *ten thousand* royals for my murder."

The others regarded him warily. "Too risky, Surchatain. Someone may take it seriously," Thom objected.

Henry looked at him. "Then offer five hundred thousand royals for my demise."

"There's not that much gold in all Lystra!" Vogelsong sputtered.

"Exactly," Henry replied. "Anyone with enough awareness to plot the murder of a Surchatain would realize that. Then how shall our real enemy make his legitimate offer distinct from the mad propositions cluttering the taverns?"

Again a silence. "It is clever," Thom admitted. "But still risky."

Henry shrugged. "Did you expect to appoint me Surchatain and then keep me under glass? It is my lot to be tested. Ares told me this plainly, and in front of you all."

Thom turned to Vogelsong. "Where are our counterfeit seals, Counselor?"

"In my chambers. I will fetch them," he replied, moving to the door in rustling silks. Henry smiled in satisfaction, taking Sophie's fingers to kiss them, and she studied him.

After a few hours of hiking down a dusty road under a late summer sun, Faguy had stopped singing. He was entertaining no second thoughts, but knew that he had no chance of reaching the monastery before nightfall, which meant that he would make a bed for himself somewhere in the open field without food or drink to sustain him on the remainder of his walk tomorrow morning. This did not trouble him, especially; it would merely give added realism to his role as a beggar when he finally reached the Sanctum.

He did experience a qualm now and then at the thought of wild animals. Ares had long ago cleared out the wolves around Westford, but the farther afield one went, the more dangerous it was to lie down unprotected in the night.

Once, years ago, Faguy had seen a man torn apart by wolves; to this day, if he had fevers or bad indigestion, that sight recalled itself to him in nightmares. Faguy shook his head as if shaking off those night terrors. No matter what, he was determined to go where he might prove useful, and pray the Lord protect him.

He walked on as the sun descended, grateful for the aid of the stick—a fine stick, sturdy, with not a trace of splinters. And it was just the right length for him! Walking along, he was caught up in admiration of the stick for so long that, by the time he glanced up, he was startled by the appearance of a cart off the side of the road ahead—at least, in the gathering gloom, it looked like a cart, sitting lopsided.

In great curiosity, Faguy left the road to examine the thing. He discovered that it was indeed a cart with a broken axle—a fairly new cart, at that. Faguy could see fresh ruts in the turf where the cart had veered off the road upon the break.

Retracing his steps to study the tracks leading up to the wreck, he discerned that the cart had been driven most carelessly down the center of the road, no doubt very fast, and probably had broken its axle upon the sudden necessity of turning off the road quickly to avoid a collision.

Returning to the cart, Faguy ran a hand over the padded leather seat and embossed trim. It was also an *expensive* cart, the vehicle of a nobleman's son, no doubt. Faguy snorted at the father's likely reaction to his son's return on a bareback horse, with no cart!

"That cost me a hundred royals!" the father would thunder. *"I wanted a new one, anyway,"* the son would shrug.

In the midst of these imaginings, Faguy's attention was drawn to something yellow in the grass about ten feet away. He went over to look, and quickly bent to pick up a whole, unblemished golden apple.

A few feet away lay another apple, with one bite out

of it. Faguy snatched up that one as well, brushing ants from the bite mark. Eagerly, he continued to search through the grass, and found bits of sausage that had been broken apart. Wiping dirt from one piece, he tasted it, and found it quite good.

He looked back to the cart, almost visualizing the youths—for there must have been more than one—sitting in the broken conveyance for their picnic. Having never known real hunger, they played with the food, taking a bite of this or that before tossing it away, or at each other.

Faguy canvassed the whole area until it got too dark to see well. At that time, he climbed into the cart to enjoy a fine dinner of sausage, apples, oat wafers, and a little wine left in an unbroken flask. Then he settled down on the plush leather seat under a clear, starry sky to sleep.

The Sanctum was in an uproar. It had begun quietly enough, with Manworren merely glaring at Tassos while he lurched from shelf to drawer to corner in his fevered search.

As dinner progressed with no saltcellar, Manworren deserted his guests to conduct his own search in the kitchen. Nicole and Oswald, still eating, could hear his strident voice promising a lashing to the careless fool who had misplaced it.

"Tassos is the *only one* who handles the dinner ware! When will you presumptuous idiots remember that?" Manworren's voice floated clearly through the garden to the table where his guests sat.

Oswald was taking advantage of the distraction to

eat everything in sight. "More bread, Lady?" He offered her the silver bowl holding three hand-sized, fresh-baked loaves.

"No, thank you, Forcht," she replied, so he tilted the bowl into his shirt, depositing the loaves therein.

He drained his cup, then half-stood to reach for the wine pitcher. "Worthless fools! Careless dunces!" the Master's disembodied voice continued.

"More wine, Lady?" Oswald offered.

Nicole swallowed her mouthful of onion, then lifted her goblet. "No, thank you; it's still almost full."

So Oswald threw back his head and upended the pitcher over his mouth, producing a perfect stream that flowed down his throat, terminating in a few drops on his beard. He stifled a rumbling burp.

"Beg pardon, Lady." He wiped his face on his sleeve.

"No offense taken, dear Forcht," she replied. "Will you be so kind as to pass the tarts?" They paused to listen to a fearsome clatter of pots and pans from the kitchen, muted by the intervening distance.

"Certainly." Oswald carefully transferred to her hand another silver dish containing four small custard-filled pastries. In a rare act of greed (because they were so very good) Nicole took two.

Another resonant crash. "Someone will pay! Someone—" The Master's tirade was aborted, and there followed a stark silence. Nicole and Oswald paused, looking at each other.

A flash of brown past the garden door caught her eye. As she leaned over to look, Oswald turned to the garden window, and saw two more robed figures shoot from the kitchen door to that of the transept across from it.

He and Nicole regarded each other, then simultaneously rose from the table and exited the Master's quarters into the apse. They went only as far as the transept crossing to look down the nave.

Through the open doors at the end, they could see the robed figures frantically accosting the weary visitors that had settled down in the travelers' court for the night, it being now just twilight. Amid indignant protests, their belongings were searched and scattered.

With mounting astonishment, Nicole watched the outraged visitors scramble to gather their property. Then the gates of the court were opened, and the travelers tossed out one by one.

Nicole touched Oswald's arm, directing his attention to Tassos, emerging from the east corridor of the monks' quarters. He turned down the nave to enter the west corridor. "He failed to search his own rooms," Oswald whispered.

"So now he is searching ours," she returned in like voice.

Detecting movement behind them, Oswald turned to glimpse shadows pass across the stained glass windows of the apse. "They are searching everywhere," he noted.

Over the next half-hour, while daylight slipped away, the two visitors watched brown figures flit like frenzied ghosts through every corner of the Sanctum.

Nicole observed two enter the vestibule, and presumably the empty leprosarium—and come out again straightway, holding their sleeves to their faces in protection of what leprous vapors might remain. But contracting leprosy was, apparently, preferable to what would happen to all of them should the saltcellar not be found.

Glimpsing a light in the garden, Nicole went to the transept door, standing open, to watch a monk with a candelabrum rifle the basket of yarns beside the tapestry frame. Finding nothing but yarns, he took his candelabrum to every bush and flower bed, searching.

Another monk brought a spade to begin digging any place in the bed that looked to have been recently disturbed. Oswald, coming to her side, muttered, "They'd dig for a long time before finding anything *I* chose to bury."

It was now almost completely dark. The two visitors watched Manworren emerge from his quarters with both hands full of candles. "Light!" he shouted. "I want every corner lighted!"

As monks rushed forward to take the candles he brandished, he brushed past his lady guest with neither acknowledgment nor apology. She lifted an eyebrow at her bodyguard, who smiled grimly.

Shortly, the whole nave and apse were ablaze with the light of scores of candles in wall sconces with reflective bronze backs. Tassos, entering from the now-empty travelers' court, called to his superior, "Master Manworren!" The Father was disquieted enough to forget protocol and hurry to meet him.

They stood just across from the entrance to the west corridor. Manworren swung around to scan every inch of the lighted church as Brother Tassos reported, "Master, all the quarters have been searched. The leprosarium, the brew house, the stables, have all been searched.

"The garden is being dug up, but it may take some time . . . to. . . . Master, what is it?"

Manworren's piercing gaze had traveled past his visitors in the transept to settle on a glint of gold above the retable. They turned to follow his gaze, but could not see what he saw. Tassos studied the altar and retable, but was likewise in the dark. "What do you see, Master?"

In a hollow voice, Manworren commanded, "Bring me a ladder."

8

Brother Tassos blankly repeated, "A ladder? What may we fetch it for, Master?"

Father Manworren began stalking back up the nave toward the apse, so Tassos followed.

Turning back to the brown robes that stood by hesitantly, Tassos gestured at them as a group. "Bring the stepladder from the bell tower!" Two monks, moving swiftly to comply, collided with each other. Meanwhile, a third hurried out the north transept door.

In seconds he returned, bearing the stepladder. "Brother Tassos, it wasn't in the bell tower! It was sitting just outside the door here."

As if unhearing, Manworren took the short ladder and spread its legs in front of the altar. Monks began gathering in the apse and nave to watch in silent apprehension. Oswald and Nicole remained where they were in the crossing, also watching with all apparent curiosity.

Manworren mounted the stepladder, which trembled underneath him. Grasping the retable, he reached over the top and brought out the saltcellar. A stricken silence attended him as he descended the ladder, gripping the precious receptacle.

Scores of eyes went back and forth between the purloined saltcellar and its late hiding place. One set of eyes, brown and luminous with laughter, watched from under a hood on the edge of the horrified group.

In the midst of this silence, Nicole said, "I've quite finished the duck, Father."

"Surchatain Henry and Lady Sophie." Georges' sonorous voice announced the ruling couple precisely as the eighth tolling echoed away, signaling the commencement of dinner. Sixty guests standing behind their chairs bowed as Henry escorted his wife into the banquet hall and sat her at the head of the table.

Taking his seat beside her, he waved for the wine steward almost before his guests could be seated. "No stinginess tonight, good steward! Fill them till they overflow!" he ordered.

Giles quickly looked up, for Valley wine was expensive—but seeing as the palace owned the vineyards, there was little objection that even the Steward could muster.

In literal obedience, the wine steward carefully filled each goblet just to the rim. This required great skill on his part, but not as much skill as did lifting such a goblet to one's lips without spilling wine on one's expensive clothing.

Vogelsong observed, "The Surchatain is in high spirits tonight."

"Yes, Counselor; I am." Henry confessed that fact, but not the reason for it: the idea that someone took him seriously enough to offer five thousand royals for his murder thrilled him.

And even now, at least twenty counterfeit letters were being sneaked into public houses all across Westford, offering outlandish and conflicting rewards for Henry's assassination; for finding Lord Fancsali (who was dead) to crown him Surchatain; and for proving that the world was flat. The last geographical challenge was Vogelsong's idea, for he had recently acquired translations of Pythagoras, Aristotle, and Ptolemy for the library.

Continuing his theme, Henry explained to the Counselor, "If you were married to the most beautiful woman on the Continent, you'd be in high spirits, too."

Blushing, Sophie tossed her head with the fabulous crown of silver vines, gold leaves, and alexandrite grape clusters dangling over her ears.

Fortunately, Henry did not compound his unintended slight with an apologetic glance toward Vogelsong's wife Elida; as a matter of fact, Henry had probably forgotten that Vogelsong was married.

But Renée, sitting at Elida's left, snorted mildly. Here was an interesting lapse on Renée's part, considering her intense interest in dinner seating. Given that Faguy was supposed to be sitting at her left, it would seem inevitable that she would notice his absence. However, being preoccupied with scanning the dress and placement of other people at the table, she did not.

Part of the reason was that Doctor Savary, who normally sat to Faguy's left, knew that he would not be at table, so unassumingly moved up to his seat, and everyone down his side of the table followed suit. So all that Renée detected, at the time, was that there was a male to her left, as there should have been.

In response to Henry's boast, Ben, sitting at his right hand around the corner of the table, cleared his throat in disagreement. Bonnie, across the table from Ben, cooed and wiggled at her husband.

That got Renée's attention. She leaned forward to sharply study her protégée, who wasn't wearing a lick of makeup. This was troubling, and the lady sat back to debate with herself how to address it.

Servants began bringing out peas, glazed sops, and crustades—custard pies with spiced minced veal. Thoughtfully stabbing at the sop with her fork, Renée turned to address a comment to the person she had assumed to be her husband. That is when she noticed the aberration.

Staring at the doctor who was unaccountably sitting beside her, she bristled, "What are you doing there?"

Hunched over his bowl, he glanced up. "Eating."

Wulfredia issued a melodious giggle; Renée bypassed the affront to glance around the table in sudden awareness that someone was missing. "Where is Lord Faguy?"

Savary sat up. "He went to the Sanctum." Henry, Thom, and others at the head silently noted that.

"He needed some peace," an unidentified wag commented.

A ripple of mild laughter went around the table. Incensed at both the laughter and the illegal absence, Renée sputtered, "He can't go anywhere! He's my husband!"

Giles, across the table from her and one seat down,

was quick to take advantage of the opening. Daubing at the corner of his mouth with a linen cloth so as to display the fine ruby ring recently acquired for his pinkie, he said, "Dear Lady, I suppose you did not receive my assistant's report? Oh, dear. The notary who married you and Lord Faguy was operating illegally. You are not married at all."

Renée stared at him, speechless, while Stengi, down the table, murmured confirmation.

"How inconvenient," Elida purred with just enough venom to win Renée a few sympathizers among those who resented Vogelsong's sudden airs.

She did not respond, for the apprehension was sinking in that Faguy, rather than take steps to correct the problem, had taken steps away, hastily. Then again, she knew that he had come to her door this afternoon; but what, precisely, had passed between him and Maddie, she didn't know. She hadn't cared to ask.

Regarding his sister's chalky, bloodless face, Henry looked around the table for a diversion. "Lord Roschlau!" he called, and all heads swiveled toward the lord, who practically jumped up. "How goes it with the pamphlet sales?"

Roschlau cleared his throat, then admitted, "Exceedingly well, Surchatain. I am . . . most grateful for the Surchatain's patronage. Word of your kind approval has spread across the city like fire. I have received orders which warrant a second, larger printing, and a single order of fifty copies for the university. In addition, I have received requests for copies from Eurus, and. . . ."

As he went on and on about the success of the story

of his unsuccessful venture, Lord Guibert watched in growing disgust. Then he considered: if a failure sold well, what would the market be for the story of a success? And he began to compose in his head the text of his own pamphlet: *The history of the greatest mining success in the history of Lystra began on an otherwise uneventful summer's day. . . .*

Following Father Manworren's successful recovery of the saltcellar, the Sanctum settled down a bit, although the gates were not reopened to the dislodged travelers. Nicole and Oswald withdrew to their rooms for the evening. She carried a lighted candle, as it was dark as pitch in the corridor.

Immediately upon entering the inner room, they noticed the disarray of their possessions, which had been thoroughly searched.

"Is anything of yours missing, Lady?" Oswald grunted, leaning down to pick up a flint box that had been opened—as if a saltcellar could fit inside it.

"No, Forcht," she said, retrieving articles of clothing scattered about. "You carry our coin purse, and that is the only thing we have of value."

He stopped. "Hold the light down to my pack, if my lady will." When she did, he said, "My skinning knife is gone. And the axe."

They looked at each other, and Nicole observed, "I think the dear Father does not trust you with anything that could be used as a weapon."

"Then he'd have to cut these off," Oswald said, raising his fists.

This she wryly acknowledged, then said, "No

matter," adding under her breath, "we shouldn't need the tools, as we won't be leaving any time soon."

Looking out the door down the empty corridor, she gestured with a whisper, "Let's see if it remains open." She took the candle out of the room.

Oswald followed her the few feet to the north end of the corridor, to the door to the wash house. Quietly, she tried the latch, and found it bolted again. "Oh!" she breathed in aggravation.

He shook his head. "We should have known that they'd check it, Lady."

Though disappointed, she agreed, and they returned to their rooms.

They were settling down on their pallets—Oswald in the outer room, eating the bread from his shirt, and Nicole in the inner, with the door open between them—when they heard the quiet grating of a bolt being drawn and a door opening.

Nicole looked up to whisper, "Someone just opened the door to the wash house."

A few seconds later, the door between Oswald and the corridor began to creak open. He and Nicole stared hard at the widening crack in the flickering candlelight. Oswald stood, raising the candle to illumine the doorway more completely.

At the entrance of a hooded monk, Nicole leapt up to throw herself on him with kisses. He wrapped his arms around her and she pushed away the obstructing hood to reveal the lined face and deep scar. "Ares, sleep with me tonight," she breathed.

He looked to be considering it. "Would you rather I sleep with you or get rid of Manworren?" he asked.

"Both," she said.

He chuckled, glancing up at Oswald, who, out of deference, raised his face only when he was addressed. "Excellent placement of the saltcellar, Forcht. What does Brother Tassos have in his room?" Ares asked in a low voice.

"Ah, a rosary under the cot, and an ivory diptych in his bookcase, Surchatain," Oswald whispered.

"Very good," Ares said while Nicole snuggled in his arms. "Then I'm off."

When he disengaged from her, she uttered a disappointed protest. "Shh!" He grinned. "Just a little longer. I have much to do tonight." He added to Oswald, "The corridor is now open at both ends."

"Surchatain," Oswald acknowledged. Ares kissed his wife, flipped his hood back over his head, and melted into the dark corridor. Oswald sat to finish off his bread.

Going back out through the deserted wash house, Ares felt along the wall for the door to the east corridor. He opened it noiselessly, turned into the corridor, then opened the door to Tassos' outer room. It also was black as a moonless night, but since he had been through these rooms earlier, the layout was imprinted on his memory.

Entering the inner room, he paused to listen to Tassos' snoring. Then Ares approached the cot and leaned down to whisper, "Tassos. Tassos."

"Uhh." Without the aid of light in his eyes, the monk did not come fully awake.

"Tassos, you are a thief," Ares whispered.

"Uhh?"

"You are a thief, Tassos."

"Oh, no, no," he mumbled.

"Yes, Tassos, you are a thief. Look under your cot," Ares whispered.

"Uh?"

"Look under your cot," Ares repeated.

While Tassos muttered some unintelligible reply, Ares slipped back out the door to the corridor, thence to the wash house, to see to his other tasks.

Early the following morning, the Sanctum bells began tolling the hour of prayer—with immediate and disparate effects on the residents. Nicole, awakened by the ringing, sat up to listen a moment. With what rhythm and grace the bells were rung!

Suddenly smiling in the darkness, she breathed a prayer of thanksgiving. "Thank you for my darling Ares. Thank you for this beautiful place. Thank you for cleansing it."

Beyond her doorway, Oswald opened his eyes at the ringing and looked around the still-dark room. He muttered to himself, "Wonder what else he's been up to?"

As the bells continued tolling, Tassos awoke from troubled dreams. He pulled himself up to a sit, stroking his face, and murmured, "Who started ringing the bells in the morning?"

Then his hand froze over his face as he recalled something—or thought he recalled something—from the night before. Was it merely a dream? Or a warning spirit? There was only one way to tell.

He took up the unlit candle from his bedside table and carried it to the wash house, where embers lay smoldering in the fire pit. Tassos lit the candle here, then hastened back to close himself in his inner room, taking care to shut both doors.

Hesitantly, he got on his knees beside the cot to extend the flickering candle underneath—and gasped. With trembling fingers, he loosed the precious rosary from its hiding place and studied it. "No," he breathed. "It cannot be. How have I done such a thing?"

When the bells continued to toll, Manworren sat bolt upright on his feather mattress and roared, "Find out who is ringing those infernal bells and STOP HIM!"

The monk on night watch at his bedroom door obediently ran out of his chambers. Hampered by the fluttering robe, he stumbled around the outside of the apse in faint daybreak while the bells continued to sound.

What madman is ringing the bells? We shall soon know. No one has been authorized to ring the bells for matins since—Here he paused in his stride, an icy fear creeping over him. *No. It cannot be.* Resuming his run, he rounded the corner to the entrance of the bell tower, wrenched open the door, and ran inside.

Panting, he stopped to let his eyes adjust to the darkness. No one was here. But the vibrations from the swing-chimed bells, all three of them, still hung in the air; their ropes still quivered.

He touched a trembling rope in mild awe, then stepped to the staircase to look up—all was dark and still. Because he sensed a presence nearby, he began to hesitantly climb the treacherous, open-sided stairs.

Then his hands went cold. *It no earthly ringer; it is Gruse, the leper ringer, come back to his beloved bells*—So the monk thought, and truly believed.

Stumbling back down the stairs, the monk backed out of the bell tower in haste. And the phantom rose from his hiding place on the stairway, just ten steps up from where the monk had stood.

At the abrupt cessation of the bells, Tassos blinked. He still sat on his cot, staring at the jeweled rosary, lustrous even in feeble candlelight. *I must do something. I am not a thief. I must return it to the Father.*

Buttressed by these thoughts, he slipped the rosary around his neck, then donned his robe to hide it. *I will return it. I would not harbor anything stolen from Master Manworren.*

But then the acknowledgment rose from his conscience: the rosary was not the Master's. It had been donated by a wealthy patron who intended it to be sold and its proceeds used to care for the lepers. The Father had simply put it away in his jewel box. Master Manworren was the thief.

With these grim thoughts, Tassos left his rooms, candle shaking in his hand. He went directly to the Master's quarters. Letting himself in quietly, he glanced around the outer room. Given the morning light streaming in through the eastern window, Tassos was able to extinguish the candle. He eyed the door to the sleeping chamber warily—the Master was habitually a late sleeper. No doubt, he was still abed.

Catlike, Tassos crept to the fine ebony box and opened it. Again glancing at the door, he swiftly removed the rosary from his neck and laid it in the box. He was sifting through the treasures, trying to see if anything else might be missing, when he heard, "What are you doing, Brother Tassos?"

He spun to see Father Manworren eyeing him from the door of his sleeping chambers. Tassos bowed. "Master, after the regrettable events of yesterday, I thought it wise to conduct an inventory."

The Father narrowed his eyes at him. "Yes, Tassos. That is an excellent idea. Have my breakfast made, then we will begin such an inventory. Together."

Faguy awoke early from a restful night on the long, leather-covered cart seat, intending to resume his trek to the Sanctum at once. Stretching and yawning, he stepped out of the cart to relieve himself a little ways off from it.

He was hungry, certainly, but not nearly as hungry as he would have been without the excellent meal provided him last night. He hiked up his pants and paused, wondering if he might be able to find something more in early daylight that he had missed in yesterday's twilight.

So he began foraging in the general area of his previous discovery. Sure enough, he soon located two more fat apples. Tucking one in his pocket, he began eating the other as he set southward on the road again, twirling the excellent stick before setting it to its task.

Nicole was not terribly surprised when an invitation from Manworren to breakfast did not appear. "I've fallen out of favor," she pouted to Oswald.

"Flesh and blood can't compete with gold in the Father's eyes," he muttered, rummaging through their pack. "They didn't see fit to take our provisions." He brought out gingerbread, currants, and a cord of dried venison.

Following a less sumptuous, but more peaceful breakfast than what Manworren provided, they returned to the garden. Its plantings had been slightly disturbed by the search efforts of the previous evening, so Oswald went around tamping dirt back down around roots and refilling haphazard holes.

Nicole took up her station at the tapestry frame, surreptitiously watching the activity beyond the open kitchen door. Oswald reclined in his position under the medlar tree, from where he could see directly through the window into the Father's receiving room.

A few hours later, well before noon, Faguy was surprised to see the Sanctum come into view already. He picked up his stride to the front gates—and was astounded to find them shut and barred. Some consternation rose in him: had it closed? Were Ares and Nicole gone? Would he have to return to the palace?

Then he saw the welcome sign posted to the side, and read it thoroughly. With that, he felt justified in knocking. So he rapped smartly with his stick on the gates, and continued to knock until he heard a bolt sliding back on the other side.

The gates were opened just enough for a brown-robed monk to look out. "What do you want?"

Faguy closed his gaping mouth at the uncouth welcome and said, "I am a traveler desiring benefit of the shelter that Surchatain Ares provided here."

"Eh." Reluctantly, the brother opened the gates narrowly, and Faguy entered the courtyard to see it devoid of visitors.

While he was looking around in bewilderment, the

monk began a retreat to the church entrance, leaving the gates barely open, at least. Faguy caught at his wide sleeve. "And may I have a bite of bread, Brother? From the store that Surchatain Ares provided for wayfarers?"

The monk gave a long look at his repeated invocation of the founder, but grunted, "I will bring you what's left over."

"Thank you, Brother." Faguy released his sleeve to sit on the edge of the well and draw up the bucket.

Shortly, the monk reappeared with a trencher of brown fries—brown bread seasoned, dipped in egg batter, and fried. Taking the trencher with appropriate expressions of gratitude, Faguy tasted a piece, then stared at the departing monk in wonder.

This excellent stuff is the leavings? How do they contrive to eat so well? He finished off the bread, then sat in the shade of the deserted courtyard to watch and listen.

At the palace at Westford, someone else was up early—for her. Given her busy evening schedule, Renée seldom got out of bed before noon. But the bells had just sounded ten when she emerged from her bedchamber to have Maddie assist her in making her toilet.

Sitting at the vanity before her mirror, the lady opened a porcelain jar to critically evaluate its contents. "I'm getting low on chalk, Maddie."

"My lady's been using more of it lately," the maid observed, taking up her long blonde hair to begin brushing it.

Renée looked at her in the mirror. "Well then, you need to go buy more, don't you?" she said coolly.

"Yes, Lady," Maddie said, expressionless.

Renée continued to eye her in the mirror, then casually asked, "What did Lord Faguy want?"

"Lady?" Maddie paused brushing to look at her in the mirror.

"Lord Faguy. When he came to the door yesterday afternoon. What did he say?"

The maid made a contemptuous face. "Nothing. I told him you were busy and he went away."

Renée's eyes did not leave her face. "That was my husband, Maddie."

The quiet tone got the maid's attention. "Yes, Lady."

"From now on, I expect you to treat him with the deference due his rank," Renée said.

Maddie's eyes widened at this unprecedented demand. "Yes, Lady. But I understand that—he's—"

"Gone," Renée exhaled, looking away. Her eyes evaluated something midair, then she adjusted the luxurious silk robe around her. "Summon Bonnie."

The change of topic caught Maddie by surprise. "Bonnie?"

"Yes, Bonnie." Renée's eyes flicked back to the mirror. "It has been brought to my attention that the Captain's wife needs to acquire some backbone."

"Yes, Lady." Maddie put the brush down on the vanity and departed the room.

She was gone for quite a while, during which time Renée applied her makeup, experimenting with new rouge and eye shadows. Finally, the maid returned, alone.

When Renée turned in displeasure from the mirror, Maddie hastily curtsied and said, "Pardon, Lady; she says she's a married woman now, and won't be summoned like a child."

Renée took a deep breath to compose herself, then said in a steely voice, "Where is she?"

"In her quarters, Lady," Maddie replied.

Renée waved impatiently, ordering, "Help me dress," and Maddie flew to her wardrobe.

In less than a quarter hour, the lady emerged from her quarters, perfectly attired and coifed. As she floated down the corridor to the Surchatain's wing, she reminded herself not to be overly harsh with her young protégée—Bonnie simply dissolved under her rebuke. The girl had to be reoriented to her priorities *gently*. And the first thing she had to learn was not to let a husband rule her.

Reaching the door of the chambers that Bonnie and Ben shared, Renée instructed the sentry, "Announce me."

He knocked. Hearing, "Enter!" he stepped into the room and intoned, "The Lady Renée."

Any response, if there was one, seemed to be a . . . giggle? The sentry paused, and Renée swept in past him. As always upon entering this room, she faltered.

It was big. So vast, so capable of holding comfortably all the treasured furnishings that were now crowding Renée's own cramped quarters. This suite was larger than either the Surchatain's or Surchataine's suite, and the only things that made theirs more desirable were the garderobe and tub built in. But this suite, with its marvelous windows, was now occupied by a couple who could no more appreciate it than her hostler Jack and his wife.

Hearing chatter from the bedchamber, Renée snapped out of her envious reverie. She reminded herself firmly to be gentle with the impressionable young girl, then went to the doorway and looked in.

Bonnie was standing over a pile of dresses on the bed. Her wardrobe stood open, and two other girls were arguing with each other. "No, take the red! It's terribly outdated, but it's got gold trim, and Meuer will give you a good price for it—enough to get *two* new dresses!" Meuer was the seller of quality second-hand goods in Westford.

"She doesn't *want* to get rid of the red, you goose—the Captain favors that one! Don't you remember he said she looks like a temptress in it?"

"He meant *whore*, you pathetic—"

They suddenly broke off their argument to look at the intruder. Bonnie turned. "Oh, hello, Aunt Renée," she said mildly. Then she turned back around to muffled snickers.

"What are you doing?" Renée asked.

"Getting rid of old clothes so I can buy new ones," Bonnie answered with a toss of her head. "The red goes." And the girl who had been arguing against it gathered it up to toss it victoriously onto a heap of similar rejects.

Renée glanced at the costly gown, crumpled in disgrace on the floor. It was one that she had bought for Bonnie personally just last winter.

"Why are you doing that, darling?" Renée asked, flicking a condescending glance at Bonnie's dress auditors to turn their laughter against them. "Just tell Giles what you need."

Louder snickers. "That worked so well for *you*, didn't it?" one girl muttered.

"What?" Renée demanded.

Bonnie elbowed her friend, then explained, "I told you, Aunt Renée—one of the last things Papa did before he left was have Giles put me on an allowance. The only one who can change that is Henry, and he won't."

"Well." Renée assumed a superior air, smoothing her upswept hair. "Since he is still my little brother, I will have to work on him for you."

She paused to make sure Bonnie understood who was still her most powerful friend in the palace. "By the way, I was sorry to see that you didn't get your makeup back last night."

Now the girls fairly guffawed, and angry red flashes actually appeared across the lady's vision. "Be quiet!" Bonnie shouted at her friends—but she was fighting the laughter herself.

Pressing her lips together to contain it, she turned seriously to her mentor. "I didn't want to wear it anymore. Ben says it makes me look like an old woman." And the unanimous expression of the three youthful, makeup-free faces that gazed at the lady said, *Like you.*

"I see," Renée murmured. "Well, then." She turned to leave, and the haggling over which dresses to take to market resumed behind her.

With quiet dignity, the lady returned to her chambers and sat at her vanity. Whispers of gossip about old ladies who used chalk rolled over her like morning mist. She stared at her reflection for long minutes, then went to the washstand and dampened a soft cloth. Sitting again, she used the cloth to gently wipe one half of her face clean.

She studied the contrasting sides for some time before cleaning the other half of her face. Then she looked down at the nearly empty porcelain jar, and set it aside.

Her maid entered the suite with fresh laundry. Renée stirred. "Maddie."

"Yes, Lady?" She paused in putting up the clean clothes.

"Have Jack outfit my carriage. Make sure he takes a hamper from the kitchen of the best they have on hand. And help me pack."

"Pack, Lady? For a day trip?"

Renée's blue eyes narrowed thoughtfully. "Possibly. But for possibly longer. I need simple, yet elegant clothes. No dancing dresses. And sturdy shoes. No jewelry. And . . . no makeup."

Maddie looked perplexed. "Where could my lady possibly be going that you don't want your jewelry and makeup?"

"To the Sanctum, Maddie, dear," Renée purred, studying her own clean, suddenly young-looking face in the mirror.

9

Horrified, Maddie exclaimed, "The Sanctum! That nasty leprosarium? Oh, no, Lady—you simply mustn't! It isn't healthy or safe. It's not a proper place for my lady at all. There are no men, only monks and lepers! I don't want to go!" In her blathering, the uppermost thought in her mind finally slipped out.

Renée regarded her in mild humor. "You aren't going with me."

The maid paled at the rebuke. "Not going with you . . . ? I have to! I'm your personal attendant!"

Renée rose from her vanity to open her massive wardrobe and begin pulling out the clothes she wished to take. "Why should I need a personal attendant at a monastery, which will be chock full of men eager to wait on me hand and foot? No, I shall take only Jack."

Then she paused at the wardrobe. Reaching another section, she began yanking out a flurry of expensive dresses.

"What are you doing, Lady?" Maddie gasped.

"These I want you to take to Meuer right away," Renée instructed. Gown after gown in the most sumptuous colors, with the most elegant tailoring and trim, landed on a pile in the middle of the floor.

"Meuer? Isn't he the second-hand seller?" Maddie asked dubiously.

"Yes. Quickly."

Dazed, the maid began picking up the deluge of fabulous gowns. Two was all she could hold at once, though ten more lay piled around her. "What . . . how much does my lady want for them?"

"Nothing. You're to give them to him," Renée said briskly, critiquing the mountain of silks and satins. For good measure, she pulled two more dresses out of the wardrobe—one that she had not even worn yet.

Maddie stared at her as if watching the lady's mind finally crack under all that makeup. "*Give* them to him? Why? That means he will sell them cheap, and drive down the price everyone else might get for their dresses."

"Exactly. Maddie, dearest, take them *now*," Renée uttered, and the maid hastened to scoop them up.

Maddie summoned two other servants to assist with the transport of the gowns. While they packed the dresses properly in light cotton sheeting and loaded them onto a cart in the courtyard, a line began to form at Meuer's shop.

Meanwhile, Renée packed her own bags. She required only three, so severe was her paring down of necessities. Then she dressed herself in elegant yet subdued travel clothes, with only a stunning feathered hat for adornment.

She debated the contents of her purse, finally settling on the trivial, portable sum of seventy royals. The purse itself she secured on a silver chain around her waist, which allowed the purse to lie hidden in the folds of her skirt. She lifted the lid of the chamber pot to drop the rest of the coins, over a hundred, inside.

Then she reclosed the pot with a sigh. How inconvenient that her little brother should discover the hiding place for her gold. While he would never take any himself, he was unable to keep his mouth shut. She must think on that.

Renée stepped into the corridor to gesture to a sentry. "Take my bags downstairs." With a quick bow, he entered her receiving room to stare dismally at the large, overstuffed brocade bags.

From the corridor, her icy voice wafted back into the room. "Are you coming, darling?"

Inhaling, he bent to hoist the largest bag on his shoulder, the next largest under his arm, and the third in his left hand. Then he tottered out toward the curving stone stairway.

Less than a half-hour later, the lady and her bags were departing the palace courtyard accompanied only by her driver, Jack. She settled back under the silk-fringed top of the one-horse carriage, watching with approval as other, ruder conveyances made way for hers on the road.

Adjusting her hat to completely shade her face, she murmured, "You should have known you couldn't escape that easily, darling Faguy."

Raising her voice to deaf Jack, she leaned forward to thump him on the back. "Make him step lively, Jack!" He looked back questioningly.

"GO FASTER!" she shouted. He nodded, flicking

the whip over the horse's back, and the carriage lurched forward.

Father Manworren pushed back from his excellent breakfast of eggs fried with onions. "Now then, Brother Tassos," he said to his sweating assistant. "Let's you and I begin our inventory, eh? And let's start with the ebony jewel box."

Tassos was mouthing a labored reply when a cry came to their ears. In the garden, Nicole and Oswald heard it and looked toward his window.

Shortly, no less than three of the Brethren, cowl hoods down on their shoulders, came rushing in a blind panic into the Father's quarters, all crying at once, "Master!" "In the leprosarium—" "You must come—"

"What? Stop this jabbering and tell me what the problem is!" he snapped.

One, pale and trembling, said, "Father, the builders entered the leprosarium this morning to resume the reconstruction, and then fled, crying to high heaven. They said—there was—and then we went in to look, and, there was—You must come see it!"

"Bah! Fools!" Gathering his brocade lounge-robe around him, the Master stalked out of his quarters down the nave, Tassos trailing him. Nicole and Oswald looked at each other, then leapt up after them.

By the time the Father had reached the door to the vestibule, a sizable crowd of brown robes was at his heels. "Open it!" he ordered Tassos, who brought out his keyring with shaking hands to unlock the door. After some fumbling, he succeeding in getting the door open.

The Father brushed him aside to enter, throwing

open one of the inner doors. While the monks hung back, Nicole and Oswald slipped in behind him to look.

When Manworren yanked aside the curtain, even Nicole, sturdy as she was, gasped. Because the south doors stood wide open, the light fully illumined every corner of the large room, empty but for one explicit display. Oswald studied it in frank admiration, and the remaining Brethren who dared peek through the doors stood paralyzed in fright. Tassos stepped full into the room, gazing.

The blackened, charred remains of a skeleton dressed in a clean white leper's shroud sat up against the south wall. Its lower jaw, barely hanging onto the skull by burnt ligaments, hung loose in silent, macabre laughter.

The bones of its feet and lower legs that protruded from the shroud were crossed at the ankles, left over right, in a casual, rakish attitude. Its left arm was folded across its shrouded ribcage to provide a base for the elbow of the right arm, the forearm of which stood upright. Of the clawed fingerbones on the right hand, the index alone pointed upright, to the ceiling.

"It is a sign. A warning," Tassos breathed. "He is warning us that heaven is watching."

"It is a jest," Manworren uttered through clenched teeth. "And we have a jester in our midst." He turned to scrutinize all who were behind him, including Nicole and Oswald.

Unflinching, she returned his scrutiny. "What human jester would risk contracting leprosy to stage such a wretched joke?" she asked.

At this reminder of the contagion, the others began

falling back away from the doors, shoving each other to get out of the vestibule. "Stop! Return at once! Remove that thing!" Manworren shouted.

No one obeyed, so Oswald shrugged. "I will."

The Master eyed him. "So you are not afraid of it, eh?"

"No," Oswald said flatly, "since you know I'd never leave the lady's side to do such a thing, nor would she have a hand in it."

Manworren lowered his eyes at the unarguable logic —his guests were not responsible for this outrage. Then he grunted, "My gratitude to you, then."

Oswald barely inclined his head, then asked Nicole, "Will my lady wait in the garden till I return?"

"Of course, Forcht. Be sure to stop in the wash house on your way back," she replied, and he bowed to her.

"Permit me to escort my lady back to the garden," Manworren said, attempting to reprise his role of host.

Nicole averted her eyes noncommittally. The Father's brocade robe, secured around his paunchy middle with a slippery red silk sash, was gaping open at the chest and the legs, exposing far more white flesh and greying body hair than she ever wanted to see. So she walked ahead of him quickly to her bench in the garden. Tassos followed pensively.

Nicole took her seat on the stone bench, pulling the tapestry frame toward her. Manworren paused. "Would the lady care for some refreshment?"

"No, thank you, Father," she replied, glancing up.

Tassos came forward to hand her the pillow that had gotten misplaced the previous evening. "Thank you,

Brother Tassos," she said warmly. Nodding diffidently, he turned to the Master's door.

Opening the door, he yelped in distress. Manworren rushed to the door, shoving him aside. Nicole jumped up from the bench to look.

The three stared into a room that had been turned upside down. The precious contents of the ebony jewel box had been thrown across the floor and the box itself upended. Drawers in the sideboard stood open, emptied of their silver and gold ware, which were also scattered like trash. Fine linens had been tossed from their cubbyholes to rest on furniture or floor.

Despite the disarray, all that had been ruined (that Nicole could see at a glance) was the salt. The saltcellar had been emptied in a pile on the colorful rug, then feet had trampled the salt before the golden container itself had been dropped upon the remains. The imprints of sandals, which all the monks wore, were clearly visible in the salt.

Studying the disorder, Nicole discerned Ares' touch at once. Nothing had been destroyed except the salt, and there was probably nothing taken; it had all been simply —exposed. All the hidden treasures had been discovered, and a judgment rendered as to their relative worth.

While Tassos gazed around the room, he felt a flood of relief. Anything that was missing could now be ascribed to the vandal that had struck when Tassos himself was with the father in the leprosarium.

It suddenly occurred to him: *The bell ringer, the vandal here and the prankster in the leprosarium—the same person is doing it all. Or . . . has convinced others that enough is enough. There is rebellion in the Sanctum.* The identity of the ringleader was almost a secondary question; it was apparent that the simmering outrage had found a vent. And this thought filled the brother with a quiet thrill.

"Upon my word," Nicole said, looking around. "Who knew that there was so much wealth here? My offering of a royal now looks to be a drop in the ocean." Seeing Manworren's jaw working furiously, she returned to her garden bench.

Eyes glazed in anger, the Father gestured to Tassos. "Get all this picked up."

The Brother knelt to begin collecting precious jewels. "Shall I inventory everything, Master?"

"Eh," he grunted. While Tassos watched, he went to his bedchamber and shut the door.

With a heavy heart, Tassos resumed picking up all the valuables. He had been present when many of these items had been donated. This solid gold bracelet, exquisitely chased—he remembered the widow who traveled all the way from Eurus to lay it upon the altar and pray. With tears in her eyes, she had prayed aloud for the blessing of this gift to the praise of the Heavenly Father.

Only after she had left did Tassos discover that once she had been very wealthy, but the bracelet was the very last of her worldly goods. Having discovered the comparative value of the life above, she had divested herself of everything she owned and entered the abbey.

Tassos continued gathering rings, loose gems, necklaces (including the rosary) and other ornaments into the ebony jewel box, then returned it to the sideboard. He replaced the gold ware and silver ware; counting the utensils, he found them all there.

He refolded the linens, separating out a few that would require rewashing. Then he took up the rug and shook out the salt on the east grounds. Before replacing it, he fetched a broom and swept up the errant grains from the polished wood floor.

When order was restored, Tassos looked around uneasily. Everything appeared to be here, but . . . he felt something to be missing. He did not know what it was. Tentatively, he noted the saltcellar in its hallowed place; he opened drawers to recount gold ware a third time. It was all there.

Hesitantly, he returned to the ebony box to sift through its contents again: the rosary, the small jewelry and precious gems—how easy they would have been to steal and resell! but here they were! Then there was—

Tassos froze. The diptych. The ivory diptych was missing. With a panicky glance toward the still-closed bedchamber door, Tassos began a methodical search of the floor, looking in corners, under furniture, shaking out every rug and basket. It was not here.

Pale and perspiring, he quietly left the Master's chambers. At work on the tapestry, Nicole glanced back through the window as he passed into the apse, then went down the nave toward the east corridor of the monks' quarters. He looked around deliberately before taking a lighted candle from its wall sconce, then went down the corridor and let himself into his quarters, closing the door firmly behind him.

He set the candle down on the washstand in front of the mirror to intensify its light. Then, standing in the doorway between the two small rooms of his suite, his sunken eyes swept slowly over every modest stick of furniture. In the inner room, he canvassed the washstand, the ewer and bowl, the bed; in the outer room: the table, the chair, the bookcase—

His heart pounding in fear, he knelt before his precious books. The Master did not care for books, except those that were decorated with gold leaf, but these volumes were worth more to Tassos than any amount of gold. His thin, trembling fingers ran over each spine, gently withdrawing one book after another to lay them aside on the wooden floor.

His worn copy of *Confessions* fell over, and there was revealed—Tassos' heart stopped.

Slowly, he pulled out the miniature diptych, opening it to regard the delicate carving. Then Tassos slumped on the floor in despair, clutching the diptych to his chest with one hand and holding his head with the other. What to do? What was there to do?

Belatedly, with the disturbance of balance on the shelf, another book fell open on his knees. And Tassos did what came naturally to him: He looked at the words, and read until his mind was clear.

He closed the book and calmly replaced it on the shelf, then regarded the delicate diptych resting in his hand. How fragile it was, how easily crushed under a brute heel. "Like a conscience," murmured Tassos. "Or a sense of purpose, crushed under the weight of cravings. Well, my friends—"

He straightened, addressing his precious books lined up just so. "Forgive me for regarding your physical bodies to be worth more than your souls. I see my error,

which has been gross. I will not continue to abide in it."
Gripping the diptych, he got to his feet.

At Westford, Henry strolled around the first floor of
the palace with Commander Thom. The young
Surchatain made a point of looking in side rooms,
poking his head into the audience hall, even checking the
infirmary—"I count a total of twenty people," he
announced.

"Twenty-two, if you number the servants who just
entered the infirmary," Thom amended.

"That's one-third the number usually milling around
here," Henry said.

"That is correct," Thom admitted, regarding Henry's
satisfied smirk. Raising a tentative hand to his beard, he
murmured, "I wonder how long a ghost can keep them
away."

"When that wears off, we can invent a monster,"
Henry proposed. He found it gratifying to talk without
having to shout to be heard—and risk being overheard.
The only other discernable voices came from two maids
lounging in a doorway, gossiping.

Thom looked troubled. "We have no need to invent
monsters; they will present themselves in one form or
another."

He paused, and Henry eyed him, waiting. "I am not
convinced that the letters have answered our. . . ." When
Thom lowered his voice, he was drowned by the maids'
laughter.

Henry turned in irritation, for he couldn't help
hearing: "—and as soon as I leave, who should show up
but the Lady Bonnie with those uppity friends of hers—

they aren't even titled! I hung about to watch as she brought in a trunk full of dresses—and with all my lady gave him—*gave* him—he just told the Lady Bonnie, 'I'll give you two royals apiece for them.' 'Two royals!' she screeched like a banshee. 'This one alone cost thirty!' Well, he was firm, so in the end—"

"Do you have any idea what Lady Bonnie will do to you when she hears you've been down here mocking her?" Henry asked in only half-joking horror.

She and the other maid spun toward him, having been obviously unaware of his presence. Stiffly, the talkative maid curtsied with, "Pardon, Surchatain," and headed for the stairs. While Henry was watching this maid, the other servant took the opportunity to disappear.

"I haven't dismissed you," Henry said to the first, scrutinizing her, so she faced him with hands folded submissively in front of her. "Wait a minute. You're Sister's maid Maddie."

"Yes, Surchatain," she said, curtsying again.

"You can't say you don't know what *Sister* will do to you when she finds out you've been down here making fun of Bonnie," Henry said, awed by such recklessness.

"Pardon, Surchatain, but the Lady is not here," Maddie said.

"Where did she go?" Henry asked.

"To the Sanctum, Surchatain."

Thom glanced at her and then deliberately turned away as if disinterested. After the moment required to recover, Henry nodded to her. "You may go."

He watched her trot up the curving stairway, then

eyed Thom in dread. "She went after the runaway husband," he whispered.

"Apparently so," Thom conceded.

"Poor man," Henry said in sympathy. "Should we send a regiment to his aid? The Red's not busy today, are they?"

Thom hesitated. "Lord Faguy has made his bed, and now must lie in it. I am more inclined to wonder what she will do upon finding those who preceded him down there." That is, Ares and Nicole.

Henry looked off in sudden alarm. "Oops."

For the rest of that morning and into the early afternoon, Faguy sat in a shaded corner of the travelers' court, watching. He saw very little; a few travelers stopped by to rest or draw water from the well, but, as it was too early to stop for the night, those few who stopped soon left again.

An interesting question, and one that he pondered at length, was why there were no travelers in the courtyard when he arrived this morning. Even if they had all left by the time he arrived, he should have encountered most of them on the road. Had the brown-robed brute that greeted him this morning turned them all away? Had the Sanctum closed itself to travelers? If so, he must discover why.

He watched several monks go in and out the front gates with tools or other burdens. One monk carried out candle holders to clean.

Watching him indifferently scrape off the wax onto the ground, Faguy blinked in surprise. Good candle wax was expensive, and any prudent householder would save the scrapings to remelt into new candles.

As that monk was working, another passed by, then paused to speak to him. The first pushed back his obscuring hood to reply while keeping a wary eye on the door to the church. Neither noticed Faguy in his corner, but he was not close enough to hear what they said. It was clear from their troubled faces, however, that they were not exchanging benedictions.

With the passing of noon, something interesting did come about. A nicely dressed merchant drove his cart into the travelers' court. Climbing down from his seat, he went to the church door to rap on it with the handle of his driving whip.

Faguy sat up to watch as the door was opened, and a monk leaned out. Faguy was able to hear the merchant say, "Good afternoon to you, Brother! Kindly tell Father Manworren that Goss, textile master, has brought a fine selection of the newest, most luxurious fabrics for bed and boudoir—"

"Not now," the monk hissed, waving. "He cannot see you today."

This was unpleasant, and evidently unexpected, news. Forcing a smile, Goss replied, "I've come at his invitation, Brother. I don't mind waiting a while, but the Father knows that this is far out of my circuit. I cannot just drop by."

"Go away!" the monk snapped.

Grimly, Goss half-turned to his cart. "Good day to you, sir. Kindly tell the Master that if he wishes to see my goods, he must come to my shop in Westford."

The monk shut the door on him, and the textile master left with mutterings and a sharp crack of the whip. Upon leaving, he kicked one gate almost closed. Faguy sat back thoughtfully.

Some minutes later Oswald entered the front gates, striding toward the church door. Faguy scrambled up, poised to call out to him, when another monk exited to intercept the Second. So Faguy melted back into the shadows to watch and listen.

"What did you do with it?" the monk asked.

"Committed him to the Sea," Oswald replied, correcting the pronoun, "and not to the garbage pit where he had come from. You shouldn't be disposing of your dead there; they're not buried, nor properly cremated; they'll draw rats and breed disease," he lectured.

"The garbage pit!" the other exclaimed. "That scoundrel of a gravedigger—"

"If you held prayers over your dead, you'd know what became of them," Oswald chastised him.

The monk had no reply to that, so Oswald made as if to go around him into the church. The monk snapped to attention. "Where are you going?"

"To bathe," Oswald said, pausing.

"Go around to the wash house, you filthy mercenary," the monk rebuked, possibly in retaliation. Nodding, Oswald turned to exit the gates again.

The monk reentered the church, and Faguy sat back to digest *that* scene. All of the monks he had seen thus far were exhibiting disturbingly worldly attitudes. And, the Second was obviously not here in his capacity as officer of the Lystran army. So there was subterfuge afoot. "Interesting," Faguy murmured.

Over the course of his vigil, he noted one particular

monk who came into the traveler's court just to look. The first thing he saw, evidently, was the outer gates barely opened. Hastening across the court, the monk opened them wide.

Upon reentering the court, he scanned it and saw the lone visitor for the first time. Approaching with a bow, he said, "Welcome to the Sanctum, guest. My name is Brother Tassos. Do you require anything?"

"No, nothing, Brother, thank you," Faguy replied in surprise, taking note of the other's long, set face. "I am only resting before resuming my journey."

"You have no baggage," Tassos observed.

"I am begging my way, Brother," Faguy admitted.

"Then stay as long as you require, friend. This is a place of refuge," Tassos said with vehemence.

"As Surchatain Ares intended," Faguy replied, watching him.

"Do you know the Surchatain, sir?" Tassos asked, glancing at his worn work clothes.

"I have seen him and heard him speak," Faguy said. "He is a God-fearing man."

"We should all fear God," Tassos said, his look of determination more pronounced. "I shall see that you do not lie down hungry tonight."

"Thank you, Brother Tassos."

With a nod, the monk headed back toward the church, and Faguy sat back to think about *that*.

Then a movement caught his eye; he looked to the gates where a handsome horse and carriage had just entered. Tassos, at the church door, turned to gape at the newcomer before hastening into the nave, obviously to inform someone.

Faguy sank back in terror, recognizing the carriage, the driver, and, most ominously, the passenger, Glancing around wildly for escape, all he saw was the door to the stables, a long ten feet away.

Not daring to breathe, he watched the driver climb down from his seat and let down a step on the other side of the carriage. While the passenger rose to descend the step with her back to him, Faguy skittered to the stable door and slipped inside.

Then, heart thumping, he watched out of a crack between the boards as the hostler drew water for the horse and the lady looked around the courtyard.

A voice behind him said, "Well, hello, Faguy." Clutching his chest, the poor man spun to look at the speaker.

10

Still clutching his chest, Faguy gasped, "Surchatain Ares."

"Shh." Eyes glinting, Ares quieted him with one hand while the other rested on the handle of a shovel.

In the hot, smelly work of shoveling manure from the stalls, he had taken off the monk's robe altogether. It lay within easy reach, draped over the side of a stall. However, Faguy did not notice it for staring at Ares' work clothes. They looked much like what he himself wore. Suddenly he was transported years back to a storm in Prie Mer, and a Surchatain who shoveled debris like a common laborer.

But in the shock of seeing Ares here, now, employed as a stableboy, Faguy blurted the first thought that crossed his mind. "Surchatain—I smell—you smell—"

"Like a woman. I know," Ares said, sniffing his arm. "I was compelled to bathe in the wee hours of the morning, and found myself privileged to use the bath water of a lady." Ares smiled briefly at the thought. "Now, who did you see out there?" He nodded toward the courtyard.

Faguy lurched back to the crisis at hand. "The Lady Renée," he replied in a strangled voice. "I had married her," he admitted, shame-faced, "then discovered that the notary was unlicensed, so, finding myself—unattached, came to see how I might assist you; but now she has also come—and—"

Ares regarded his pallor humorously. "And Jack will be stabling her horse shortly."

Faguy flailed a little. "Surchatain—"

"Shh!" Ares hushed him again, reaching over for the monk's robe. "Come with me."

Renée accepted a cup of wine from Jack (*not* well water) and sipped it while scanning the courtyard. Since it was deserted, her prey must be in the church, then. Very well. He would be easy to find.

She smoothed her dress, then caught Jack's eye and gestured toward her bags. He touched his hat and proceeded to unload them right there in the middle of the court.

About that time Brother Tassos flew out of the church, but paused on the steps to compose himself. A few other monks had found something in the travelers' court that required their immediate attention as well, though what that could be was not readily apparent. While they stood in a tight group doing nothing, none of them dared look the formidable creature in the face.

Summoning the courage for which the Polonti are famous, Tassos approached Renée to bow deeply. "Welcome to the Sanctum, Lady. I am Brother Tassos. How may I be of service to the lady?"

She eyed him through slitted eyes, fanning her

luscious bosom. "Thank you, darling—Tassos, is it? I am Renée of Westford, and I require the best room you have, whether it is available or not. I also need a porter or two." She gestured unnecessarily to the large bags on the ground.

"Certainly, Lady." His voice cracked, and he cleared his throat.

Tassos waved to a couple of loitering monks, who came forward to stare at her bags before hoisting them. Once Jack had satisfied himself that the bags were on their way inside, he began unharnessing the horse from the carriage.

"Please follow me," Tassos requested of the awesome lady. She gestured for him to lead, and he turned to stumble up the steps into the church. Renée glanced at the monks following to make sure they were carrying, not dragging, her luggage.

Entering the nave, she glanced around, then Tassos opened the door to the west corridor of the monks' quarters—the same corridor that housed Nicole and Oswald. "Here are our travelers' quarters, Lady," he said without conviction.

Renée looked into the dark, narrow corridor, sniffing, "Am I to be thrown in prison, darling?"

"No! Of course not!" Tassos protested in horror.

Another monk hurried up to murmur, "The Master says he is ready to see her." He did not look directly at the object of his message.

"That's better," she said smugly. "Lead me to him," she instructed the messenger, who bowed nervously.

In his sudden blankness of mind, he paused to determine which direction to go, then began up the nave.

Renée followed, but when the porters began milling in confusion, knocking her bags against each other, she beckoned them curtly. So her luggage trailed her, as did Tassos.

She was escorted into the Master's receiving room, where he stood resplendent in white robes and gold brocade. Nicole, glimpsing movement through the window, turned from the tapestry frame. But she was totally forgotten by Manworren the moment he laid eyes on the newcomer—elegant, blonde, with blue eyes and naturally crimson lips.

He bowed low to effuse, "Your servant Father Manworren is deeply gratified and honored by the visit of such a person to our humble abode. May I ask the name of the beauty who has appeared like a vision to me?"

Renée, carefully evaluating the room and its contents, did not reply. Tassos squeezed through a cluster of monks and bags to say, "Master, this is Lady Renée of Westford."

"Lady Renée!" Nicole exclaimed, entering the open garden door. "What a happy coincidence! Do you remember me? Nouri of Venegas? We met at the spring fair in Crescent Hollow." Which they did, in fact—17 years ago.

Renée regarded her plain dress, then replied, "Darling Nouri. Of course. How could I forget?"

Nicole came up to her and Renée leaned forward to kiss the air beside her cheek. "Where is that beastly husband of yours? What was his name—Dimitry?"

"Dimitry isn't with me, dearest," Nicole murmured. At that time Oswald entered the room behind her, studying the new arrival, and Nicole explained, "I came only with my bodyguard, Forcht."

More or less clean, Oswald bowed, and Renée eyed him sardonically. "I'm so glad you managed a little excursion without the beast," she purred.

Manworren endeavored to regain the new visitor's attention. "Lady Renée, may I offer you refreshment?" He snapped his fingers at gawking monks, who then hastened to begin setting the table.

"Nouri and I will be delighted to accept," she said.

"And Forcht," Nicole added.

"Of course," Renée said, then went to the door of the bedchamber and opened it.

Looking in, she muttered, "I suppose this is the best you have." A haze of delight encompassed the bedazzled Father as she ordered, "Put my luggage in here."

The bag handlers began to comply, but Tassos stopped them, sputtering, "Master, it is unseemly for a woman to stay in your room!"

"There now; don't worry, Tassos, darling." Renée puckered her lips at him. "The Father has no intention of allowing baseless gossip to sully my honor. He's staying somewhere else. Maybe one of the charming little suites you first showed me."

Manworren began to blink rapidly. Taking stock of his bedchamber again, she went on, "I require fresh bathwater—rose scented is best, but if you haven't any dried petals on hand, I will accept almond milk and saffron.

"I require someone at the door constantly—Forcht, darling, you'll do—and a changing screen, of course. And *warmed* towels, darling—there's nothing so horrifying as drying off with cold towels. Nouri, dearest, you wouldn't mind lending me a hand, would you? You're such a dear."

The two women paused at the bedchamber door, and Renée let her eye fall on the magnificent oak table. "I will be ready for dinner in an hour, dear Father. Maybe two. You are so kind." After Nicole had preceded her into the room, Renée shut the door, and locked it.

At Westford, Lord Davignon and his nephew Lord Hetrick had just been ushered into the Surchatain's receiving room. Awaiting them there were Surchatain Henry, Commander Thom, Counselor Vogelsong, Second Paramore, and Captain Ben.

"Thank you for coming on such short notice, gentlemen," Henry said mildly, studying them. Old Davignon was pale and trembling; Hetrick was steady but grim. "You had some news for me?"

"Yes, Surchatain." Davignon inclined his head. "A report from my man, my steward, Joslyn. But an hour ago, he was at the wine seller, Weingert's, to pick up my week's order. My man was the only one there, and while he was waiting on Weingert, who had gone down to his cellar, he heard murmurings from a side room. Joslyn is a good man, quick on his feet, so he went to the door to listen.

"And he heard spoken: 'Tonight we move. Henry will die.' And something more about dinner. He could not distinguish what was said, for Weingert came up with my order, and Joslyn had to step lively to not give suspicion.

"But Joslyn is a quick thinker, and told Weingert

that he had instructions to deliver gifts of a bottle or two from me to several of Weingert's other customers, and he asked if there were any others there. He said he thought he heard someone in the side room. So Weingert cursed and went to that room, and Joslyn said it was an empty storage room with the outer door standing open!"

Lord Davignon continued nervously, "Joslyn said Weingert told him that he kept the outer door unlocked for the vinter to deliver when he was otherwise engaged, but rascals had been using it as their gaming room."

Davignon wiped his brow while the others watched silently. "The rebellion has gone beyond letters, Surchatain. They are planning to strike very soon. You will forgive me, Surchatain? I feel a fever coming on. I fear I may not be well enough to appear at table tonight. I beg your forgiveness, Surchatain." He was sweating profusely.

Henry nodded. "I see that you are already quite ill. I am grateful that you summoned such strength to come warn me. Go home and take to your bed now."

"Thank you, Surchatain." Davignon bowed deeply. "Thank you." Then he hastened out.

Hetrick followed slowly. At the door, he turned back to say, "Your forbearance toward my uncle's illness is appreciated, Surchatain. I, however, am quite well. I will be at dinner, and I will be armed."

"I would have liked," Thom said abruptly, "to have heard from Joslyn himself."

Hetrick lowered his eyes. "We . . . are looking for him," he said heavily. "He gave us this report, and went out to resume his duties, and . . . we are looking."

Henry nodded, and Thom's chin came up minutely.

With a bow, Hetrick also departed. Thom shifted his eyes to the window, and there they stayed.

The administrators contemplated this bit of news. "I have not seen such overt defiance since Surchatain Ares came to the throne," Paramore observed.

"That is true," Vogelsong whispered, staring at him.

"If they are plotting to attack at dinner—" Ben suddenly looked at Henry. "We must remove the Chataines from harm's way."

"How?" Henry asked. "Lock them up? Forbid them to come to dinner? And what do they tell their friends, who then speak to other friends, who then create a city-wide panic?"

Vogelsong, still staring at Paramore, was struggling with possible logistics. "How shall any number of armed men hope to enter at the dinner hour and successfully attack a hall full of soldiers?"

Thom suddenly took his gaze from the window. "They have someone on the inside," he said. The others looked at him as he addressed Henry. "One of your administrators is a traitor. There can be no other explanation for such boldness."

His fellow officers absorbed that. "Well, then," Henry said quietly, "I suppose we'll find out at dinner."

With Surchataine Nicole ensconced in Manworren's room, Oswald would allow no one else to wait on the newest arrival. He himself brought in buckets of steaming water for her bath, took out the chamber pot, and brought in towels and scented soaps.

Then he stood at the closed bedchamber door to make sure that no one got close enough to overhear any conversation between the Lady Renée and the Lady Nouri.

While brown-clad brothers replenished the saltcellar and began preparations for an early dinner, Manworren fretfully flitted around his receiving room. Once or twice when he presumed to approach the door of his unreachable inner sanctum, Oswald expanded like a great, bearded puffer fish to block him.

Manworren pleaded, "I desire to inquire whether the lady needs anything."

"The lady makes her needs known without inquiry," Oswald replied.

A moment later, Manworren exploded, "How am I to prepare my own toilet?"

A corner of Oswald's lip turned up, but Tassos, hearing, bowed. "The Master is welcome to use my own humble room, if he requires it."

"Bah!" Manworren brushed the offer aside, but minutes later gave up and exited his receiving room.

Tassos waited a few beats, glancing at Oswald from under his brows. The bodyguard's gaze remained straight ahead of him. So Tassos slipped something small and white out of his robe and put it into the ebony box. Again he glanced at Oswald, who saw nothing but potential disturbances to his lady's peace.

With a despondent sigh, Tassos left in the direction of the kitchen, and only then did Oswald's eyes follow him.

Perhaps a half-hour later Manworren reappeared, damp behind the ears, to pace between his quarters and the kitchen barking needless and contradictory orders.

Despite his interference in the preparation, dishes

began appearing on the table: mutton in verjuice (cider vinegar), pea soup, white herbs, and figgy. A half-dozen robed and hooded monks brought in the savory dishes and then stood against the wall to await further orders.

The moment that all was ready and at the peak of flavor, as if by a miracle the door opened and Renée and Nicole emerged. They came to the table with light, chatty laughter; Oswald drew out Nicole's chair and Tassos seated Renée.

Slightly flustered, Manworren took his own chair, and Oswald sat. Then the wine bearer came forward with the flask. Since he was hooded, Nicole's eyes fixed on his hands, but it was not Ares.

Preparatory to speaking, Renée tossed her head in her old manner. Oswald, despite himself, smiled; he appreciated a finely executed bloodletting.

"*Dear* Father Manworren," she said, fixing him with her luminous blue eyes, "you are unspeakably kind to offer refuge to such a poor unfortunate as myself. When my beastly little brother ascended to the throne, I was made unwelcome—"

"Your brother?" Manworren cried. "You are sister of the new Surchatain?"

"Why, yes," Renée said through gritted teeth at the outburst. "As I was saying, when he—"

"Threw you out of the palace?" Manworren cried again, clutching at his chest.

As much as Renée did not like to be interrupted, she knew how to ride a current. "With hardly anything but the clothes on my back," she affirmed, daubing at dry eyes. "So here am I: deserted by a faithless husband, alone, bereft—"

"Not as long as I breathe, Lady," he said passionately. "You shall require nothing from anyone else, for I shall be protector and provider, your shield against the world, your fortress from the host that rise against you, though they may ascend from the pits of Hades itself!"

"Um hmm," Renée mumbled, having picked up her fork to begin eating during his speech. Oswald and Nicole had done likewise.

While Manworren watched, spellbound, Renée swallowed and said, "That would be lovely." She critically examined the gold fork in her hand, then raised a brow indifferently and continued eating.

"That was our vow," Tassos said quietly.

Everyone looked at him in surprise as he stood in the place of a servant behind the Master's chair. "'To protect the helpless, defend the weak, succor the suffering, pray with the dying.' That was our vow upon the opening of the Sanctum. Surchatain Ares administered it to us himself."

The monk standing against the wall behind Tassos raised his head minutely, and Nicole's eyes fixed on him. Although every square inch of skin was covered, she knew him at once. It was Ares.

"Go bring bread, Brother Tassos," Manworren uttered, glaring at him.

Tassos did not move. "You have perverted our vows and our purpose," he said.

"So it is you," the Father said, sitting back. "You filthy Polonti, you are our little jokester. Do you understand that if I turn you out with anathema upon you, you will be as a leper to the rest of the world? You will starve beside the roadway, and travelers will take to the fields to avoid your rotting body."

"So be it," Tassos said. "I am not a thief."

"Wonderful," said Manworren. "Give me your keys and get out. I will write up the document of anathema tonight."

With a bow, Tassos surrendered his keyring and departed through the door to the apse. Unnoticed, the monk against the wall slipped out into the garden.

The Master, feeling his importance, turned back around in his chair, bracing one elbow on its scrolled arm as he raised a gold goblet to rest against his lips. He eyed his newest guest, who appeared to have melted in his direction. "I love a man of power," she uttered.

"I am the master here," he admitted with a slight grunt, setting down the goblet precisely beside his plate. "Oh, we have reformers who worm their way in from time to time, but I have a special tool to render them— sterile, so to speak."

"You intrigue me," she confessed, leaning forward to display her cleavage to its best advantage. "Tell me what tool that would be."

He smiled coyly. "Why, you have just seen me exercise it, Lady. Anathema is a powerful deterrent."

She withdrew a bit. "It's dangerous," she observed. "One too many complaints, and someone from Westford comes down to see what you are about."

"Oh ho ho! Someone from Westford," he said scornfully, leaning forward so that his white silk tie dangled in the verjuice. "I have seen to that, as well, for I have a friend in the court at Westford. He sits at the Surchatain's table."

"Now you toy with me," Renée protested, heaving her bosom to detract attention from Nicole's sudden start. "Had I such a friend, I could revenge myself upon my brother."

Manworren uttered, "My friend has become yours, Lady."

Suddenly, he seemed to regain awareness of his other two silent guests, adding, "We will speak of this later." When Renée inhaled in anticipation, he let his eyes travel freely down her neckline.

In his room, Tassos sat before his bookcase, drawing out the volumes one by one. He caressed their covers, opened them to read a line or two, then replaced them tenderly on the shelf, recalling how he felt upon reading the words in them for the first time.

He thought far back to his discovery of books in the great library of Eledith, and how he had grown to love learning there. In that library is also where he had heard of the vast libraries in Eurus and Westford, so had made the difficult, dangerous journey to see them.

But upon discovering that Polonti are roundly scorned in Eurus, he fled south to Westford. There he was treated better, but not much—not because he was Polonti, but because he was a vagrant.

Had he any fighting skill, he could have attached himself to a traveling merchant or joined the Lystran army; but all he could do was read and write. So he became a monk.

And it was the greatest honor of his life to be chosen as the Master's assistant upon the opening of the Sanctum. At last, he had found his calling, and served in the Sanctum with his whole heart. It seemed certain to him at that time that he had been led to this work by the Crucified One.

But the euphoria did not last; the snake entered the garden. The little changes the Master began to make here and there—dispensing with the bells at matins, keeping back a donation or two for "emergencies"—finally caused him to raise questions of conscience.

But the Master was not Master for nothing; he knew what to do to silence his troublesome assistant. He bought Tassos' own compliance with gifts of books. And it worked; oh, yes, it worked very well. Tassos buried himself in their precious pages and closed his eyes to all else.

Reflecting on the insights—more than that, the very love that these little books had imparted to him—caused his eyes to water, for now he must leave them. The curse of anathema allowed him to take no possessions, nothing but the underclothes he wore. Even the robe—the mark of a monk—must be stripped from him.

And to give the anathema teeth, the Master administered it with a brand on the back of the hand. That it was often confused with a leper's brand only enhanced its effectiveness.

Sighing, Tassos replaced the last book on the shelf. As they were bribes, it was only fitting that they should be withdrawn from him in punishment for accepting them. But they themselves were not evil, for they had rekindled in him the courage of his race to defy a traitor to the One True Master.

Standing, Tassos leaned on the doorway of the inner room, and his gaze landed on the mirrored washstand.

Considering the incongruity of it, he smiled wryly. When the woman who owned it had come here as a leper, she brought it with the rest of her movables.

The table and chairs she used, but the mirror had become a horror to her. She had begged Father Manworren to make use of it elsewhere. Since it was not a fine enough piece for his quarters, and lesser monks were not entitled to such vanities, the Father had decided to break it up for firewood without telling her. He would not even bother trying to sell it, for by then he was already quite wealthy.

But the woman desired to know that everything she possessed, regardless how trivial, was put to good use; therefore Tassos took it. And before she died, he was able to tell her truthfully that it was faithfully serving its original purpose. Now, his smile faded as he reflected that it would certainly be chopped up.

His outer door began opening, and a brown figure slipped into the small room. Tassos turned, commanding his heart to be submissive as he looked to the monk's hands for the document that announced his doom.

But those hands instead reached up to draw the hood back from the wearer's head. In shock, Tassos regarded the deep scar creasing the face, and mild eyes studying him. "Surchatain Ares," he whispered.

"Hello, Brother Tassos. Shall we talk?"

The monk's jaw dropped, then he shut his mouth in composure. "I am at your service, Surchatain."

"Excellent. Come with me."

After Manworren had prevailed upon Renée to allow him to use the chamber pot in his bedchamber, and was in the process of doing so, Renée drew Nicole out of the hearing of the one monk who remained in the receiving room.

"Change of plans, darling," Renée whispered. "As much as I would love your company tonight, I must allow our patsy to think he will sleep with me, to loosen his lips about this traitor at my brother's table."

"I quite agree," Nicole whispered. "Ares was here tonight, and left after Tassos. I will try to make sure someone is near your door to get a message to him."

"Very good," Renée replied.

They both turned as the Master, reeking of perfume, came out of his bedchamber rubbing his hands. "Well, then." His eye rested coolly on Nicole and her bodyguard.

She took the hint. With a curtsy, she said, "Thank you for the excellent dinner, Master Manworren. Please excuse me for the evening."

"Certainly." He nodded, satisfied.

Turning to the hooded monk against the wall, he barked, "Empty that chamber pot, and be quick about it!"

Faguy nodded deferentially. He was careful not to let his face show, but Renée never looked toward him as he went into the bedchamber to fetch the pot.

Outside in the nave, Nicole whispered to Oswald, "Please see if you can find out what has become of poor Brother Tassos. And then hasten back. I have promised Renée a messenger at the door to get word to Ares when she finds out who is Manworren's accomplice at the table."

Oswald paused. "As you say, only, I do not care to

leave my lady unattended in this treacherous place."

"Greater matters prevail, dear Forcht," she said, chin lowered. "I am not alone." So he escorted her to her room in the west corridor, then went off on his errand.

Renée settled herself on the gilded, brocade loveseat, accepting a cup of wine from the Master's eager, slightly trembling hand. The monk who had left with the chamber pot now returned it to the bedchamber and stood silently against the wall of the receiving room to await further orders. Neither Renée nor Manworren so much as glanced his way.

"How divine you look, dear Master," she murmured.

He lifted his double chin to look down on her. "Rarely has a vision like you passed before these poor eyes," he intoned.

A little gasp escaped her, and she turned her face away. "So you say, but I can believe not a word of it. Were I so desirable, my husband would not have abandoned me. As there is nothing in me that any man would find appealing, my attempts to win his favor were all pathetic."

So saying, she raised slender white fingers to her quivering lip. Beneath her hand, the top two buttons on her bodice had mysteriously come unfastened.

Manworren tossed aside his goblet and threw himself to his creaking knees before her. "That man is an idiot!"

"No, it is true!" she cried. "I am no longer young and beautiful. But what is worse—"

Her face inexplicably changed, and her breathy act disappeared. In truthful self-revelation, she said, "I let my maid lord it over him. That was inexcusable. I should have insisted he be treated with the honor he deserved." The brown figure against the wall stirred.

"Any man would be honored by your very presence!" Manworren insisted.

Renée snapped back into character. She looked down on him at her knees and breathed, "No, your kindness blinds you, darling. I am mean and selfish. I take advantage of people who are too good to respond in kind." Her eyes widened at the second truth that had unaccountably slipped from her lips.

"I won't hear such slander from you!" Manworren cried, pressing his odorous mouth to hers. She winced, but allowed him to kiss her with her mouth firmly closed. The monk began swaying slightly against the wall.

She broke away, pushing Manworren firmly back with a coy smile. "You play with me in my pathetic state, raising my hopes to trust you before dashing them to pieces on the rocks."

"No, Lady," he moaned. "What can I do to convince you of the depth of my desires?"

"Oh, I have no doubt of your desires," she said wryly, regarding him. "I merely seek reassurance that once you have used me to your satisfaction—when you have drunk to the dregs and lay back satisfied—"

"Yes, yes!" he cried.

"—That you will remember your promise to befriend this poor, wretched creature who has come to seek shelter in your breast," she said.

He stared at her blankly, so she explained, "You promised to help me gain leverage over my despicable brother."

"Yes," he breathed, "yes, I will." But right now he was engrossed in her bodice.

Renée expelled an impatient sigh, then forced his head up to look him in the eye. "I need proof of your good intentions before I give myself *fully* to you."

"Proof," he panted, his thinking processes now totally disengaged.

"Who is your friend at the court?" she demanded.

"My friend at the court?" he repeated blankly.

She sat up in disgust, shoving him off her. "It is as I thought. You were lying to take advantage of a poor, friendless woman."

"No!" he cried. "My friend is the very Steward of the palace, Giles."

"Giles?" she repeated skeptically.

"Yes! He comes himself to tell me what Ares, and now Henry, is doing. I pay him for information, and he makes sure that the Surchatain receives only good reports from inspections," Manworren panted.

"Giles," she muttered. "I never liked him." She looked toward the door. "Excuse me, darling. I need—"

As she started to rise, he forced her back down to the loveseat, a hand firmly around her throat. "You will go nowhere at present, Lady."

II

With Manworren's hand tightening around Renée's throat, she thrashed and gurgled. She attempted to get her fingers up to his eyes, but he was pressing his body so hard upon hers, she could not get a hand free. Apparently, he had decided that he would have her even if it meant killing her in the process.

Suddenly the weight was lifted, and the vise removed from her throat. Gasping, Renée watched Faguy, hood down on his shoulders, heft Manworren off the floor in a rage.

He threw the Master into the nearest wall, then bent down and seized him by the splendid robe. Lifting him with both hands, Faguy pounded the silver head again and again against the wall, shouting, "Go!" to her.

Renée scrambled off the loveseat and ran out into the apse. Seeing no one, she stumbled on down the nave, looking. Finally she stopped where she was and began screaming, "Nicole! Nicole!"

Numerous brown forms began appearing in the nave. Scanning beyond them, she seized on a tall, bearded figure striding up the nave toward her.

Running to him, she gasped, "It's Giles. The man says his friend is Giles, Oswald."

Brows contracting, Oswald nodded. His eyes went to her throat, marked with bright red handprints, and he asked, "Are you all right?"

"Yes," she said with a toss of her head. "My husband is here." And she turned in a swirl of skirts to hurry back to the Master's quarters.

Entering, she found Faguy picking himself up from one knee, touching a bloody lip. The east door was open, and Manworren was gone.

"Darling! What happened? Where is that beast?" she cried, hurrying to him.

"He fought back," Faguy said, "and ran out." He nodded to the open door as he got to his feet.

"Oh, my poor dear," she murmured, drawing into his chest. "Let me tend you." He looked down at her. Twining her fingers in his, she led him to the bedchamber, then shut and locked the door.

Out in the stables, Oswald had just delivered the news to Ares, sitting in a stall with Tassos. "Giles is Manworren's ally at the palace?" Ares repeated in disbelief.

"That's what she said he said," Oswald replied with a shrug. "She extracted the information at some cost— the prints of his hands were plain on her throat."

Ares started to rise. "Where is he?"

"Being tended by the lady's husband," Oswald said with a tight smile. "But, if I may say, the Father is not our main worry at present, Surchatain."

Ares sank back to the hay, looking through the

dusky stable to the back wall with its grey and splintered wood. "Giles," he murmured.

As Tassos seemed to be on the verge of speaking, Ares asked him, "Do you know anything of this?"

"Yes, Surchatain. I was often present when the Master met with him," Tassos affirmed.

"It was Giles?" Ares asked in stubborn disbelief.

"Yes."

"What happened when he came? Tell me how their meetings went," Ares said.

Tassos raised a nervous hand to stroke his face. "The Steward would ride down in a lavish carriage and the Master would present him a gift of gold. No business was discussed at first; they always insisted on being served dinner," Tassos said.

"As at dinners in Westford," Oswald muttered.

Tassos mutely denied knowledge of that, then continued, "Afterward, when I served the wine, they would bring out papers, and a ledger. The Master would tell him who among the Brethren was making trouble—asking too many questions or raising questions of conscience. They would talk far into the night. Several nights I fell asleep standing against the wall before I was dismissed.

"The Steward would leave the next day, taking back a report of the man in question having a bad attitude, refusing discipline or the like, and deserving of anathema. Giles always supported the Master's edicts, and gave otherwise glowing reports of the conditions here."

"I remember reading such reports," Ares mused. "Signed by Giles." His horse Burl, in a stall across the stable, kept looking over the railing at his master's voice.

After a moment's meditation, Ares asked, "Then what did Giles tell Manworren after my abdication?"

"He . . . told him of your poisoning, and there was much glee at the—the success of the plot against you, Surchatain," Tassos said, pale.

Ares nodded. "Go on."

"They discussed means of doing away with the new Surchatain as well. They felt it would be easy, as he is so young and inexperienced," Tassos said hesitantly. "There were . . . others conspiring with them."

"Who?" Oswald asked.

"Oh, I never heard names, sir. They were careful not to name names in my presence," Tassos explained.

"Then what were these means they discussed?" Ares asked.

"I do not know," Tassos sighed. "By that time I was always dismissed, so overheard not nearly the extent of their discussions."

Oswald began to rumble deep in his throat. "So here they were discussing murder and insurrection, and you said not a word to anyone?"

Tassos looked at him. "I was a coward." The frankness of his confession made Oswald pause. "I saw no way to make myself believed by anyone in Westford. Therefore, guilt for the Surchatain's poisoning rests on my head."

Ares asked quietly, "What proof did you have of this conspiracy? Records? Letters? Other witnesses?"

"There was no proof within my reach, and no one else heard what I heard," Tassos said.

"For you to bring so serious an accusation against the residing Master without proof would have certainly resulted in your banishment, or worse," Ares replied. "But one or two of your Brethren did find the opportunity to whisper in my ear."

Tassos asked, "When was that? When you summoned Brethren to offer comfort at the funerals?" At Ares' nod, Tassos said flatly, "No, Surchatain. The Master refused to let any of us go for fear of just that happening. The 'Brethren' he sent were imposters, allies of his, well-paid."

"Not all of them," Ares said.

Tassos gaped, then he whispered, "Leland? When he was cast out, he said that he would make his way to Westford and speak to you himself. Did he, Surchatain?"

Ares studied him. "Leland? With an X branded on the back of his hand?" At Tassos' quick gasp, Ares coolly said, "Never saw him," but his eyes were smiling.

Ares and Oswald were silent while Tassos shed tears over the courage of his friend, murmuring, "More Polonti than I. He was not afraid."

Looking out through a crack in the planking which faced the courtyard, Oswald told Ares, "There seems to be some excitement afoot. Much running hither and yon."

"You'll see to that in a moment," Ares said, meditatively sifting through the hay on the ground. Then he asked, "What do you think? Could Giles really be involved?"

The Second shrugged uneasily. "Who is to say what a man is capable of? Giles is greedy, but . . . he covets for more in the treasury, not for himself. I don't understand why he would go out of his way for gold when he wouldn't lay a hand on the treasury store."

"True," Ares agreed.

"And I don't know when he would have time for such conspiring, what with the duties the Counselor's given him—responsibilities that have always been coveted by the Steward," Oswald added.

"Also true." Ares shifted back to Tassos. "How often would he come?"

"Um." Tassos wiped moisture from his face. "Once a month, at most, Surchatain."

"And how long would he stay?"

"Just the night," Tassos said. "Sometimes they were up all of a night, going over documents that I was not privy to. The Master would often spend the whole of the following day in his bed."

"The papers you mentioned. Where does Manworren keep them?" Oswald asked.

"I do not know, precisely. They would be kept somewhere in his chambers, most likely in the bedchamber, under lock and key," Tassos replied.

They were interrupted by the clatterings of someone settling down in the traveler's court just a few feet beyond the wall. As Ares was gesturing Tassos and Oswald to a more secluded part of the stable, torchlight streamed through the crack in the planking, coloring their three faces orange-red. And Ares thought of another question that must be asked.

First, he moved them all next to Burl's stall across the stable. As they were settling down in the waning light, Ares resumed, "Now, Giles and Manworren would work on these documents at night?"

Tassos said, "Yes, Surchatain."

"By candlelight?" Ares asked again.

"Yes, Surchatain; how else?"

Ares cocked his head at the inconsistency. "Did Giles wear spectacles?"

Tassos thought for a moment. "I am not sure."

Ares leaned forward. "Think back: did you ever see him look at something written down?"

Tassos took only a moment to reply, "Yes."

"Was he wearing anything on his nose?"

"No," Tassos said immediately.

Ares and Oswald looked at each other, then Ares told Tassos, "Describe Giles."

Tassos' weary brow wrinkled. "He was . . . slight of build. Always wore very fine clothes, of course. Very dignified looking."

"What color was his hair?" Ares asked.

"Brown. Rather long. And a moustache. No beard," Tassos replied.

The other two men were silent. After a moment, Ares asked Oswald, "Can you keep matters in hand until I come back with arms?"

"Certainly, Surchatain," he uttered.

Ares stood to feel his way into Burl's stall, and the horse nickered at his approach. It now so dark that he had to find the bridle hanging on a nail by touch.

Slipping it over Burl's soft nose, Ares whispered, "I'll return as soon as I can. Keep watch over Manworren—don't let him burn anything before I get back."

Carrying nothing, not even a cloak or a robe, Ares jumped upon Burl's bare back. Oswald and Tassos opened the stable doors, and Ares set the horse to a run on the road toward Westford.

When Ares was away, Oswald nodded to Tassos. "Let's go, then." The monk obeyed.

They first went through the travelers' court, lit by a few campfires with a handful of visitors gathered around them. The front gates were barred for the night. Mounting the steps, Oswald tried the front door of the church. But this was also locked, and Tassos had been stripped of his keys.

So Oswald took him back out through the stable doors. They went around the west end of the complex to the corner room that Nicole occupied.

Feeling over the wall, Oswald located the loose boards and began removing them. "Surchataine? Surchataine Nicole?"

"Surchataine?" gasped Tassos, behind him. This was a stunning piece of news.

They heard, "Here, Oswald," and a shuffling.

He squeezed through the hole into the dark room. "The Surchatain is off to Westford, Lady. Renée has gotten Manworren to name his confederate in the palace."

"What? Who?" she exclaimed. Hesitantly, Tassos squeezed into the dark room behind Oswald.

"She said it's Giles," Oswald explained.

"Giles! I don't believe it," Nicole huffed. Seeing Tassos' shadowy form, she started, then relaxed. "Brother Tassos. That was a show of courage at dinner."

"Many thanks, Surchataine," he murmured, glad for the darkness to hide his red face.

But when he and Oswald stepped away from the

hole in the wall, enough blue moonlight shone in for the Second to begin collecting gear from both rooms.

Meanwhile, he told Nicole, "The Surchatain will unravel matters when he arrives at the palace. But it seems Manworren has papers in his quarters that we must safeguard. Please come with me, Lady." Nicole began to gather up her blanket and spare clothing.

Oswald led them out through the corridor into the nave of the church, and from there to the Master's quarters. He opened the unlocked door to the receiving room. There, he paused to note the general disarray, the east door standing open, and the candles burning down on the table.

Then he crossed the room to the bedchamber and tried the handle. It was locked. Landing a board-rattling blow on the door, Oswald shouted, "Open up!"

"Go away!" came the equally authoritative, feminine command from within.

Oswald paused, casting a dubious glance back at Nicole's shocked face. Then Oswald asked through the door, "Is Manworren in there, Lady?"

"No!" she shouted. "I'm with my husband!"

Oswald paused again, digesting this. "Where is Manworren?"

Faguy's voice answered, "He fled. I don't know where."

Oswald glanced at Nicole, then said through the door, "Then we shall await him here. Surchatain Ares said that there are important documents hidden somewhere in that room which he must not destroy."

"All right! We'll look! Leave us alone!" Renée shouted, exasperated.

So Oswald, Nicole, and Tassos made themselves comfortable in the outer room. Looking over the remains of dinner still on the table, Oswald rubbed his hands, reaching for a creamy dish. "Potatoes, anyone?"

Nicole smiled, shaking her head. Tassos looked stricken, then suddenly held up a plate.

They enjoyed the leftovers for a few minutes, then Tassos put down his gold fork to observe, "The Master may be gathering the Brethren to come against us."

Oswald snorted in reply, popping a tart whole into his mouth. Tassos further told him, "There may be as many as thirty."

"Enough to provide entertainment for the Surchataine, though if they prove too inconvenient for her to handle alone, we shall set the Lady Renée upon them," Oswald grunted.

But upon consideration, he got up to shut and lock the east door before sitting again. Taking up the gold pitcher, he offered, "More wine, Brother Tassos?"

"Yes, thank you," he said, extending a matching gold cup.

Half an hour later, the door to the bedchamber suddenly opened, and the three in the receiving room sat up. Renée and Faguy came out, carrying a locked box and a ledger which they placed on the table.

"If there are secrets, they are in here," she said briskly. Oswald studied the box, then went to the sideboard for a heavy gold candlestick. This he raised preparatory to knocking off the lock.

"Wait," urged Tassos. "Before you destroy it, let me see if I can find the key." Oswald complied to lower the candlestick, and Tassos hurried into the bedchamber.

Minutes later he returned with a gold key. "See if this fits," he said, handing it to Oswald.

The Second took the key, placed it in the lock, and turned it. Opening the lid, he extracted a sheaf of parchments. The others gathered around to look through them.

Raising a page, Nicole gathered her brows in puzzlement. "It's in another language."

"No, Surchataine, I do not believe so," said Faguy, who was perusing another sheet. "It is a cipher—I would hazard to say a Caesar cipher. I've known many a merchant who kept his books in code to protect himself against competitors, creditors, and the tax assessor."

"A Caesar cipher? What is that?" Nicole asked.

"A simple substitution cipher, Surchataine, in which each letter of the message is replaced by a letter which is a set number of places down in the alphabet," Faguy explained.

"According to the historian Suetonius, Julius Caesar used it to communicate with his generals on the field. He used a key of three, replacing each letter with the one three places down. Thus A becomes D; B becomes E; C becomes F, and so forth. It was effective simply because most barbarians who might intercept such messages were illiterate. However, it is easily broken," he said, regarding the parchment.

The text that he was studying looked like this:

IBXAZ HTAXV CDGP TPI TATTE CTSAJPV
HTAGPJF PWRDG RXGPY

except the words were arranged in a vertical column

rather than a horizontal line. Interspersed between them were ink stamps of a seal which depicted a woman holding a lily.

"How thrilling, darling. You are too clever," Renée purred in admiration.

"Can you interpret it?" Nicole asked him.

"Perhaps," Faguy murmured, with the expression of a man who certainly believed he could but did not want to appear over-confident. "I will try." And they all sat around the table to watch.

The mood at the palace table was somber tonight. Sophie did not know the precise reason for it, other than the growing tension from the anonymous letters. The most Henry had said about them was to assure her that all would be well, but she knew he was worried about something, because he had spent hours on the roof this afternoon.

She also noted how many soldiers were lining the banquet hall tonight—easily three times the usual number. Then when she looked down the long row of tables, she saw that several people were missing from the lower end. Since the courtiers and merchants she knew personally were here, she couldn't be sure who was absent, but at least ten were unaccounted for.

Ben cleared his throat at Henry—the Surchatain started out of a pensive reverie to wave for the wine steward, who came forward to begin pouring for the silent guests.

Bonnie was staring dully down the table, where Giles sat in Renée's former place. Bonnie missed her mentor deeply, and regretted her earlier rudeness, especially since Meuer had been so stingy with payment for her dresses.

With his usual acumen, Georges had juggled the seating at the upper table after the departure of Renée and Faguy. On Henry's side of the table in descending order sat Ben, Thom, Deirdre, Paramore, Father Birondo, Oswald's wife Evangeline, and Giles' assistant Stengi.

On Sophie's side of the table sat Bonnie, Vogelsong, his wife Elida, Giles, his wife Genevieve, Doctor Savary, and Wulfredia. Bonnie accepted her cup of wine listlessly, then let her lowered eyes linger on Giles' brocade suit trimmed in leopard.

Had Giles realized that her gaze had settled on him, he would have been thrilled. Unfortunately, given Bonnie's habit of looking sidelong, not straight on, it was Elida who was left with the impression that Bonnie was staring at her. Only Vogelsong sat between them. But every time he leaned back, Elida saw Bonnie's eyes cut toward her.

Something in the oppressed woman snapped. After having played the mouse to Renée's cat for years, Elida had thought that finally, with that lady gone to the Sanctum, she herself would enjoy a peaceful, happy dinner. Who knows but that she might drop a clever word or two? Or build up her husband with some astute observation?

But now Ares' daughter, who was no longer Chataine but merely the wife of a *captain*, was giving her, the Counselor's wife, the evil eye in Renée's absence—! Elida could endure it no longer. Tonight, the mouse would roar.

So the next time Bonnie turned her lusterless eyes down the table, Elida was ready. She glared back at the Captain's little wife with the focus of a lightning bolt. The wine cup which a servant placed at her elbow went unnoticed. Bonnie averted her eyes to her plate, and Elida felt the thrill of conquest.

But a moment later Bonnie looked back. Elida almost missed it because her foolish husband the Counselor was leaning forward to sip from his cup so as not to spill a drop on his elegant suit. But when he put his cup down, Elida sprang again to the challenge, turning in her chair to fix her rival with a deadly stare.

For long moments the two were locked in visual combat—haphazardly, to be sure, for Bonnie was still looking sideways, and they both had to adjust for the Counselor's movements. Why could he not sit still in his chair?

Then Bonnie blinked. Her focus seemed to change as she turned to look straight at Elida, who narrowed her eyes to slits in the fierceness of battle.

Bonnie said, "Counselor, is there something wrong with your wife's eyes?"

Everyone looked at Elida, who hit the unseen cup with her elbow just enough to splatter wine on her best dress. As she grabbed at the cup to keep it from toppling, Vogelsong leaned over in alarm. "My dear, have you taken ill?"

"No, not at all," she whispered. "Just a little warm. It's nothing," she said, frantically daubing spots with her napkin.

Heaving a sigh, Bonnie murmured, "I miss Aunt Renée. The table's just dead without her."

There were some acknowledging smiles, but Ben glanced at her in dismay. She told him, "You warned me it wouldn't be any fun tonight. You were right."

Looking around, she asked, "Does anyone know when she'll be back?" No one knew.

"I miss Mama and Papa," Sophie said in such a quiet voice that no one heard her but Henry. He turned and took her hand to kiss it in reassurance.

When she smiled back at him, she saw the sword at the side of his chair. Its scabbard had been strapped to the chair leg, the hilt within easy reach when he was sitting down. Her mouth dropped open—bringing weapons to the table was such an affront to their guests, she couldn't imagine what prompted him to do it. As she raised her eyes to his face, she saw a pensive, cautionary look in his grey eyes. So she held her peace.

Servants began bringing out apprayleres—mock pitchers made of pork, cheese, bread and spices, molded together and baked. Since they were real containers, they held broth for the plates of roasted duck that appeared alongside.

Although the guests were used to the dinner magic worked under Georges' supervision, the apprayleres evoked murmurings of admiration as the diners poured out the broth on their meats and then broke the pitchers apart to eat them.

Absently, Henry picked up the small pitcher and broke it before draining it, creating a fist-sized puddle on the table in front of him. Before anyone could notice, Sophie moved her appraylere to rest on the puddle, hiding it.

"Surchatain, may I speak?" inquired Lord Guibert.

"An accident," Henry said hastily, wiping his hands on his linen napkin. "What? Certainly, go right ahead."

Dark glances were cast up and down the table at the egregious breach of decorum in allowing any conversation to commence before the food had been properly appreciated. More than one guest noted to himself that Ares would not have countenanced it. But Ares was no longer here. . . .

"Thank you, Surchatain. I wished to introduce my lord to the pamphlet I shall be printing on the success of my bluestone and copper mining venture in western Lystra, and the riches I amassed from it," Guibert began.

"Excellent," Henry said blankly, staring at the door beyond him. Although it should have been obvious to anyone that the Surchatain heard nothing of what Guibert said, a few of the guests glanced at Lord Roschlau's reddening face.

"May I read a line or two from it, Surchatain?" Guibert drew a wad of parchment from his coat.

"Of course," Henry said, still demonstrating no apprehension of what this conversation was about. His attention had been drawn to movement in the antechamber to the hall. He tensed, watching the anteroom fixedly.

Thom turned his head just enough to see out of the corner of his eye over his right shoulder. Under the table, he tugged on his wife's dress to induce her to scoot forward as far as she could. Then he rested his hand on the short blade hanging at his hip.

Ben, sweat on his upper lip, looked across the table at his wife. He was too far away to protect her in a sudden fight.

Guibert began reading, "'The history of the greatest mining success in the history of Lystra began on an otherwise uneventful summer's day. I had taken shelter from the blazing sun under the awning of the excellent wineshop of my friend Lord Weingert—" He paused to nod toward the wine seller seated down the table from him—"when I chanced to note a vagrant, certainly ragged and unprepossessing in his appearance, who nonetheless wore on a string around his neck a large and unquestionably fine, though unpolished, turquoise stone of at least—'"

"Lord Ares," Georges suddenly announced from the entrance to the antechamber.

The effect of Ares' appearance in the hall was as a sudden storm that breaks the heat of just such a day that Guibert had described. Interrupted, the lord looked up in displeasure, but as it was truly Ares taking a stand at the lower end of the table, Guibert bit back his objection.

Some guests had to look twice to recognize their old Surchatain, whose salt-and-pepper beard obscured part of his scar. Also, he wore rude work clothes rather than dress blacks, which Henry now wore.

Thom, Paramore, Ben, and the other captains rose simultaneously from their seats; Henry looked up with undisguised relief.

"Papa!" Bonnie cried.

"Papa," Sophie whispered, pushing back her chair.

"Forgive the intrusion, Surchatain," Ares said formally, bowing to Henry, which alarmed the young Surchatain. "Be seated, Lady Sophie," Ares added in a lower voice, as she appeared ready to cross the room to him.

First, Ares' eyes swept the soldiers standing at attention around the hall. Returning his attention to Henry, Ares said, "I have come to advise you that there is treachery at your table."

Startled courtiers looked around; Thom exhaled gently. Henry placed his elbows on the arms of his chair and leaned forward in mild interest. "Say on, Lord Ares."

Ares began walking up the length of Sophie's side of the table. "The Lady Renée, at great risk to herself, uncovered the fact that a high person at this court has been in the habit of making monthly visits to the Sanctum, where he received bribes to falsify reports, and conspired to overthrow you."

A stir passed around the table, with some uttering subdued exclamations while others watched Ares warily. At the mention of Renée, tears appeared in Bonnie's eyes and Elida slumped.

"Sister has her uses," Henry admitted.

"Quite so." With a dry smile, Ares paused behind Wulfredia's chair. She turned to watch him, as everyone else at table was doing.

"Steward Giles," Ares said.

The Steward, three seats up from Wulfredia, straightened. "Surchatain? Er, excuse me. Lord Ares?" His look was attentive, curious, and placid.

"Please take Lord Guibert's manuscript and read from it," Ares said, nodding.

"Certainly, sir. Hand it up here, would you?" Giles gestured down the table, and Guibert's manuscript was passed from hand to hand until it reached the Steward.

While the whole table watched silently, Giles

fumbled in a side pocket of his coat to withdraw a brocade spectacle-case. He opened this leisurely, pleased to be the center of attention without trying, for a change.

From the case he took out a pair of gold-rimmed spectacles. Placing these on his nose, he peered at the script, cleared his throat, and began, "'The history of the greatest mining success in the history of Lystra began on an otherwise—'"

"Giles, how long have you worn the spectacles?" Ares asked almost tenderly.

The Steward looked up, blinking. "Why, for a few years now, Surchatain. Lord. Ares. I don't really need them during the day, of course, but the candlelight is just not sufficient for the eyes anymore."

"Yes, I knew that." Ares smiled as if personally vindicated. "But not everyone does. A witness at the Sanctum identified you as the traitor—"

"I beg your pardon!" Giles huffed.

His wife, next to him, exclaimed, "That is a lie!"

Ares held up his hand. "Peace, Lady Genevieve, I realize that, though the witness did not. When he said that the traitor wore no spectacles while reading by candlelight, I knew that it was not our Giles. But it was someone who *identified* himself as Giles, and signed his reports with the Steward's name and seal.

"So, Steward," Ares continued, "who made monthly trips to the Sanctum and brought back reports signed with your name?"

"Why—" Giles stared at his assistant, Stengi, across the table and three seats down.

The whole table turned to stare at Stengi. Raising his eyes coolly to Ares, he replied, "The Sanctum is in my jurisdiction. But I'm far too busy to go myself. I always send one of my assistants."

"Who, Stengi?" Ares asked.

The man paused, stroking his moustache, while the table waited. "Ah, usually Savidge or Urias."

Ares leaned down with one hand on the back of Wulfredia's chair and the other on Hetrick's chair next to her. "Summon them."

Stengi smiled. "I'm afraid I cannot, Lord Ares. Savidge is in Crescent Hollow, and Urias was dismissed from service some time ago."

Ares smiled. "Then we must bring up our witness to look at your face and say whether the man who conspired to overthrow the Surchatain was you or not."

Stengi erupted, "That fool Manworren? He is an idiot, a dolt, a sot—"

"Yes, he is. But how do you know this, Stengi?" Ares asked.

There followed a strained silence. Stengi began, "Because—the reports—"

Giles interrupted indignantly, "The reports were always favorable to Father Manworren. I read them carefully."

"As did I," Ares said, straightening. "It always raised suspicions in others"—he glanced up the table at Thom, then Father Birondo—"that the reports were uniformly favorable to the Master, especially when there were so many petitions from him for anathema on various Brethren."

Stengi sat back and looked at Ares for a long time. Finally he said, "It makes no difference what you do with me. The die is cast, and changes will be made whether you wish it or not. I am not alone."

"Oh, that I also know," Ares said. "Father Man-worren was even more a fool than you think, and you were greatly mistaken to trust him in any measure. He left behind documents that the Second Oswald is—"

"Now! Strike now!" Upon the startling revelation that Ares possessed written proof of conspiracy, the shouted command came from someone at the table and several people jumped up from their chairs. One overturned a lower section of table on the unfortunate guests across from him, burying a half-dozen of them in linen, tableware, and spilled food.

Under cover of this distraction, while screams and shouts erupted in the hall and soldiers converged on the table, another guest whipped a knife from his belt and threw it toward the head of the table.

Glimpsing the thrown knife, Ares wheeled to watch where its point might land. In this instant, shielded by the confusion, a third conspirator thrust a knife into Ares' unprotected side.

At the sudden searing pain, he whipped back to regard in surprise his assailant's satisfied expression.

12

hile Oswald, Nicole, Renée, and Tassos sat around the table watching Faguy pore over the parchments, a quiet knock sounded on the door to the apse.

The group quickly looked up; Oswald rose to walk over to the door and open it. Three monks stood meekly outside. One began a nervous petition: "Please excuse us, friend, but we were looking—"

"Brother Degani?" Tassos called, craning his neck.

Oswald stepped back to allow the three to enter the room. "Brother Tassos," murmured Degani. "We had thought you were already under anathema."

"I would have been, were it not for the intervention of Surchatain Ares," Tassos said. "Does anyone know where Master Manworren is?"

"He and another brother took horses and rode north in great haste," Degani explained.

"Who went with him?" Tassos demanded.

"Brother Bernard," Degani said.

"The pretender," Tassos scoffed. "If he is a monk, then I am a Surchatain. What did they take with them?"

"Naught that we could see," Brother Degani replied.

Tassos told the guests, "I fear that they have ridden to Westford to summon armed assistance from their conspirators."

"So has the Surchatain ridden to Westford," Oswald grunted, coming back to the table to reclaim his seat. "So we'll see which set of arms arrives first. Now then, Faguy, this cipher of the Father's interests me. Can you break it?"

"If I have time," Faguy said a little pensively. Regarding his sometime wife's adoring gaze, he cleared his throat. "I will need scrap parchment, quill and ink," Faguy said, spreading out a little.

Tassos immediately rose to find the necessary items in the Father's desk and place them before the cryptologist, then sat back down. Brother Degani spoke quietly to the two other monks, who left. He then stood behind Tassos' chair to watch.

"All right, then," Faguy said, dipping the quill. "The first sheet, that with the columns here, appears to be of primary importance. You will notice that on subsequent sheets, the same words are repeated with numbers next to them. So let us decipher what appears to be a list, and go from there. We will begin with the first column of nine words." These were:

IBXAZ HTAXV CDGP TIPI TATTE CTSAJPV HTAGPJF PWRDG RXGPY

"Now, we see first that our encoder—presumably Father Manworren—is careless or cocky, for he took no trouble to disguise the number of letters in each word; apparently, the first word is of five letters, the second five, the third four, and so on. This gives us a valuable reference point, if we can indeed count on it," Faguy lectured while Renée watched in admiration.

He glanced at her, then continued, "When we count the total number of letters in these nine words—"

"They are forty-seven," Tassos said like an eager schoolchild. "Oh—pardon me."

"Not at all. Have you seen this writing before?" Faguy asked, his eyes keen.

"No, friend. But the cipher interests me, so I counted while you talked," Tassos said innocently.

Oswald's lip curled slightly, and Faguy colored. "Yes, well, forty-seven," Faguy said, writing that down.

He looked over the list again, then resumed, "A brief examination tells us that one cipher—**T**—stands out for its frequency. We note that **T** appears"—he counted —"seven times of the forty-seven, disproportionately more than the others.

"Since we know that the most commonly used letter in our language is E, we are going to assume that the cipher **T** has been used for the letter E. So if we begin structuring the words that way, we have—" Faguy wrote:

_ _ _ _ _   _ E _ _ _   _ _ _ _   E _ _ _   E _ EE _

_ E _ _ _ _ _   _ E _ _ _ _ _   _ _ _ _ _   _ _ _ _ _

The others looked at this beginning doubtfully. Faguy went on, "Now, let us assume that our cocky encoder merely used a cipher wheel to encode his text. That is, if the cipher **T** stands for the letter E, then the cipher **U** would stand for F, and so on. Like this." And he wrote two alphabets, one next to the other:

P — A
Q — B
R — C
S — D
T — E
U — F
V — G
W — H
X — I
Y— J
Z — K
A — L
B — M
C — N
D — O
E — P
F — Q
G — R
H — S
I — T
J — U
K — V
L —W
M — X
N — Y
O — Z

"The left alphabet here represents our cipher text, and the right is the alphabet of our message. So let us try it, and see what we have," Faguy proposed, redipping his quill. "We locate **I**—the first cipher of the first word—in the left alphabet, and see which letter it corresponds to."

"That is T," Nicole said, looking over his shoulder.

"T. Yes, it is. Thank you, Surchataine." While the others looked on, Faguy quickly deciphered the first word to read, "tmilk." He paused to look at it.

"'Tmilk'?" muttered Oswald. Tassos sat back in disappointment.

Faguy studied the stubborn cipher for a few minutes. "Well. He has either added false letters, or—ho, now! I see my error."

The others sat up in renewed interest as he redipped his quill. "Because there are seven of the **T** cipher, I assumed that to be E. However, there are six of the **P** cipher, which could just as easily be E. Let us rearrange our alphabets here and try again."

So saying, he wrote out two new alphabets, matching up **P** in the cipher alphabet with E in the message alphabet. Then he carefully deciphered the first word to read

"'Xqmpo'?" Oswald muttered. "I think I like 'tmilk' better."

Tassos regarded Faguy in sympathy. "The Master is clever. Because he is coarse and wicked does not mean he cannot cover himself."

Faguy blinked over the nonsensical text, aware of Renée's silent gaze. Redipping his quill with resolve, he said, "Indeed he is. Still, I am certain it is a Caesar cipher. We shall attack it with brute force."

Although the term sounded promising, the onlookers soon discovered that it involved Faguy's writing out long charts of letters which he compared to each other, one at a time. Since this was not very exciting to watch, the group began to lose interest.

One by one, they drifted away from the table to get something to eat or drink. Tassos excused himself to visit the latrine, but returned straightway. Still Faguy labored over his charts.

Oswald began nodding in his chair, then sat up abruptly to look outside. "The Surchatain will have reached Westford by now," he observed.

Faguy nodded, but kept working. Brother Degani slipped out to see if any of the Brethren had news. Nicole continued to sit quietly at the table. She looked to be deep in thought, or listening, as she was not attending Faguy's labors.

But Renée was. Although it was imperative that Faguy get the text deciphered as soon as possible because of whatever was happening in Westford, he was motivated not as much by looming catastrophe as by her steadfast attention.

Half an hour later, Faguy had his head in his hands, despairing over the gibberish in front of him. Oswald and Nicole were seated at the table while Tassos stood on watch at the garden window. They were silent, thinking of the critical minutes inexorably burning away, but knowing better than to whip a beast that is already on its knees under a too-heavy load.

Renée lowered her eyes to the worksheets scattered across the table, then she blinked. "'Tmilk,'" she said. "That is 'Klimt' backwards. He is that horrible little cousin of Lady Tate's who is always peering around corners."

It was as though lightning hit the group. Oswald and Nicole sprang up; Tassos threw himself back down to a chair as Faguy seized his first pair of alphabets.

Following "Klimt," Faguy deciphered the next word to read, "Giles." "Manworren has written a list of conspirators," Oswald said.

"Perhaps," Faguy said, splattering ink as he hastily redipped the quill.

Irritably, Nicole said, "No. I do not believe it. Not Giles."

"Why not?" Renée asked.

"He is not bent that way," Nicole said stubbornly. "He would not betray Ares. I will never believe it."

"Should a man have anyone to believe in him as you do, Lady, he would never go astray," Tassos murmured.

"As it happens, the Surchataine is right," Oswald grunted, with a long glance at her. "We knew it was not Giles when the brother here said he saw no spectacles on him and described him with brown hair. The Steward is almost as vain about his silver hair, what he has left of it, as a woman. And he couldn't read anything without his spectacles."

As they absorbed that, Oswald concluded, "It was probably Stengi, using Giles' name and title, to protect himself in case he was found out. So, Faguy, who's next on the list?"

Faguy required another ink bottle at that point—his fourth of the evening—then set the quill to parchment once more. Tassos rose from the table to leave the room briefly, returning with Brother Degani. Meanwhile, Faguy moved on to the third word, which translated to "Aron."

"The jeweler?" Renée said in dismay. "Oh, this is too painful for words." But she did not seem surprised by the possibility.

The remainder of the column translated to "Tate," a lady who had been particularly demanding of special privileges; "Peele," "Gaulden," "Quarles," and "Rocha," all discontented nobles who were well known to the palace, being nightly dinner guests, and "Jaric," a newcomer to Westford whom no one knew anything about, except that he dressed well.

With that, Faguy said, "Given that 'Giles' is a pseudonym, it does indeed appear to be a list of conspirators, beginning with the most involved. Therefore, I would hazard to guess that these are lists of payments from the Father." He tapped the second parchment, that with the numerals.

"Payments?" Renée bristled. "Why should he pay them?"

"Let us say rather, investments," Faguy amended. "That is, he was diverting gifts made to the leprosarium to support rebellion against the throne."

"'Support rebellion'?" Nicole asked. "How?"

"Well, the money would be routed to the conspirators in Westford to buy arms, hire mercenaries, and pay bribes. It is not cheap to remove a Surchatain," Faguy said with downcast humor.

"If that can be established, then this is proof of treason," Nicole said quietly. Which was punishable by death.

"Yes," Faguy said, and dipped the quill in the inkwell again. He paused to look at Renée and murmur, "Thank you."

She puckered her moist lips at him. "We're in this together, darling." He cleared his throat, wiping the excess ink off the quill.

He worked a little longer in deciphering more names, which only reinforced their first assumption about what they had. Oswald began to get restless. "This information must go to the palace at once. The Surchatain will be in conference with them by now. Given this proof, he will arrest these named, then have the rest of the parchments studied.

"But we must act quickly—once the traitors realize they have been exposed, they will strike recklessly. They won't unseat Henry, but they could do great harm."

Faguy stood, gathering up the parchments with ink-stained hands. "I will take them."

"Wonderful idea, darling." Renée also stood, ordering Brother Degani, "Take out my bags and wake my hostler to ready my carriage at once. Speak to him in signs; he's quite deaf." Tassos rose with a gesture to Degani, and they both hurried to retrieve her belongings from the bedchamber.

Faguy paused, clutching the parchments, and she eyed him humorously. "Or were you going to walk them to Westford?" she posed.

"No, you are quite right, Lady," he admitted.

She sidled up to him, toying with his frayed collar. "And then tomorrow we can find another notary."

He blinked. "All right."

While the Sanctum's gates were opened to allow the fast departure of Renée and Faguy, driven by Jack, Nicole watched with a hazy sense of disquiet. "Is it well, Oswald? Do you think Ares arrived in time?"

"Oh, yes, Surchataine. All is well," he said.

She turned back up the golden nave with a sigh. "I'm very tired."

"Go rest in the Master's bedchamber, Surchataine. I will keep watch."

"Thank you, Oswald." She glanced at him with grateful eyes before proceeding up the nave. At the altar she paused. Troubled, she laid a hand on its burled wood. Then she shook her head and exited to the Master's quarters.

While the blood seeped through the hole in his shirt, Ares stared at Lady Tate. She drew back the knife preparatory to striking again, more effectively. In the instant that he regarded her, his eyes communicated: *Why? I gave you what favors you asked of me.*

And her eyes replied, *It was not enough.*

The next instant, Wulfredia, glimpsing the blood and the knife, shot up from her chair. She grabbed a large pewter platter, scattering the fried vegetables it held. Wheeling with a cry, she slammed the platter into Lady Tate's face. The lady's head snapped back at the blow. She tottered, dropping the knife, then fell straight back onto the marble floor.

"Surchatain!" Savary gasped at the blood. He snatched up a linen napkin to attempt to press it against the wound. But Ares was taking stock of the larger situation: the rebellion had been immediately quashed.

Stengi was being held tightly between two guards; another soldier's booted foot had clamped Lord Gaulden's head to the floor, and Captain Crager was withdrawing eight inches of bloody blade from someone else's limp form. Guests were surfacing from under dishes and overturned chairs, breathing heavily, looking around.

With palpitating heart, Ares looked to the head of the table to see what had become of the thrown knife. Henry was standing, sword in hand; Sophie was sitting in shock. Where was the knife? Ares scanned others at the front anxiously; he saw blank faces, but no blood.

As if prompted by a word in his ear, he suddenly fixed on the appraylere sitting in front of Henry's place. Sticking straight out from the pitcher was the knife, its point buried in the baked pork mixture. "Again You have saved us," Ares whispered.

"Papa!" Sophie screamed.

The table suddenly awoke to the fact that the old Surchatain was injured, what with the doctor anxiously daubing at the blood covering his side to assess the wound.

Thom rounded the table at a run; he stopped to take in Wulfredia still clutching the platter and Lady Tate unconscious on the floor with a bloody nose.

"Get him to the infirmary," Savary barked.

"No," Ares objected. "It is not serious. But this is: I have left the traitor Manworren at the Sanctum with the Surchataine still there. Thom, I need fifty of the Blue in saddles at once."

"Fifty riders! Summon the Blue!" Thom shouted over his shoulder, and Captains Fawler and Sankary sprinted out of the hall. "I shall lead them, Surchatain," Thom said, eyeing Ares' drained face.

"Come if you will," Ares said, moving away from Savary's ministrations.

"Surchatain, you must not ride. You must come lie down until I can stop the bleeding," Savary insisted.

Ares paused, weighing a response. "I would not override your instructions, Doctor, except that the peril is so great. I beg your indulgence. I must ride."

He turned toward the door, but Henry stepped up to block his path. The two evaluated each other a moment, then the young Surchatain said, "Let me ride with you."

"You may," Ares said.

He took another step, only to find his firstborn at his side, weeping. "Papa, please go lie down."

He leaned over to kiss her forehead, then that of her sister behind her. Looking at one, then the other, he whispered, "I must ride back to your mother. Do you understand?"

"Yes, Papa," Sophie said, broken, but Bonnie turned to fling herself on her husband.

Ares eyed him, but allowed Henry to give the order: "Captain Ben, I leave you and Captain Fawler in charge of the palace defenses until we return." Wordlessly, Ben saluted. He then turned to instruct that the rebels be taken down to the dungeon.

In minutes Ares was on Burl with fifty of Lystra's finest gathering on horseback behind him. He had been detained only by Savary's insistence on wrapping a belt of cotton tightly around his midsection to help staunch the bleeding. While the horses danced restlessly on the torchlit cobbles of the courtyard, soldiers opened the creaking, iron-banded gates.

"Forward!" Ares shouted, digging his heels into Burl's sides.

On his right rode Henry, on his left, Thom.

Immediately behind them rode the Second Paramore, Captain Sankary, and fifty of the Blue.

Thom and Henry carried torches, as did ten of those following, but the night was still quite dark. The horses were compelled to gallop blindly down the southbound road that they knew by heart, the riders gathering in a tight formation to avoid the ditches alongside the road.

They passed the fields where the Greens had made their heroic stand against the Qarqarian invaders seventeen years ago—the fields which always raised a lump in Ares' throat. Those young boys, now glorified, seemed to hover among the stars, watching their earthly comrades pound toward the Sanctum.

Suddenly there was an oncoming carriage in their path. Ares cried a halt; there followed collisions, confusion, and a smattering of riders thrown into the meadow bordering the road. The carriage horse reared in fright, but its driver was skillful and the carriage was not overturned.

When order was somewhat restored in the ranks, Ares called, "Who goes there?"

"Get out of my way!" came the enraged response.

"Lady Renée," Ares said in illumination.

Astride his horse, Thom brought his torch to the side of the carriage so that the principals could see each other. Faguy began urgently, "Surchatain, we have— dear Lord, you are bleeding!"

"I am all right," Ares said, perspiration streaming down his face. "What do you have?"

"We have found the papers of Manworren's which appear to be a list of conspirators and payments. The Second Oswald was insistent that they be brought to your attention at once, and acted on at once." Faguy waved the sheaf of parchments bound with a silk cord.

"What of Manworren?" Ares asked, gripping the reins while Burl danced.

"He escaped—Tassos was convinced he rode to Westford to gather arms, which is why the Second was so adamant that we bring word to you at once. He was sure they would attack the palace tonight," Faguy said.

Ares blinked. Breathing heavily, he asked, "How long ago did Manworren leave?"

"Hours, Surchatain. He will be in Westford now, making the rounds of these friends!" Faguy exclaimed, shaking the sheaf.

"Thom. Henry." Ares turned on Burl's bare back. "You must escort Faguy and Renée back to the palace. Send soldiers to these houses at once. Put them under house arrest until charges can be formally brought. Make sure everything is done legally and in order, but *do it now*."

"Surchatain." Thom saluted. His eyes watered as he took a long look at Ares' greying face, then he wheeled his horse to cry, "Make way for the carriage! Back to the palace! Rear troops about face and ride!"

The riders fell back for Jack to urge the jittery horse forward, flanked by the officers. Ares watched their training manifest itself: in minutes the dark road had swallowed up the soldiers, the hoofbeats fading to a distant drumming.

A waning moon peeked out from behind the clouds as Henry alone sat on his horse next to Ares. Henry said, "Nicole is safe, Ares. Oswald is with her. There is no reason for you to ride on to the Sanctum tonight."

Ares turned his head, and Henry watched his chest laboriously rise and fall with each breath. "I do not know that. Manworren may deliver his message, then return to take vengeance. Oswald is only one man. He may not be enough. I must be there."

When Ares kicked Burl, Henry kept abreast of him. Rather than argue with him, Henry said, "Then I will ride with you."

Ares reined up. "Your responsibility is with your office, to preserve order and peace. You cannot do that from the Sanctum. You must go back to Westford now." Ares kicked Burl again, decisively enough to elicit a neighed objection.

Stubbornly, Henry stayed at his side. Ares wheeled on him. "You can't follow me on this road, Henry!" In a whisper, he added, "You will come later."

Henry dropped his head, wiping his eyes, while a sudden gust scattered blond curls across his brow. He nodded, turning his horse northward at a gallop.

Ares closed his eyes, steeling himself against the growing pain. This time, Burl did not wait for the goad of the heels to leap forward into a gallop. Ares gasped, drawing up his knees, then put his head down to ride.

Even at such a pace, it was several more hours to the Sanctum, and Burl had to slow now and then to make sure his way was clear on the dark road.

Ares did not attempt to guide him, but trusted the horse to take him where he needed to go. And he needed to go to Nicole. He must make it back to her. The pain grew intense; and the blackness—had the night become that much darker? But Ares rode on. He had to.

To keep himself conscious, he prayed, as he had

done constantly over these last three days. "You will bring good from this," he whispered. "You will enable Henry—unh!"

He grunted in pain as Burl stumbled over an unseen obstruction. But the horse regained his footing, and Ares gasped, "I beg—that You enable Henry to rule wisely, with honor, and justice—that you safeguard my precious daughters, and my wife, the light of my life. . . ."

He looked at the black shape of the abbey rising on the hill at his left, but Burl seemed to know that this was not their destination, and galloped on. "The children here, these orphans—grow them to be mighty in Your love, and truth—to walk in the light of Your truth. . . .

"Save Lystra from the lawless," he groaned. "Preserve her in Your peace." Spent, he laid his head on the rippling neck, gripping the mane to stay astride the broad back. And the hooves pounded on.

There were gates. And shouting that sounded a great distance off. Burl danced in place, then moved forward again. When the horse trotted into the travelers' courtyard and lowered his head, Ares fell off.

The lights brought him around—there were flaming torches around him, and campfires burning low here and there. *Which battleground is this?* Ares thought, rousing himself. *I must fight—but where am I? On the plain south of Westford?* He looked around at the boys being slaughtered on his right and his left while the dripping sword hung heavy in his trembling hand.

The Poison Greens? Suddenly he was on the black horse, surveying the fighting around him. He reached back into his quiver time and again to pick off Qarqarians the moment before they could deliver the death blow to a Lystran soldier on the ground.

Hornbound? All at once he was encased in a ring of fire, waiting for Ulm's army to come crush the remnant of rebellious slaves.

Then doors were opened in front of him, and he looked into a brightly lit nave. *No. This is a church,* he realized in relief. *I must go in to pray.*

Shoving aside strange, unwelcome hands, Ares staggered up the steps to enter the doors. Bracing himself on the entryway, he blinked up the candlelit nave. *Nicole is here. She is here somewhere.*

Rasping for breath, squinting to focus, he somehow placed one foot in front of the other to walk up the nave. Did he know this church? It had such a long nave, extending such a great long way from the entrance to the apse. The columns, too, were crooked, jumping out erratically in his path.

As he advanced, he focused on the windows in the back, of Christ in battle, Christ on the throne. How brightly they were lit! How they shone.

Almost blind, he stumbled into something, the feel of which told him was the altar in the apse. He had made it; she was close by. She would not be far from the altar.

Exhaling, he reached out his hands, extending himself to lie across the altar, and there he closed his eyes.

I3

The first sensation that Ares experienced was that of bells. He heard bells tolling matins. It was a sweet sound, a sound that a soul new to heaven might hear. He listened contentedly, gratefully, until other sensations asserted themselves on his awakening consciousness.

He smelled Renée's perfume. *Then I am not in heaven*, he thought, disturbed. There was something wet on his face. His gut ached sharply.

He opened his eyes blearily to see Nicole sitting beside him. She looked calm and beautiful as she regarded him in satisfaction. He spat out something that tasted like wet cotton.

"I would rather not die at the site of Renée's latest conquest," he mumbled.

"What?" she laughed, stroking his head.

"I assume that I am in Manworren's bed, and the reminder of her presence is making my head ache," he muttered. Watching her remove the thin, wet strip from his pillow, he asked, "What is that?"

"It is an invention of the doctor's to wick water to someone in a deep sleep, who cannot drink on his own," she said, moving the small bowl of water from beside his head to his lips. "Drink."

Groaning, he lifted up enough to drain the bowl before lying back down. "How have you acquired the doctor's knowledge?" he asked, feeling on the sheet for her hand.

She took his fingers to kiss them, leaning over him. "From the doctor. He followed you down from Westford."

Ares studied her. Smiling, she explained, "The Brethren alerted Oswald at once when you came, but we might have lost you had the doctor not arrived. He said the wound is not deep, but you lost much of your necessary humors."

Ares sighed, tentatively feeling the bandage over the wound. "Lady Tate was the one who stabbed me," he murmured, still offended.

"Of course," she briskly, and he looked at her in surprise. "You would not sleep with her," she added. His brow creased at the revelation of the lady's motivation. "The doctor also said that her stabbing you is what saved your life. Had it been a man, you would not have survived."

Oswald came in from the outer room, saluting. "Surchatain," he said, then waited for instructions as if the change in locale and circumstance was irrelevant.

"Where is this doctor who defied my orders?" Ares asked coolly.

"What orders were those, Surchatain?" Oswald replied. "No one remembers hearing you order the doctor to stay at Westford, and Surchatain Henry ordered him to follow with medicines to see that you were tended, so when the doctor finished his duty here, and gave the Surchataine instructions for your care, he returned to the palace to see to the traitors' injuries."

At this, Ares pulled himself to a sit, looking out to the morning sunshine. "What has transpired over the night?"

"A great deal, Surchatain. I just sent back the latest messenger from Westford." Oswald paused to find a beginning point. "Of those who attacked at dinner last night, Gaulden and Aron are in prison. Stengi is in prison. Quarles is dead; Lady Tate has not yet awakened, and the doctor does not believe she will."

Ares looked aside contemplatively. "Lord Roschlau was not among the conspirators?"

"No, Surchatain. Whether he was made agreeable by the palace's sponsorship of his pamphlet, or was simply a toothless barking dog all along, it seems clear he never conspired against you. His name appears nowhere in Manworren's records. Lord Faguy was up all the night translating them," Oswald replied.

Thinking, Ares straightened with a grimace. "The question is: are they reliable?" Nicole handed him another cup of water with a command in her hazel eyes; he complied to drink it down.

"The Counselor feels they are proof enough for arrest. He sent out sealed warrants for all so named, and they were brought in throughout the night. There were Klimt, Peele, Rocha, Jaric, that I can remember—"

"What of Manworren?" Ares asked.

Oswald nodded. "He was caught with Spechler, the false notary. They were taken in the very act of arming mercenaries. They're also residing in prison, and may stay a while. Without Faguy's translations of the lists, we'd 'a' not known who we were looking for till they had killed Henry."

Ares' gaze sharpened. "That was their plan? To kill Henry?"

"Certainly, as it had been to kill you. Faguy determined that Lord Quarles had paid a large sum of money to the poulterer," Oswald replied.

Nicole looked up quickly—the poulterer had used his access to the palace kitchen to poison Ares twice. He had also attempted to poison Henry and Sophie, and had succeeded in poisoning the Second Rhode.

"I see," Ares murmured, sinking back down. In exhaustion, he closed his eyes again, and Oswald quietly withdrew.

It was several hours later that Ares awoke with a different sort of pain in his gut: hunger. "Lady," he murmured, lifting himself with effort at the aroma that had brought him to consciousness.

Nicole had just set on the bedside table a plate of venison roasted with carrots and onions, lightly seasoned. It was the kind of plain food that Ares had always preferred. She indicated her desire to feed him, but he took the plate and fork to eat for himself.

As he was finishing, Oswald stuck his head in the door. "Surchatain, you have visitors."

"Show them in," Ares said, handing off the plate to his caretaker.

Two large men stepped into the elegant bedchamber, and Ares regarded the tired, sweaty faces of Henry and Thom. Nicole rose, smiling.

The Commander appraised Ares' healthy color and

alert demeanor, then glanced at her to murmur, "I will ever regard you as a miracle worker, Lady."

"It was the doctor's doing," she demurred.

At the sight of Ares alive and breathing, Henry was unable to speak for a moment. After an aborted attempt at a jest or two, he finally blurted in defiance, "I did follow you. Only later."

"And sent the doctor after his runaway patient. Savary is a stubborn fellow," Ares observed.

Henry plopped into the chair beside the bed; Thom drew up a second for himself. Ares asked the Commander, "What is happening in Westford? How are the people reacting to the arrests of so many prominent nobles?"

"All is quiet," Thom said wryly, "and any fears we had of a popular revolt seem to be put to bed. Stengi's relatives have come out with evidence against him; the other nobles in prison appear to have been abandoned. No one has come to see them; no one has sent a letter. Evidently, they did not have wide support for insurrection."

Ares nodded, his eyes traveling over the luxurious appointments in the room without seeing them. Wincing, he leaned forward. "Instruct the Counselor to proceed cautiously, according to the strict letter of the Law. Any conviction of treason must be on overwhelming evidence, not simply that of Manworren's records—they are just as likely to be wrong as not.

"If the evidence against anyone is not compelling, you must release him. You must give them time to call witnesses and present a defense. Any evidence that Stengi presents against anyone is to be disregarded—he knows that he is facing death, so he will attempt to take down with him anyone he hates. If we err in our judgments, it must be on the side of mercy."

"That may result in the release of a traitor, who will then resume his designs," Thom noted.

"The alternative is to put the innocent to death, which will cripple Henry's reign," Ares said. "Let God see to the invisible; let us act according to what light He gives us."

Thom stood. "I will relay these instructions word for word."

Henry remained seated. He blinked, then glanced up self-consciously at Thom and Nicole. "May I . . . have a word with him alone?"

Smiling, Nicole crossed the room to take Thom's arm. "Come, Commander; let me show you the leprosarium, and tell you what little surprise Ares left for us there."

"Surchataine," he acquiesced, glancing back to the bed with the shadow of a smile.

Henry waited until they had left the Master's chambers altogether, then turned to his surrogate father to study the humorous eyes and ghastly scar. "I thought you were going to die," Henry said.

"So did I," Ares said, shifting.

Henry looked down to the sheet, blankly picking at a loose thread. "I don't know if I can carry on when you pass."

"You have to," Ares said. "For Sophie's sake. For your children's sake. For those who come long after your bones have turned to dust."

The serious grey eyes softened a little. "Will you

come back to Westford, then? After the doctor gives you leave to ride?"

Ares inhaled contemplatively. "No," he said. "I rather like it here. Nicole loves the garden, and it is close to the Sea. No, I think we will stay."

Regarding him, Henry assumed a bargaining air. "Sophie wants badly to see you."

"She may come for a visit, with a bodyguard," Ares countered. "And Bonnie, if she wishes."

Henry snorted, "Bonnie may be a little busy for a few days. Sister is taking her out to buy dresses—and who knows what else. Ben is not happy."

"Throughout eternity, some things never change," Ares said.

"AND, Sister and Faguy went to another notary to get properly remarried this morning. They demanded to see his license first," Henry related.

"Love is stronger than sanity," Ares observed.

Henry chortled, "But you should see Maddie—now all of a sudden she's curtsying to him and calling him 'Lord Faguy.'"

"Ah." Ares smiled.

"Speaking of insanity, a fellow showed up this morning with irrefutable proof that the world is flat! He demanded a hearing!" Henry laughed.

Ares looked confounded. "Why? That is absurd. What could he hope to gain from an impossible position?"

"Well, because of the—" Henry paused while Ares watched him. "Because someone issued a challenge to prove it, and, I suppose he assumed that, of course, someone at the palace would know something about it."

Ares listened to this deficient explanation while trying to decide whether he really wanted to know the full story or not. Then he decided that it did not matter if he knew. It was time to let go.

A shadow filled the doorway, and they both looked up at Brother Tassos. "Oh—pardon, Surchatain. I had not realized—"

"I'm done with him," Henry said, standing.

He looked down on Ares, and the old Surchatain looked up at his replacement. For the first time, Ares saw it: the conviction in Henry's face that this was his calling to perform, and somehow, he would do it. By the grace of God, he would do this. With a silent nod, Henry turned and left.

"Come in, Tassos. What is on your mind?" Ares asked.

"Surchatain, forgive my presumption. Many of the Brethren are wondering . . . what will become of us, and what you will do with the Sanctum now," Tassos said.

"Why, I wish to rededicate it to the purpose for which it was originally built, Brother Tassos. And I wish you to be Master," Ares said.

Tassos looked stunned. "Not you yourself, sir? As Master?"

"No. Merely a guest," Ares said, easing back in satisfaction.

"And—the leprosarium?" Tassos asked.

Ares sat up. "I want to reopen it, Tassos. I want to collect all the lepers who were turned away, and I want you to find those who were turned out under Manworren's anathema. Compel them to come back."

Tassos began to blink rapidly. "I know where some

are, Surchatain. They have been in hiding nearby. Only . . . Leland. I do not know where Brother Leland is now."

"Father Birondo knows. He has been hiding him for quite some time," Ares said, readjusting the pillow under his back. "Furthermore, I see ample means in this room alone of funding their care for a great while to come. So go get them."

"Surchatain." Tassos bowed in gratitude.

But as the new Master turned away, head swimming, Ares remembered something. "Oh—Tassos."

"Sir?"

"I am the one who had placed the rosary and the diptych in your rooms," Ares said.

Tassos regarded him quietly for a moment. "And the saltcellar—?"

"Yes, that was my doing, also," Ares confessed.

Tassos studied him, then lowered his head and laughed. "I see, Surchatain. Yes, I certainly see." He paused to contend with a sudden inner conflict. "Surchatain, may I . . . keep the books?"

"What books?" Ares asked.

"Father Manworren bribed me with books to keep silent about his actions. I was prepared to relinquish them, but. . . ."

"Where did they come from?" Ares asked.

"They were gifts from donors—"

"For use at the Sanctum," Ares finished.

"Yes," Tassos said.

"Then who better to use them than you?"

Tassos hesitated. "I will, with the Surchatain's permission."

"I am not Surchatain, but permission is granted you," Ares said a little impatiently.

"Thank you, Surchatain. Will that be all?" Tassos' mind was already back at his book shelf.

"Yes," Ares sighed, settling back. His side hurt. "You are dismissed."

Moments after Tassos had hurried out, Nicole returned to reseat herself at Ares' bedside. "Henry has collected Thom to ride back."

"Good," he said, twining his fingers in hers. "They have much hard work ahead of them."

They sat quietly a moment, then he said, "Nicole, do you want to go back to Westford?"

She looked at him in mild alarm, then murmured, "If you go back."

"That does not answer my question."

"Is it necessary?" she asked.

"That also does not answer my question."

"No," she said. "I want to stay here, but only if you are here also."

He pressed both her hands in his to bring them up to his face. "Then you and I will stay; Henry and Thom and Vogelsong can take care of Westford. Sophie will probably come visit soon, but it may be a few days before we see Bonnie. Renée is taking her shopping."

Nicole expelled a laugh, then laid her head contentedly on his chest. She rested there a moment, then murmured, "Do you hear it? The Sea?"

Ares' brows lifted minutely; no, the surf was not audible from here. "Yes."

"Then I want nothing more," she sighed.

There passed a few days while Ares and Nicole made themselves at home in the Sanctum. There passed a few weeks while Manworren's goods were cleared out and sold; the leprosarium refurbished; and old friends reunited.

There passed a few months while the administrators at Westford struggled over questions of law and judgment. Lord Quarles had been killed by Captain Crager the night of the uprising—Quarles had thrown the knife right in front of the Captain's face.

Lord Peele died later of wounds suffered then, as well. Lady Tate died without ever waking, but her cousin Klimt was merely banished, as it could not be proved that he had been anything but a lackey. Lord Davignon's man Joslyn was never found. The consensus was that he was dead, but no one would admit to his murder. Lord Aron, the jeweler, disappeared from prison and the face of the Earth.

Manworren, Bernard, Spechler, Stengi, and Gaulden went to trial. Manworren's trial, coming first, was most memorable.

With funds from an unknown source, Manworren acquired an advocate from Crescent Hollow who was a skillful researcher and compelling orator. This man spent the greater part of the trial elaborating not on his client's activities, but on those of the Westfordians.

Specifically, the lawyer exposed in detail the outrageous duplicity of the Surchataine Nicole in gaining illicit entry to the Sanctum with her "friend," the Second Oswald. Ares, in the observers' gallery, listening to the besmirching of his wife's honor, was seen to bleed continually from his scar. (Nicole had excused herself from the gallery that day.) Nonetheless, he listened quietly, but Oswald had to be removed from the hall.

Next, the lawyer turned his attention to Ares' shocking subterfuge in stealing treasures meant for the sustenance of the church, in impersonating a monk and betraying confidences, and, most appalling, in defiling the sanctified leprosarium with the contagious body of a dead leper. All during this exposition, Manworren sat listening in grieved sorrow, occasionally raising a hand in forgiving benediction toward his persecutors.

Palace officials at Westford quietly panicked upon seeing this presentation begin to sway the nobles on the jury. Public opinion tilted in favor of the besieged Master, especially when the lawyer recounted the events of the final evening, when the poor monk was subjected to the advances of the lascivious widow Renée. Upon attempting to flee her wicked suggestions, he was set upon by her lover—NOT husband—the penniless hanger-on, Faguy, before escaping with his life.

In the front row of the observers' gallery, Renée very much enjoyed this part of the trial, but honest Faguy might as well have been burned at the stake for the suffering it caused him. And Vogelsong, in charge of the prosecution, appeared helpless to counter such testimony.

But others had not been idle during this one-sided exposition; Father Birondo, though nearly blind and very unworldly, called upon agents both human and divine to arrange for a rebuttal.

Therefore, on the last day of testimony in Manworren's case, the Father brought into the great hall a score of men with brands on their hands. One at a time, beginning with a certain Leland, they testified as to the circumstances of their anathema, branding, and expulsion from the Sanctum. Fellow Brethren still at the Sanctum also gave their testimony about these events.

Brother Tassos, in testimony that amounted to a public confession, recounted with tears sins that made the listeners' hair stand on end. Manworren dropped his facade of holiness to sneer at his former subordinate, and by the end of the day, his lawyer had disappeared.

Manworren was convicted of Treachery by an Intimate and hanged.

His associate Spechler, still incensed over Stengi's revoking his notary license over a few royals, provided hours of testimony against the remaining conspirators which did not help his case. In short order, he and his associates Bernard, Stengi, and Gaulden were tried, convicted, and likewise executed.

But when the relatively unknown Jaric came to trial, he proved by means of letters to his sister in Eurus that he was acting on his own to disrupt the conspiracy, and the only reason he failed was because a key contact lost courage and did not follow through with their plan. After much discussion as to Jaric's fate, Thom engaged him as a spy for Lystra and sent him to Qarqar.

With the successful culmination of the trials, the province reverted to its natural state of engaging in business. Henry settled into the rulership, always wearing the dress blacks at council meetings or open audiences. Thus the days passed.

These combined days stretched into weeks, which rolled into months, which strung themselves together into years. Year after year passed, and as the great snowbanks on the mountains are built from the accumulation of one snowflake upon another, so the increments of time gathered slowly, imperceptibly, until upon this spot of Earth was left only the foundation footings of the church that anchored the Sanctum.

Westford had passed away; the site of the palace, ancient in Ares' day, came to be covered by concrete parkways and tall buildings. But the Sanctum foundations lay exposed in open meadow. And one day, a group of visitors gathered on this spot.

Their leader crushed out a cigarette under his foot as he talked on his phone. "Look, it's a ten-hour flight back; there's no way I can pull everything together for a lecture in Chicago on the twenty-third. I've got term papers to grade and a mandatory faculty meeting. . . . Well, they'll just have to reschedule. Later."

Pocketing his phone, he turned to the two dozen students following him and raised his voice. "Okay, this is our last stop for the day, so we'll make this short and sweet—Caldwell, put away that iPod or I'll flunk you on class participation for the day. Okay—shut up, people! Now this is a minor site; we wouldn't be here but for the recent discovery of a funerary stone."

A soft groan rose from the group, half of whom were checking messages. A number of the young women were slapping or scratching their bare legs in the knee-high grass, and a few threw up their hands to head for a tour bus in the distance.

The leader, meanwhile, ducked under a nominal rope barrier to stand over the stone. It lay flat in the earth, apparently in the middle of the ruins. His students, some extending recorders, clustered around him on the outside of the rope while he continued to lecture.

"From the shape of the outer walls, being in a cross, we can ascertain that this was a small cathedral, probably mid-fourteenth century. The stone was located in the apse, probably under the altar. Excavations are scheduled to start next month, and they're hoping to find relics. Maybe gold, but certainly—"

"May we see the stone, Professor?" one young man asked.

"Don't interrupt, Palmer. Okay. Like I said, minor site, but the stone bears reference to a barbarian chieftain that I've rather come to appreciate. This was Ares—"

"Spell that, Professor?" Palmer requested. He was tall and slender, with curling blond hair and gray eyes. But what made the other students snicker was his taking notes with a pen, on a pad. Of paper.

"A-R-I-E-S," the professor said impatiently. "Now, this chieftain didn't accomplish anything important, but he's still interesting." The professor, a smoker who still made time for the gym, lit a cigarette and began to pace around the stone as he talked.

"He seized power in his little district by butchering the previous ruler, as well as his entire family, which was the normal method, historically, for ascension to the throne. He quelled numerous uprisings by a combination of craftiness and wholescale slaughter, as dictated by the code he followed, known as The Law of Roman. This code provided for absolute sovereignty of a dictator, and was widely recognized as an authority for hundreds of years."

A young woman raised her hand. "Could they read?"

"Good point," the professor replied, pointing at her with his cigarette. "No, for the most part, but they were very superstitious, and any reference to the Law was supposed to invoke some kind of magic power. Also, they did have a few scholars who were able to read and write, and whom Ares relied on to give him what he needed from the Law to achieve his ends.

"Of course, if his advisors wanted to keep their heads, they did what he said. He commonly employed torture and beheadings. And he made judicious use of his daughters," he added with a wink at another young woman in low-rise shorts, who laughed nervously.

Smiling, he took a long drag on the cigarette and continued, "Ares possessed some sort of physical deformity—historians are far from agreement as to what that was, specifically; I've taken the position that it was leprosy—I'll unveil the evidence for that in the paper I'm presenting at the symposium—"

"Give us a hint," one girl coaxed.

"Why should you listen to me?" he asked, again smiling.

"Because you're the expert on barbarian cultures!" she exclaimed.

"Not Dr. Baxter?" he baited. The group hooted and he smiled. Palmer was silent. "Well, one big clue is the site you're standing on. There are some external references to the fact that Ares established this for the care of lepers. No way would he have done that if he weren't one himself."

The students nodded at this obvious logic, and the professor continued, "This disability, whatever it was, sent him into fits of insane rage which inspired terror and awe in his subjects. Hence his long rule."

"Professor, what does the funerary stone say?"

"Palmer, if you don't shut up, I'm swear I'm flunking you out of the class. Okay. During his rule, Ares' little district enjoyed an economic boom that allowed for remarkable stability over hundreds of years. It never really experienced decline, per se, until the population was assimilated by the changing dynamics of the larger political sphere and ceased to exist as a separate entity." Palmer's pen was still during this summation, which he had already read in Dr. Baxter's book.

The professor continued, "Nonetheless, some excellent examples of art and artifacts from this period, along with a sizable portion of The Law, have been recently unearthed. They are on display in the university library."

Palmer's hand shot up. "Professor, has the Law been translated? Is it accessible to students?"

The man looked ready to explode, then suddenly relaxed. "Okay, Palmer, I know you just have to get out all your questions. That's what kiddies do."

He paused for the group to have a laugh at Palmer's expense, but as the young man looked undeterred, the professor explained, "The physical copy is under glass, but a translation with notes has just been uploaded to the university website. I'll try to take a look at it before the symposium."

He checked his phone. "Okay, that's all we have time for here. To the bus, people; time for happy hour."

The young man, Palmer, made eye contact with a young woman in the group, who exhaled and shook her head firmly. He continued to stare at her until she dropped her shoulders in reluctant consent.

The students turned to head for the wheeled speck in the distance. With their departure, only the breathing of the wind and the calls of meadowlarks remained, so the site was quiet once more.

For a moment. Rising up from kneeling in the tall grass, Palmer looked at the departing group, then tapped the shoulder of the girl at his side. "Okay, we've got maybe five minutes."

While she rose, brushing grass and dirt from her bare legs, he crept under the barrier to the site, waving her over. "Palmer! I don't want to get in trouble!" she protested.

"You won't, if you do this quick. Look, Sophia, you're the only one here who's studied dead languages. I just want you to look at the stone and see if you can read it," he urged, glancing back at the diminishing crowd.

With an exasperated sigh, she looked down on the exposed stone. It had been finely chiseled into a rectangle about three feet in width and two feet in height. Engraved on it were the words:

Ares † Nicole
Veritas Lux Mea

"Look at the spelling of his name," Palmer said, writing in his pad. "Nicole. Wife? Mistress? Horse? Never mind; I'll figure that out later. Can you read it?"

"It's Latin," she said, staring at the inscription. "It means, 'The truth is my light.'"

"Is that from the Bible?" he mused.

She blinked. "It can't be. You heard the professor; this site dates from the mid-fourteenth century. The Bible was written by the Southern Baptists in the eighteen-hundreds to defend slavery. I thought you knew that from Dr. Dickerson's class."

"Oh," he said. "No, I—slept through most of his class."

They both stared at the stone a moment. Sophia knelt to run her fingers across the engraved lettering. "He was a good man," she whispered.

Palmer looked back at the bus while the wind scattered blond curls across his brow. "Okay, we gotta hustle. But I'm going to skip happy hour to go look up that translation of The Law. I want to know more."

Sophia stood up. "So do I."

They darted back under the barrier and began running toward the idling bus. Suddenly the two stopped and stared at each other. "Did you hear that?" he whispered. "Like—a laugh?"

"It was a friendly laugh," she insisted. "A chuckle."

"Like . . . we're on the right track." He inhaled. "Okay," he said decisively. "Let's go."

Glossary

For food items, see the Appendix.

alexandrite—the gemstone chrysoberyl, which changes
 color according to the light in which it is viewed

amanuensis (a man you EN sis)—a secretary

anathema (ah NATH e ma)—generally, a curse or
 someone cursed; here, the formal expulsion of a
 member

Ariel (AIR ee ul)—great-grandfather of Ares

Ares (AIR eez)—former Surchatain of Lystra

Aron, Lord—the dominant jeweler of Westford

Athian (A the an)—Lord Backvold's son, who
 challenged Ares for the throne

Auer (OW er), **Lady**—a noblewoman of Westford who
 enticed her nephew Athian to challenge Ares for the
 throne

Backvold, Lord—a nobleman of Westford whose son
 challenged Ares for the throne

Ben—Captain of the Blue Regiment of the Lystran
 army; husband of Ares' daughter Bonnie

Bernard, Brother—a counterfeit monk at the Sanctum

Birondo (beer ON do), **Father**—the priest in the palace at Westford

Bobadil (BOB a dil)—Ares' grandfather, who lost the throne of Lystra when he was murdered by his Commander Talus

Bonnie, Lady—16-year-old daughter of Ares and Nicole, twin sister of Sophie and wife of Captain Ben

Burl—a fast horse from the stables at Westford

Calle (kail) **Valley**—province west of Lystra, famous for its vineyards and fairs, which Ares annexed after defeating its Surchatain in battle

Carmine (CAR men)—former Counselor at Westford, ex-husband of Renée, now deceased

Cedric (SED rik)—son of the usurper Talus; father of Renée and Henry; was murdered as he attempted to execute Ares

Chatain (sha TAN)—son of the ruler of a province; the feminine is **Chataine** (sha TANE)

Crager (KRAY ger)—Captain of the Red Regiment of the Lystran army

Crescent Hollow—capital of Calle Valley before that province was annexed to Lystra

crux—a gold coin minted in Scylla

Davignon (da VEEN yon) **Lord**—a nobleman of Westford

Deirdre (DEE dra)— (1) wife of Roman the Great; (2) Commander Thom's wife

diptych (DIP tick)—a carved or painted object of two flat panels attached at a hinge

Druella (dru EL ah)—formerly maid to Chataine Melva, now Magnus' wife and Surchataine of Scylla

Eledith—capital of Polontis

Elida (ell EE da) **Lady**—Counselor Vogelsong's wife

Eurus (YUR is)—capital of Scylla

Evangeline—wife of the Second Oswald

Faguy (FAH gwee), **Lord**—a long-time ally of Ares, a native of Prie Mer

Fancsali (FANK sah lee), **Lord**—a rich adventurer from Scylla who was murdered by a slaver

Fastnesses—mountain range forming the partial border between Lystra/Qarqar and Scylla/Seleca

Fawler (FOLL er)—Captain of the Green Regiment of the Lystran army

Forcht (fort)—Oswald's alias upon entering the Sanctum

garderobe (GAR de robe)—a water closet, indoor commode

Gaulden, Lord—a discontented noble of Westford

Genevieve (JEN e veeve), **Lady**—Steward Giles' wife

Georges (JEOR jes)—dinner master at Westford

Giles (hard g, long i)—the Steward at the palace of Westford

Goss—textile master of Westford

greenstone—turquoise gem of inferior quality to bluestone turquoise

Guibert (GWEE burt), **Lord**—a nobleman of Westford, newly rich from mining copper and blue turquoise

Henry—Surchatain of Lystra, husband of Ares' daughter Sophie

Hetrick, Lord—a young nobleman of Westford, nephew of Lord Davignon

Hycliff (HI cliff)—once-famous port city on the coast of Lystra, now run down

Jack—groom (or hostler) at Westford who usually drives Renée

Jaric—a new arrival to Westford who dresses well

Joslyn—Lord Davignon's steward

Klar—Surchatain of Eugenia

Leland (LEE lund)—a monk turned out of the Sanctum

leprosarium—a refuge for lepers

Lystra (LIS tra)—province once ruled by Roman the Great, then by his descendant Ares, then by Henry

Maddie—Renée's maid

Magnus (MAG nus)—Surchatain of Scylla once married briefly to Renée

Manworren (MAN wor en)—the monk in charge of the Sanctum

Melva—former Chataine of Qarqar

Menchal (MEN shel)—Lady Sophie's maid

Merle (murl)—head laundress at Westford

Meuer (MYUR er)—the quality second-hand seller of Westford

Nicole (ne COLE)—Ares' wife, mother of Bonnie and Sophie

Ninian (NIN ee an)—Lady Bonnie's maid

Nouri (NUR ee), **Lady**—Nicole's alias upon entering the Sanctum

Odea (oh DAY ah)—the outpost in desolate far western Lystra on the border with Eugenia

Order of Preaching Brethren—the order of monks who serve at the Sanctum

oriel—a projecting room on an upper floor, or an upper-floor bay window

Oswald—Second in Command of the Lystran army under Commander Thom

Paramore (PAIR ah mor)—the junior Second in Command of the Lystran army under Commander Thom

parapet—the top portion of a castle wall, behind which runs a walkway

Passage—the river marking the boundary between Lystra and Scylla

Peele, Lord—a discontented noble of Westford

Pia, Lady—a courtier at Westford

Poison Greens—the notorious mountain range dividing Lystra and serving as a boundary between western Lystra and Qarqar

Polontis (po LAWN tis)—mountainous province far northeast of Lystra, home of the hardy, courageous, but unsophisticated **Polonti** (po LAWN tee)

Prie Mer (pree MARE)—small coastal town, Nicole's birthplace

Purdy—former overseer of livestock at Westford and childhood friend of Nicole's

Qarqar (KAR kar)—mining-rich province northwest of Lystra

Quarles, Lord—a discontented noble of Westford

Renée (ren AY)—Henry's 36-year-old half-sister

retable—a raised shelf or ledge above and behind an altar for holding candles, vases, etc.

Rhea (ray), **Lady**—an old flirt at the court of Westford

Rhode (road)—Second in Command of the Lystran army who gave his life to protect Henry and Sophie

Roman—the first great Surchatain of Lystra; author of Roman's Law; great-great-grandfather of Ares

Roschlau (RAUSH law), **Lord**—a discontented nobleman of Westford

royal—the basic monetary unit traded on the southern coast of the Continent; the value of one gold royal equals fifty silver pieces

Ryal—Commander Thom's 12-year-old son, Henry's page

Sanctum—Lystra's monastery/leprosarium established by Ares

Sankary (SANK air ee)—Captain of the Gold Regiment of the Lystran army

Savary (SAV a rie), Doctor—the physician at Westford

Scylla (SILL ah)—the province to the east of Lystra, ruled by Magnus

Seleca (SEL e kah)—once-great province to the northeast of Lystra, now riddled with slave markets

Socius (SO shus)—amanuensis to Counselor Vogelsong

Sophie—16-year-old daughter of Ares and Nicole, Henry's wife

Spechler (SPECK ler)—illegal notary in Westford

Stengi (STEN ghee)—Giles' assistant

Surchatain (SUR cha tan)—the ruler of a province; the feminine is **Surchataine** (SUR cha tane)

swing-chimed bell—a bell rung by a rope attached to a lever which itself is attached to the headstock; the precursor to full-circle ringing.

Talus (TAL us)—the Commander who murdered Surchatain Bobadil (Ares' grandfather) and seized the throne of Lystra; Renée and Henry's grandfather

Tassos, Brother—assistant to Father Manworren at the Sanctum

Thom—Commander of the army of Lystra

toilet—the act or process of bathing, dressing and grooming

tonsure—to shave part of the head upon entering a religious order

trebuchet (TREB you shet)—a war machine which flings heavy projectiles over great distances at fortress walls

Ulm—usurper of the throne of Qarqar who went to war against Ares

Van Laeke (lake)—a member of the Red Regiment of the Lystran army

Venegas (VEN e gas)—a small coastal town in Scylla

Vogelsong (VO gel song)—Counselor at Westford

Weingert (WINE gert), Lord—the premier wine merchant of Westford

Westford—capital of the province of Lystra

Wulfredia (wool FREE dya)—assistant to Doctor Savary

Yonge (yung)—a Captain of the Lystran army; the officer in charge of the outpost at Odea

Appendix

Regarding the Surchatain Who Became a Monk

"[Ninth-century Bulgarian king] Boris himself surrendered his crown to his older son Vladimir and, after having educated his younger son Simeon as a monk, embraced the monastic habit himself. His peaceful devotions were violently interrupted when Vladimir apostatized and the nation with him. Thus Boris put aside the habits of the monk for his former vocation as a warrior, soundly defeated Vladimir in battle, had him blinded and imprisoned, placed the monk Simeon on the throne in his stead, and returned to his monastery to take up again the uninterrupted course of his prayers."

From William R. Cannon, *History of Christianity in the Middle Ages* (Nashville, TN: Abingdon Press, 1960), p. 121.

Regarding Medieval Foods

Many of the foods cited in this book are taken from Volume 1 or 2 of Cindy Renfrow's *Take a Thousand Eggs or More: A Collection of 15th Century Recipes,* 2nd edition (Unionville, NY: Royal Fireworks Press, 2003).

Following is a chapter-by-chapter list of dishes and the page numbers of their recipes in Cindy's books.

Chapter Two

flampoyntes bake—ground pork baked in a pie with cottage cheese, pine nuts, ginger and gillyflowers: Vol. 1, pp. 136-37

prenade—spicy chutney served with fried dough chips: Vol. 1, pp.161-63

rapeye—spicy-sweet, crunchy applesauce: Vol. 1, pp. 72-73

Chapter Three

bolas—plums stewed in spiced wine, served in pear halves: Vol. 1, pp. 202-03

broth saake—chicken broth with wine and numerous seasonings: Vol. 1, pp. 108-09

maumenye royal—pork served in a sauce of almond milk, spices and pine nuts: Vol. 1, pp. 158-59

fritters—apple rings battered and fried: Vol. 1, pp. 176-77

Chapter Four
vyaund leche—a soft cheese made with beer and honey:
  Vol. 1, pp. 42-43

Chapter Seven
tarts—pastry with custard filling: Vol. 2, p. 547

Chapter Eight
glazed sops—a sauce over toast made with onions, olive
  oil, wine and almond milk: Vol. 1, p. 7
crustades—custard pies with spiced minced veal: Vol. 1,
  p. 115
brown fries—brown bread seasoned, dipped in egg
  batter, and fried: Vol. 1, p. 219

Chapter Ten
white herbs—a dip made of herbs, almond milk, honey,
  and rice flour: Vol. 1, p. 59
figgy—fig and wine pudding: Vol. 1, p. 167
verjuice sauce—cider vinegar with ginger: Vol. 1, p. 123

Chapter Eleven
appraylere—mock pitchers made of pork, cheese, bread
  and spices, molded together and baked: Vol. 1, p.
  253

Regarding alphabets

The alphabet used by Faguy in deciphering the Caesar cipher is modern. In addition to the letters we know, the Middle English alphabet contained the following characters:

> æ, named "ash," later replaced by **a** or **ae**
> ð, "eth," replaced by **dh** and later, **d**
> ȝ, "yogh," replaced by **y**
> þ, "thorn," replaced by **th**
> ƿ, "wynn," replaced by **w**

A thorough discussion of Middle English can be found online at http://en.wikipedia.org/wiki/Middle_English.

A Meeting, Circa 1981

The recording angel Muthlabben took his place in front of the group assembling before him, over a hundred people. "Order, please, everyone. I know that many of you have left weighty duties to come today, but your input is vital."

He paused to watch one woman, blond and content, settle on the floor with toddlers playing around her. "Deirdre, yours too," he said gently.

"I'm listening," she replied, reaching out to catch a baby falling over her knees. Her husband Roman watched with quiet satisfaction. Another woman sat beside her to assist with the overflow, and Deirdre flashed her a smile. "Thank you, Bettina."

Muthlabben lifted his eyes to sweep the group, who watched patiently but without great expectation. "I have excellent, wonderful news. We have a located a chronicler for your story!"

Some of his audience gasped, clapped, or laughed in delight, but many looked skeptical. Basil murmured, "Why do I sense a downside around the corner?"

"'Downside'?" the angel repeated in offense. "No,

no. The writer is perfectly willing, enthusiastic, well-educated and—and—"

"Second-tier?" Vogelsong suggested.

"Margery Allingham had a full plate already, as you well know," Muthlabben snapped.

"She was just a suggestion," Vogelsong sighed.

"Man or woman?" Nihl asked curtly.

When Muthlabben hesitated, Nihl groaned, "Is she up for the battle scenes?"

"I'm sure she'll handle them adequately," Muth-labben said.

"How are her research skills?" Paramore asked dubiously.

The angel blinked. "Developing," he said, and half his audience groaned. "Come now, people, don't be ungrateful," he chastised.

"Forgive us," Roman said, and the room stilled in respect. "We have been waiting a long time for good news. Just tell us that she will tell the story truthfully."

"Yes!" Muthlabben said. "All that she receives, she will record with great faithfulness. There will be many impediments and tests—"

"Impediments?" Nicole repeated in alarm.

Oswald rumbled, "In what form? Will her books be seized? Burnt? Will she suffer torture and martyrdom for our story?"

The group looked to the angel, who cleared his throat. "Ah, no. No . . . burnings of any kind. She'll be mostly . . . ignored."

The souls gathered here were mostly too polite to issue raspberries, but Giles murmured, "That *is* hard."

"And you mustn't discount the difficulties of

preserving data in rapidly changing retrieval systems," Muthlabben argued to a host of blank stares.

Roman said, "Please just tell us the drawbacks so that we may quickly decide whether to vouchsafe our story with her."

Muthlabben spread his hands in conciliation. "She is young and relatively green. She is not the most original wordsmith. She will entertain unrealistic expectations for the commercial success of her efforts. But she will love your story, and you."

While the group considered this, Muthlabben nodded to Roman. "Your part of the story will comprise only three books. She does not have the courage to chronicle your sorrows and suffering."

Deirdre looked up. "I understand that. However, can you see that my husband's consolations to me are recorded?"

"Yes, Deirdre. They will be, at least the most crucial parts," he promised. Reluctantly, he added, "Others of you will not be portrayed as completely as we would like. Some matters she will be unable to see into."

Carmine smiled pensively. "That is a hazard of our finite minds," he murmured.

Muthlabben looked at someone else far back in the room. "She will comprehend only a piece of your story, Chiacos."

With characteristic Polonti brevity, he observed, "A piece of the truth is better than none at all."

The group considered that, some nodding, and Muthlabben hastened to add, "But she will also make revisions that better address your circumstances." Chiacos raised an eyebrow.

Nicole regarded him thoughtfully before turning back to the angel. "You said she will love us."

"Oh, yes, my dear." Muthlabben smiled. "Your own story will encompass nine books, beginning with you and ending with you."

Bonnie, beside her, snickered, "If it's a woman, then it's not Nicole she loves best."

Many glittering eyes turned to a figure who seemed to be wearing black. He smiled mildly. "As a matter of fact, I have already visited her."

"When, Ares?" Nicole asked.

"In the night. But she will not remember it for years yet," he said.

Thom demanded, "The question I have is: will she write our story so as to honor God?"

Muthlabben acknowledged him with a tentative nod. "The final answer to that must come from the Crucified Himself. All I can tell you is that she will try. She will try."

His repeated assertion hung in the air while the souls present considered it. Then he said, "I need your word on this now. Everyone here must agree to give her the story, or it will not be given. So who is for aye?"

Numerous voices spoke their approval, and the angel tabulated the votes with a glance. As the voices trailed off and then died, his eyes found the solitary holdout: the only one who did not approve yet. Everyone turned to look at her.

Renée, sitting back, said, "Tell me what she does with me."

Muthlabben pursed his lips. "You are her secret mirror. She will be exasperated and adoring of you. The more you are attacked, the more she will write of you."

"Perfect," Renée purred. "Then I also consent. Only —you must forbid her to write cf me when I am old."

"No," Muthlabben said.

Renée looked down her nose at him. "Beast."

"Oh, this is wonderful!" Sophie cried. "At last everyone will know how wonderfully Henry ruled!" He, in turn, looked pensive, then shook his head. Muthlabben merely cleared his throat. "But how shall she be given the story?" Sophie added.

The others looked at the angel in interest. He began to illustrate the complex process with an opening wave of the hand, but Deirdre, lifting a baby to kiss its face, said, "This little one is to be sent to her shortly. Pack the story with her."

Muthlabben, his point vacated, paused with a hand in the air. "Or, we could do that."

"At last," Nicole sighed. "At long last."

"To your duties, each of you," Roman said, turning. And the room emptied but for the angel.

Books by Robin Hardy

The Streiker Saga
Streiker's Bride
Streiker: The Killdeer
Streiker's Morning Sun

The Annals of Lystra
Chataine's Guardian
Stone of Help
Liberation of Lystra
(first published as *High Lord of Lystra*)

The Latter Annals of Lystra
Nicole of Prie Mer
Ares of Westford
Prisoners of Hope
Road of Vanishing
Dead Man's Token
Games of God and Men
In Extremis
All Mirrors and All Suns
The Laughing Side of the World

The Sammy Series
Sammy: Dallas Detective
Sammy: Women Troubles
Sammy: Working for a Living
Sammy: On Vacation
Sammy: Little Misunderstandings
Sammy: Ghosts
Sammy: Arenamania
Sammy: In Principle
(continued on next page)

Sammy: Grave Agreement
Sammy: Love Shouldn't Hurt
Sammy: The Consolation of Bucephalus

The Idecis
Unknown Name, Unknown Number: A Wimsey
Reade Mystery
Padre and its sequel *His Strange Ways*

Edited by Robin Hardy

Sifted But Saved: Classic Devotions by W.W. Melton

www.ingramcontent.com/pod-product-compliance
Lightning Source LLC
Chambersburg PA
CBHW050019180626
46810CB00002B/493